The Waiting Game

Simon Matkin

ISBN 095541940-9

Set in 12pt Bembo

Printed by the Lavenham Press, Lavenham, Suffolk

To Mum, Mandy and Chris who have helped me to find the real Philosopher's Stone.

CONTENTS

1. THE PHILOSOPHER'S STONE

Out on the highways and the by-ways all alone
I'm still searching for, searching for my home
Up in the morning, up in the morning out on the road
And my head is aching and my hands are cold
And I'm looking for the silver lining, silver lining in the clouds
And I'm searching for and
I'm searching for the philosopher's stone.

Enough of the soul-searching Van Morrison for now, although he was of course one of the Three Wise Men who guided my star. The other two members of this unlikely triumvirate were the mystical Omar Khayyam and very much down to earth Georgie Crabbe. The Irish singer, the Persian sage and the Suffolk poet. What you might call in these singularly unenlightened times a cosmopolitan dream team.

But now let's get down to what it's really all about. Work. To be more specific, work as an esteemed driver with Messrs Wells Fargo Cars Ltd, Private Hire and ostensibly Airport Specialists. Actually the only thing we were really specialists at were cock-ups. I had been with this eclectic team of eccentrics and misfits for more than three years and had over one hundred and fifty thousand miles on the clock. Thus I could truthfully give an affirmative answer to the silly buggers who kept asking me, 'do you do this job full-time mate or is it just a hobby?' However I soon learnt that a more ingenuous answer went down far better. 'No, actually I am an undercover agent for the Drugs Squad.' Ah bon, you arrogant shit for brains.

Ah arrogance, there's the rub. Some God Up There (or GUT for short) had sentenced me to an unspecified period of penance till I had cleansed myself of this particularly foul personal trait. And unlike little Jeffrey Archer I wasn't allowed to swan off to fancy restaurants and posh parties whenever I felt like it. Regrettably I still wasn't making much progress on the arrogance front as yet, so my period of penance must continue ad nauseam. So who am I as you didn't bother to ask?

Tommy Gainsborough's the name, taxiing's my game. I'm a fifty year old ex-merchant banker and former Lloyds Name. Also to my discredit is a discharged bankruptcy and a messy divorce. However, the last cut is by far the deepest and I have to admit under the greatest pressure that I am also a defrocked MCC member. How the not so mighty have fallen. My Welsh ex-wife, the lovely Megan from Meidrim, had deserted the sinking financial ship taking our two teenage boys with her to the chateau in South West France, which I had imprudently bought in her name with the laughable intention of reducing my tax liabilities. I was left with bugger all, and was now reduced to renting a scruffy one bedroom flat, albeit one with what estate agents would modestly describe as having orgasmic views over the River Bosmere and the ancient water meadows. Work and play was now back at my birthplace in the picturesque market town of Sutton Market, right in the centre of 'Le Suffolk Profond'. After twenty five years of wandering in the physical wilderness, I had returned enfin to my natural spiritual home. Parked now on the still slumbering Market Hill in the chill of the early morning awaiting my first job of the day, I gently surveyed the scene laid out before me. Or, as Georgie put it so elegantly.

> 'Describe the Borough' - though our idle tribe
> May love description, can we so describe,
> That you shall fairly streets and buildings trace
> And all that gives distinction to a place?
> This cannot be; yet, moved by your request,
> A part I paint - let Fancy form the rest.

Virtually devoid of those damned motor cars (mine excepted, of course), the ancient Market Place unfurled before me in all its period glory. First we begin with the rugged flint, fourteenth century fortress of Saint Felix situated defiantly at the top of the hill. I regret to inform you that just the very mention of this innocent church was enough to conjure up impure thoughts from my long distant schooldays of the girls' public school with the same name.

I then carried out a rather more measured assessment of this architectural extravaganza starting with the Red Lion, a fine half-timbered former coaching inn. I then let my eyes feast on the mellow brickwork of the eighteenth century Provincial Bank building which dovetailed perfectly with the gaiety of the art deco County Cinema, the Victorian solidity of the Corn Exchange and finally the rococo brilliance of the Café Gascon. On the other side of the hill were myriad period half-timbered buildings with garish modern shop fronts, fittingly ending with the handsome red brick Elizabethan Shire Hall at the bottom of the hill.

Suddenly the stentorian tones of The Fat Controller crackled over the intercom to Line 13 (that's me), interrupting my reverie.

'Are you ready to play?'

Indeed I was. I always enjoyed this delicately ambiguous question intimating that we were about to proceed either on a genteel round of golf or possibly something even a little bit erotic.

East Street to the Northern Industrial Estate, fare £3.00, the long day had begun. A single mother battling to make ends meet while grandma looks after the kids. Next Church Street to Seckford Street, fare also £3.00. A young lady going home belatedly after a pleasant evening. Sits in the back of the car. Thirdly, off to The Posthouse straddling the A14 trunk road which snaked unattractively round the town. Back into the town centre with an overkeen businessman, fare £3.50. Next a little five minute pause before the school run. Turn on 'Five Live' for The Breakfast Programme for some relaxed and informal news to suit the mood. Some footballer in the dock again accused of some drunken indiscretion. Who cares? They always get off with their fancy briefs. I'm sorry, I think I had better rephrase that last statement. I meant with their obscenely expensive QC's. If they had to present themselves before the local Magistrates with only the Duty Solicitor to hold their hands after a bit of nonsense outside the notorious Copocana Beach night-club on a Saturday night, I wouldn't fancy their chances overmuch.

This particular school run involved a circuit through the villages to pick up three youngsters and usually took up to an hour. Fare £15 on account, tab paid courtesy of Suffolk County Council of course. I would be fascinated to find out what the Council's taxi bill amounts to per annum. Very interesting reading. In fact, I would like a copy of the accounts on my desk by tomorrow morning. Investing in people my arse. More like spending like Elton John.

I wasn't at all comfortable doing these composite runs. It was never explained to us simple drivers exactly why we had to pick up these kids. Most of them appeared normal if I am still allowed to use that expression in these absurdly PC days. Anyway who the hell is normal? Certainly not those as yet uncertified lunatics still trying to start World War Three. One of the kids was obviously a bit backward (that's still safe, isn't it?), whilst one of my other charges was partially deaf. The third child seemed to have nothing wrong with him at all except to have a particular aversion to education. The latter also lived in a very desirable residence with both a pristine BMW and People Carrier in the drive. What the hell was I doing there picking up rich kids like this? There must be far more deserving cases. I'm sure this child's parents could happily or unhappily have paid for the taxi themselves if they couldn't be bothered to get off their collective cornucopian arses. By the bye, what other form of life could a car possibly convey? The Mekon and his merry green men?

I was even less comfortable with handicapped adults, especially those with mental problems. James was a regular from Headlight House, which was a day centre for those unfortunates suffering from head injuries and illnesses, especially victims of car crashes. James was a married man in his late twenties with a dazzling future in front of him, until a mindless moron wrecked his life on a pedestrian crossing one terrible Monday morning in May. Now three years later he had the equivalent mental age of a five year old and it was agonizing to behold, as he struggled to put two sentences together having manfully and independently dragged himself from his council house to the car. He was still awaiting compensation for the 'accident', as his lawyer was holding the funds and vetoing his attempts to purchase another house with the proceeds in a rapidly rising market. His magnificent wife had heart-warmingly stood by her man through it all. What the hell was I doing moaning about the vicissitudes of life? Get back on the road again immediately Tommy, and don't stop until you have passed Go and collected your two hundred quid for the day.

As if to underline the above sentiment, my next job was a pick up from the Mid Suffolk Hospital to Cumberland Street, another three quid. The fare was a regular, an elderly lady whose husband was suffering from that lingering living death euphemistically named Alzheimer's Disease. She was obviously very upset by today's visit and didn't utter a single word during the course of the journey. By now I had switched radio frequencies to Classic Gold, an easy listening station specializing in Golden Oldies which I generally found very therapeutic. Unfortunately the gentle sadness of Tears of a Clown only seemed to exacerbate the silence between us.

Luckily the next punter was a chatty and comely housewife from the Wickham estate to The Tower of Babel, more usually known as Emperor Tesco's. This monument to the modern shopaholic age was a typically low slung red brick faced pretentious pile topped off with the obligatory clock tower. Why can't we build unassuming supermarkets like on the continent, but then we wouldn't want to be too European would we? I just couldn't help noticing out of the corner of my eye that my passenger had an excellent pair of legs and that her skirt was a fraction too short. Anyway I relieved her of £3.50 which I considered very reasonable indeed when the pleasure was all mine. But as old Noel used to say, there is no harm in just looking or even thinking, just as long as you don't act. I always think that the French are much better at this sort of thing than the English. We are either aloof or lascivious, while the other half of the Entente Cordiale look at a pretty woman with just that hint of concentrated appreciation that can only be taken as a compliment. As this is the second time that the 'f' word has been mentioned now is the time to mention foreigners. The latter were just one subject on which I disagreed vehemently with most of my fellow inmates. Massive moustachioed Stack, he of Jason Leonard's physique gone to seed and one of the formidable props of the Pontypool Front Row, announced one day in The Hutch that he couldn't stand the 'Froggies'. When he answered non to my civil enquiry 'did he know any French people by any chance?', I rested my case. Not put off with that gentle put down Tonker, the other pillar of the PFR, couldn't resist a little swipe at the increasing number of local asylum seekers being rehoused in a terrace of expensively renovated council properties. My retort was that the various Afghans, Albanians and Turks amongst us were more than happy to do a lot of the jobs which no self-respecting English person would touch with a bargepole. I also added for good measure that there were enough drunks and dickheads in Sutton Market to give his Froggies a run for their money, and the cost of housing scheming single mothers far exceeded any modest amount spent on outsiders.

In case you are beginning to think my real name is Saint Maggie of Assisi in drag, I think I had better give you a little list of some of my pet hates. In no particular order of demerit are banks and building societies, celebrities, 'mistaken' policeman, political correctness and ecstatic football commentators. That should cause enough outrage for starters I trust. To end this little rant take a bow please Bob from Beyton, the nastiest piece of racist scum it has been my misfortune to have come across in all my time on The Road.

Now a slight hiccup. The Fat Controller had either over-estimated my ability to match Herr Schumacher round the inner ring road or had possibly been just a teeny weenie bit over optimistic with his bookings. Whatever, I was over ten minutes late for my next fare at The Abbey Hotel. Now the latter was by far the grandest hotel in the town with the evening's tariff starting at a cheeky £175, not including breakfast of course. The Abbey itself was an imposing Elizabethan red brick former manor house close to the town centre, with magnificent grounds and views over the town to the country and river beyond. It was therefore with a touch of trepidation that I reported to the oak panelled and hushed reception area.

> Anon, a figure enters, quaintly neat,
> All pride and business, bustle and conceit;

Malheureusement, this mini apparition wasn't very happy at all. Apparently we were en retard for an impossibly important business meeting. I got my inevitable bollocking and concomitant remark that the future of the British economy was at risk because of this catastrophe. I said that in that case, I was heading straight round to The Provincial Bank to convert my overdraft into gold. He was a bit more subdued after that. Actually I hated being late but why should one take all this crap from a little Napoleon? Stop whingeing Tommy, who said life was fair?

By now I felt I had more than earned my tea break as it was past eleven and I had accumulated the handy gross sum of some £35. However, this inalienably English human right could be vetoed by The Fat Controller if we were heavily booked or he just felt plain bolshie. My retort was that if I was cooped up in the car too long, I tended to get a trifle irritable and might just possibly let slip an injudicious word or worse to a fare. Because, believe it or not, both Hackney and Private Hire drivers were totally unrestricted in the hours they worked, so technically you could do a double shift or even a treble shift without a break if you were stupid or desperate enough. My union biased attitude was that I had no intention of ever risking my life and valuable limbs just for a few measly extra quid. Who dared mutter something about an attitude problem?

Another problem were Hackneys. Wells Fargo was a Private Hire Company which meant we could only do business by prior appointment, invariably by telephone. This meant that it was strictly forbidden for us to pick up fares off the streets as it were, or, heinous crime of crimes, off The Rank itself. However, the Hackneys in Sutton Market had no compunction about nicking our fares, especially from the railway station. Nor for that matter did Omega and Lone Star Cars, our great rivals, have any scruples about doing the same dastardly deed to us outside The Copocana Beach. Yeah, it sure was rough and tough out there on the range.

Back to breaks after that Wild West excursion, it has to be admitted that I was also a trifle indolent by nature and didn't want to pull a driving muscle if I could help it. This time I got the nod from TFC and cruised back to our illustrious headquarters, aka 'The Hutch on the Hill'. The Hutch was a dilapidated portacabin with decaying armchairs, mediaeval carpets and a tiny cubicle at the end where the squat frame of The Fat Controller could be glimpsed oozing round the corner but not, thank goodness, those sharp piggy eyes. Also in situ was The Boss, the diminutive and pugilistic Quid Carpenter himself, self evidently known as QC. As a drinking companion he wasn't a bad old bugger, but in business he just couldn't help being un peu mendacious with the shekels. Being a Monday, he was busy mugging us drivers for our desk money, a usurious twenty per cent of our gross takings for the privilege of being at his beck and call night and day six or seven days a week. My average gross income was in the region of £600 weekly for a sixty plus hour week, less one hundred pounds each for my car lease and petrol. Taking into account other expenses such as servicing, repairs and insurance, you didn't have to be an accountant to see that I didn't need an accountant.

Also in 'The Hutch' was the mighty aforementioned Tonker Townshend, a great, bald bull of a man and the real powerhouse of the PFR. A man of few words, every other one being expletive deleted. However, despite our somewhat differing backgrounds, we were both men of Suffolk through and through and behind the bluster he was a real softie, the reverse of an insult he once paid me. However pissed off I might be at any given situation, he was always ready with a pithy remark and a light up your smoke (always mine and always Dunhill). He called me Tommy the Toff which I found strangely endearing. I had invariably been an outsider in the City with their funny Masonic habits, and quickly learnt to be more at home in The Hutch than any mock oak panelled space age gherkin. Rather more derogatory in tone were descriptions from fares. The latter were otherwise known in the trade as punters, patients or, at worst, dickheads. They struck back by calling me an arrogant bastard, opinionated arsehole, a pompous prig and, sublimely, the most tedious taxi driver in the world. What a compliment.

Another problem was my accent, or as I perceived it, a lack of one. Until I started on The Road I had always considered that I spoke normal BBC English. Light years ago I had been sent away to a very minor public school situated right on the bleak North Sea and us boarders sadly got our kicks by taking the piss out of the day boys with their broad Suffolk accents. They in turn got their kicks from the local girls whom we were incarcerated away from by an Iron Curtain but that is another story. Thus I naively entered the City where all the other blokes spoke the same normal English as me as well as being equally sexually incontinent. So when I belatedly entered the real world I was still totally naive to my problem. Fares were always saying 'you don't come from round here mate,' and were somewhat non-plussed when I replied in kind.

'Actually I was born here in Sutton Market at the Mid Suffolk Hospital, you Cockney wanker.' I seemed to have an effortless talent for upsetting fares just by opening my big mouth. Georgie was shit hot on accents.

Then for thine accent – what in sound can be
So void of grace as dull monotony ?

No such problem existed for the third member in The Hutch. This was the delectable Elise, a dark haired beauty I would very hesitantly suggest was in her late thirties. Suggest was the operative word because Elise was the literal tart with a heart of gold. She also had the brainwave (or rather bodywave) of combining driving with a novel variation on the theme of driving. She was naturally top bitch by a county mile, although very little of the fruit of these very hard goings on seeped back to either QC or the IR. As for how they fitted in with Arthur Smiley's draconian Conditions for Private Hire and Hackney Carriage Drivers, God only knows. Neither must we forget the narcoleptic Local Government (Miscellaneous Provisions) Act 1976, the veritable Koran for all of Suffolk's growing clan of Muslim taxi drivers. How Elise met the dreaded Dress Code with her micro mini skirts and tight slacks was also a mystery. In this respect I would describe my own dressing as quietly conservative as long as it was black or blue. Other drivers were rather more colourful if not colour co-ordinated. Back to Elise which wasn't difficult. She had a robust Suffolk accent, was always infectiously cheerful, small breasts and a neat bum, and I fancied her like hell. Unfortunately our personal relationship was strictly platonic and I couldn't afford her professionally.

The fourth driver in The Hutch happened to be The Petty Officer, so called because though he wasn't strictly a former officer in Her Majesty's Navy, no-one could possibly deny his pettiness. With his upright posture, immaculate appearance and business-like walk he was more like a candidate for the Axis forces. Perhaps he was really a mole infiltrated by Mr Smiley to report back on our misdemeanours. Come to think of it, his alibi wasn't very solid. I had better keep my gimlet eye on him in future. Luckily Tonker was his usual laconic self as he solicitously inquired as to my health.

In fact his actual words were, 'how the eff are you, you effing toffee nosed bastard'. I must say that I always was much more at home with this form of banter than the studied politeness and double talk of the City. The majority of my colleagues were genuine and generous citizens, even if a teeny bit financially flawed and conjugally challenged, as I was of course in spades. In fact our sense of being outsiders bonded us into a far better team than eleven outstanding and upstanding individuals. Nota bene Steve and Duncan. Because the conundrum was that although we were all self-employed, we depended very much on each other. If someone had a problem with a passenger he could alert TFC with an immediate ninety nine call. All drivers were very vulnerable late at night with no partition protecting us f rom aggressive or abusive fares. I was a bit disconcerted to be told my first week into the job that the reason we were exempted from the law to wear seat belts was to obviate the opportunity of being strangled from behind with our own belt by a punter. Or to do a quick runner if things got a bit nasty.

Talking of runners, that was a perennial problem. I remember not without a rueful smile my first encounter with this unwelcome species. I took a young lad of about twelve or thirteen to Newmarket one lovely autumnal morning when GUT was in his heaven. On our arrival in that bizarre half-horsy town he disappeared into a dire tower block with the promise that he would be back in a minute when he had got the money from his mum. However, disappeared was the operative word and after more than ten minutes I realized I had been hoodwinked. Though I was out of pocket I couldn't really get annoyed when I reflected that I had been conned by a kid. What a mug. Not so funny was the next occasion when two racist louts I picked up from outside The Copacana Beach outmanoeuvred me in the wilds of Clare late one Saturday night, depriving me a fare of over £40 at fare and a half rates (i.e. after midnight). After that I learnt to take money up front if I had any doubts. Of course that didn't preclude the fare taking the fare back and the rest at the end of the journey by fair means or foul.

> And it's a hard road, Its a hard road daddy-o
> When my job is turning lead into gold
> Can you hear that engine
> Woe can you that engine drone
> Well I'm on the road again and I am searching for
> Searching for the philosopher's stone.

Yes, turning lead into gold. If Robert de Niro could do this job just for a month and turn that experience into a Taxi Driver goldmine, surely I could scribble a few notes after three long years on The Road and secure my fortune. But I was also searching for something more intangible, that much overused expression, peace of mind. Old Omar naturally puts it streets better.

> The Grape that can with Logic absolute
> The Two-and-Seventy jarring Sects confute:
> The subtle Alchemist that in a Trice
> Life's leaden Metal into Gold transmute.

In the meantime, I was back on the road again, on my long job to Stansted Airport, sixty miles, sixty quid thanks very much, for two hours effortless driving. Swings and roundabouts. The obscure long job list was entirely in the hands of QC and was the source of much antagonism. I tended to keep my head down and wait for the lottery spin of the roulette wheel. A smooth pick up from The Posthouse, a quick flash down the A14, A11 and M11, drop-off and return. My fare was a charming Irishman on his way back to Dublin courtesy of Liffey Air. He was in the electronics trade apparently, but we talked exclusively about rugby and the comparable merits of 1970's icons such as Willy John Mcbride and Mike Gibson against the current coruscating brilliance of Brian O'Driscoll and the recently retired Keith Wood. We left on excellent terms and me with a generous tip. That was the beauty of this job. You never knew whether you were going to pick up a university professor, a comedian or a dickhead.

Back to Sutton Market in time for another quick cuppa and bickie before the afternoon school run. In The Hutch this time was Leonardo the Lover, so called because of his smouldering Latin looks (Elise's words, I hasten to add, not mine), and his astounding success with members of the opposite sex. Ah well, you have either got it or you ain't. In reality he was Leonard from Leyton, but why spoil a good story with the actualité. Leonardo had that smug expression that invariably meant he had made yet another female conquest the previous night. (I originally wrote that he had scored again but this expression was ruthlessly excised by my ever vigilant editrice). Rather than look at that smirking visage any longer than was absolutely necessary, I turned my attention to Nigel, aka The Boy Racer. Nigel was an absolute nutter who frightened the shit out of his more nervous fares. He was busy regaling everybody with some outrageous recent lap record he had achieved with some unsuspecting old lady, which brought the wry observation from Sandy that it was very fortunate that her bowels weren't in full working order. Naturally this brought the whole Hutch down. Sandy was our resident Scottish alcoholic. If you have lifted even half an eyebrow as the result of the latter description, I can assure you that you haven't been living in the real world. Come on Tony, you are now formally invited to ride shotgun for me for a week and then you will be able to dispense with the services of that furtive Scottish bloke.

'Dannae make a prick of yourself again, Tommy,' Sandy sagely advised me as the conversation took a different turn.

As you can see, our chats were strictly catholic to say the least. My latest wheeze involved a plan to blow up the brand new drive-in Mcdonalds with a touch of Celtic semtex in the tradition of that great French radical José Bouvé. From the bottom of the lowest settee up piped a falsetto voice.

'You are full of high brow shit, Thomas.'

This was The Milky Bar Kid himself. He was the only driver to address me by the name on my birth certificate, and we heartily hated each others guts. The Kid may have looked only sweet sixteen but he drove like the wind as well. He also had the dubious disadvantage of requiring the assistance of a large cushion to assist him seeing over the steering wheel, which didn't do complimentary wonders for his masculinity. Luckily Eric, The Crafty Cockney and middleman of the Pontypool Front Row, relieved me of the necessity of a strangled reply to this little salvo. Eric was the typical London cabby, full of bullshit and ample of girth. However, he also had an open honest face under that terrible crew-cut and an infectious sense of humour. He also had a limitless supply of scurrilous anecdotes. In short he was the veritable anchor man of Wells Fargo and I had a lot of time for him. He always sensed when I was inclined to melancholy and could invariably extract a reluctant smile from my sullen visage. Other more uncharitable folk would utilize the deadly accurate words of Georgie instead.

He wears contempt upon his sapient sneer.

After we had quickly glossed over world affairs, women's legs and Mr Smiley's latest piece of officialdom, it was time for the afternoon return school run. After an uneventful journey, next in line was Doddy Daniel from the Mature Training Centre (MTC). We would have said in older unreconstructed times that he wasn't quite there, but we can't say that now of course. He was absolutely harmless but did make these funny brum brum motor noises which proved alarmingly infectious. At first I unforgivingly imitated him ad nauseam back at The Hutch but then, more worryingly, started to reply in kind in the car with him so it ended up sounding like something out of a Grand Prix.

Next I was landed with Big Bertha from the railway station. Talk about out of the frying pan into the proverbial fire. This old favourite eased her eighteen stone frame into my puny Peugeot and dominated not just the passenger seat but sequestered the gear box as well. Driving became a delicate and very dubious pleasure as you had to carefully engage third gear before she became wedged in and then remain in that gear for the rest of the journey, which included the particularly tricky negotiation of a set of traffic lights. The problem was that a delicate part of her anatomy had taken over first and second gears and if you were ever tempted to seek one of them, the awful realisation that you were about to be done for sexual harassment of a particularly unpleasant variety quickly stayed that errant left hand. For heaven's sake, if I am going to get done for sexual harassment let it be with Charlotte Rampling, Sharon Stone or Isabelle Huppert to make it truly worthwhile.

At this stage I must reassure alarmed female readers with the news that all Private Hire drivers in the shires must undergo a rigorous police check. I recently had to endure another of these so-called enhanced police checks, whatever that means, which just managed to reaffirm my dubious status. The only really bad incident involving women that I have heard of on this score in all my time on The Road involved a driver from Omega Cars, one of our principal rivals. This company was run by the sinister Stephano Machiavelli with his close links to the Suffolk Mafia, and not a man to be trifled with in any circumstances. The other big operator in town was Inzy Ahmed, a roly poly gentleman from a country somewhere between the Tigris river and the Euphrates. His partner in crime at the chaotic Lone Star Cars Ltd was a very tall, good looking and dark skinned gentleman who was vaguely familiar. Lone Star Cars were naturally our sole rivals for the much prized sobriquet, the biggest cowboys in town.

After Bertha finally had eased her considerable bulk out of the car, I was given a welcome respite from my exertions when The Fat Controller announced that we were clear and I could 'come on back.' That was the trouble with this job. We were either sitting on our asses or had to be in three places at once. Clients are so inconsiderate. They should come at our convenience, like women.

I thought it was time for a little doze before my final surge. On Five Live someone was slagging off extortionate taxi fares and garrulous drivers who wouldn't stop their incessant babbling. They were talking about London cabbies of course, but we were all tarred with the same brush, along with unlicensed minicab drivers. If we didn't talk we were miserable buggers but if we opened our mouths and essayed some witticism or pleasantry, we invariably seemed to upset them. My extremely vague rule of thumb was that if a fare got into the front passenger seat, it was safe to assume that they felt reasonably communicative. If they got in the back I didn't feel obliged to make conversation. The dilemma was that I always felt somewhat uncomfortable when a perfect stranger got into the car. Therefore when they got in the front I felt almost obliged to engage them in some sort of conversation which led to one or two or a score of disastrous sallies. Sometimes I wanted to literally bite off my tongue after a particularly inept remark or ill-judged attempt at a joke. When I tried to explain my dilemma to Stack one day he looked at me as if I had six heads.

'A punter is just a punter, Tommy, end of story,' he explained to me patiently as if I was a simpleton.

But if that is the case, why do all these thousands of commuters pour into London every day with a single occupant at the wheel? Because we all want our own space, don't we? Cocooned in our own world, going into the zone with our personal choice of musical nirvana, we are safe from the world. I still remember vividly my very first day on the road. Letting two total strangers into my car was a very unsettling feeling. The omens didn't appear promising. Who had ever heard of a taxi driver who didn't like people in his car? Steven Norris once described the dilemma of driving your own car compared to pubic transport (it does sound sexier, doesn't it?).

'You have your own company, your own temperature control, your own music – and don't have to put up with dreadful human beings sitting alongside you.' Nobody could have put it better, even the delectable Carly Simon.

However, I oh so gradually learnt to be slightly more accommodating, but my first love was always parcels and telephones. They never got drunk, were never rude or aggressive and neither did they pollute my car with their smell, detritus or retchings. Neither did they keep you waiting, waiting, waiting, the bane of our lives. In fact that is why I took up an old habit again, some three decades after my halcyon psychedelic years. I used to get so wound up by some of the punters that infiltrated my space that I quickly found that something considerably more chilling than a fag and a cuppa was needed to cool me down. With a joint and a bit of Van, everything was certainly going to be all right. I also took the opportunity to grow my hair again, this time with a distinguished silver pony tail, rather than dreadful Seamenesque fashion. I also rekindled an interest in magic mushrooms, the best of the bunch ironically nicknamed The Philosopher's Stone. Therefore my search for this elusive Holy Grail was both spiritual and physical as well as psychotic.

Blimey, I was so naive in those early days on The Road. One classic example of this naiveté was when TFC announced over the two way radio, 'attention, broken glass in East Street.' In the next half an hour I had two or three trips up and down East Street and kept a very careful eye out to avoid both the glass and a puncture. When I returned to The Hutch some time later I announced to the assembled company that I couldn't see any broken glass anywhere. Collapse of Wells Fargo Incorporated. Apparently broken glass was the warning slang for the fuzz, so as a former merchant banker I was self evidently a ★★★★★★. Well, you work it out for yourselves. However I was quite happy to be the butt of the troops de temps en temps, as befitted the only French speaking taxi driver in Suffolk. As they constantly reminded me, with that plum in my mouth I might as well have been speaking double Dutch anyway. Perversely it meant a lot to me. It meant that I had been accepted by this motley collection of losers, though only in the financial sense in this obsessively material world that we sadly live in. These were real people just trying to earn an honest bob or two to survive. They all said I would only last two weeks on The Road, but I had bloody well proved them wrong and earned their respect. Yes, and my own self-respect. Out of the decaying ruins of my life I was battling back in the most unexpected way. I was indeed turning a tiny piece of lead into gold.

> Up in the morning, up in the morning
> Out on the job
> Well you've got me searching for
> Searching for, the philosopher's stone.

Just seventy five minutes to the magic hour of six o'clock and another twenty four hours to my evening shift tomorrow evening. Back on the treadmill. The next pickup was back at the Mid Suffolk Hospital. The original structure was a fine Victorian building but beginning to show its age and the effects of neglect due to the usual government cut backs. Mrs P was another regular to be taken to Hintlesham Heights, a modern estate leading up to the bypass. She was the salt of the NHS, having worked at the Mid Suffolk for over thirty years except for the odd break to begat offspring. From there it was a short hop to the Sutton Market public school on the eastern outskirts of the town. This was a very minor public school with a well deserved reputation in mediocrity, except on the core subject of drugs where it scored an equally well merited A star. I had to pick up one of the cleaning ladies, a moaner of the first order, and I had long learned to agree with everything she said. Clear for quarter of an hour till Mrs H to Bingo, a charming and brave octogenarian who just went out 'to have fun and not look at four walls all evening.' Poignant.

'You can take it off now, Tommy,' wheezed The Fat Controller and take it off I did.

One hundred and twenty one pounds and fifty pence, well above par. Now comes the difficult time. Tricky business, time off. Dark evenings coming up soon. Not quite time to return to the Mill Flat, so a quiet pint or two was called for at The Rising Sun, the only remaining pub in Sutton Market undefiled by lager louts, blaring music and Brewers Tudor refurbishments. Situated obscurely down a narrow back street round the corner from my flat in the middle of a modest Victorian terrace of houses, The Sun belonged to an earlier spit and sawdust age, when nothing mattered except a good pint of bitter and good conversation, or unruffled silence if you so preferred. I was still considered an outsider in the pub after all my years away in the city and sometimes preferred to sit at a small table by the window letting the gentle hubbub waft over me. I invariably had a novel in front of me, another familiar form of escape. I found that a typically fiendish Robert Goddard plot was unbeatable for that. The Sun was a Mauldon's pub from a local micro brewery, and produced as fine a nutty bitter you could wish to find anywhere in East Anglia. Graham, the genial mine host, was a roly-poly East Ender with owl-like glasses and a good line in good advice, whether called for or otherwise. Three pints did the trick tonight and I ambled back to The Mill Flat in relaxed mood. The sun was setting fast in the west and I marvelled over the unsullied beauty of those big Suffolk skies and the peace of the surrounding meadows. Could they combine and do the trick for me?

A TV salad supper with a glass or three of ruby red Madiran wine brought the evening to an eminently satisfactory conclusion. Despite bankruptcy I hadn't managed to banish all my expensive tastes. On my return to Sutton Market I soon found a local wine supplier who kept me in ample supplies of this little nectar from South Western France. He also most conveniently offered excellent credit facilities. Ironically I had acquired this little habit in the company of that late lamented gold digger of an ex-wife. Now the Madiran had superceded her. Go Omar.

> You know, my Friends, how long since In my House
> For a new Marriage I did make Carouse
> Divorced old barren Reason from my Bed
> And took the Daughter of the Vine to Spouse.

Bitter, of course I'm not bitter after all that bitter. But I am definitely in the market for a replacement model and where is that flipping Philosopher's Stone Van keeps waffling on about?

> Even my best friends, even my best friends they don't know
> That my job is turning lead into gold
> When you hear that engine, when you hear that engine drone
> I'm on the road again and I'm searching for the
> philosopher's stone
> Its a hard road even my best friends they don't know
> And I'm searching for, searching for the philosopher's stone.

But there again, with Van, Omar and Georgie firmly on my side, anything's possible, isn't it?

2.   THE WAITING GAME

On a golden autumn day returning
Where each moment never is the same
Sometimes pure joy it comes with patience
When I'm waiting on, waiting game
When I'm waiting on, waiting game.

It was indeed a golden autumn day. The crispness in the air, the magical misty softness of the October sunlight and a cloudless blue sky. Who wouldn't jump out of bed with a lightness in their heart and a spring in their step on such a day? I wasn't on shift till six in the evening so a little pop to the coast was more than called for. It was about an hour's drive to Orford if I avoided the dreaded A14 so there was plenty of time to get into the Van zone.

The first half of the journey was mostly through flattish arable land, with the recently sown brown fields contrasting vividly with the burgeoning green of the oil-seed rape and the dark green of the mature sugar beet waiting for harvest. Plus, of course, regular rows of maize planted exclusively for the Earl of Suffolk and his merry band of bird-thirsty machine gunners. Another blot on the rural idyll. Mud on the roads. Wake up Wuffa District Council, do your frigging job.

Back to bliss. The gentle contours of the countryside, great clumps of ancient broadleaves, mellow Suffolk farmhouses and distant views to the spire of Wickham Market church, nothing is going to stop me now. When the sun is shining, I am unstoppable. On a dark and foggy morning I'm unstartable. The sadness can be overwhelming. Mais pas aujourd'hui. On through the tiny villages of Campsey Ash and Tunstall and the countryside merged seamlessly into the former Sandlings, those great sandy heathlands that once dominated all the way up to the northern tip of Suffolk. However, since the 1920's Tunstall and the adjoining Rendlesham Forests had been developed by the Forestry Commission into huge areas for timber. In my distant youth, I can still clearly remember that Tunstall Forest was particularly intimidating and forbidding with its relentless dark rows of fir trees. However, GUT moves in a wonderfully mysterious way and the Great Storm in October 1987 felled over a million of the buggers. Since then the new enlightened policy of the Forestry Commission has worked wonders converting these formerly inhospitable areas into arboreal oases of peace.

On to the unchanging ancient port of Orford with its landmark 12th century castle enjoying the finest views in all of the Suffolk Coastal AONB (Area of Outstanding Natural Beauty, stupid). It is also pretty stupid having not just one but two nuclear power stations in one of these designated areas. Then again us Suffolk folk always were a contrary lot. Down the delightful red bricked High Street to the tiny quay and the little National Trust motor boat to transport me and a handful of odd looking bird watchers for the final part of my journey across the River Ore to Orford Ness itself. This undiscovered jewel comprised a former secret atomic testing site, grazing marshes, teeming bird life and of course the unique ten mile spit and blessed silence. Could I really feel the latter as I marched past the dilapidated military buildings on to the isolated erection of a monstrous red and white lighthouse? Yeeeees! The North Sea had taken on a bewildering Mediterranean hue and I had to quickly light a joint to check I wasn't hallucinating. Back to nature. Perhaps this was what it was all about after all, as Georgie had foretold.

> Ships in the calm seem anchor'd; for they glide
> On the still sea, urged solely by the tide:
> Art thou not present, this calm scene before,
> Where all beside is pebbly length of shore,
> And as far as eye can reach, it can discern no more?

After a couple of hours gazing mystically into the vast space of sea and sky, I reluctantly trudged back across the shingle and the tarmac to the little boat again and a premonitory Don't Look Now trance across the water back to Orford. As I am very puritanical about not mixing alcohol with other substances when driving I stoically resisted the charms of a pint or two at The Jolly Sailor. Thus it was that I found myself meandering back to Sutton Market in plenty of time for my evening shift, this time passing via the reassuring woods of Rendlesham Forest, the chichi town of Woodbridge, and then off into the lowering autumnal sun. It was indeed 'a golden autumn day returning'.

Back to reality. This evening we had the dubious pleasure of Thin Lizzie at the controls. On alternate Friday and Saturday evenings she was joined by The Scarecrow who exchanged the wheel for the mike. I was indeed ready to play with Thin Lizzie a little bit. Miracles will never cease. That disgraceful piece of non PC crept past the editrice. Anyway I am not racially or sexually discriminatory in any way. I positively welcome with open arms into my car any one-legged black lesbians. Or two-legged white heterosexual ladies for that matter. But I must admit to being somewhat papaphobic, batophobic and demophobic. Quickly on.

The High Point estate to Bingo. This notorious mix of crappy sixties housing had a population comprised mostly of druggies, baddies and scroungers and was not exactly top of the taxi drivers hit parade, especially late at night. But it was not all the inhabitants' fault and to me it was a place of unremitting melancholy. Georgie was so poignantly prophetic when he observed some two hundred years ahead of his time.

> There children dwell who know no parents' care;
> Parents, who know no children's love, dwell there!
> Heart-broken matrons on their joyless bed,
> Forsaken wives, and mothers never wed;
> Dejected widows with unheeded tears,
> And crippled age with more than childhood fears;
> The lame, the blind, and, far the happiest they!
> The moping idiot, and the madman gay.

Two more town jobs in quick succession and then zero. Dead as a dodo so back to The Hutch. Being Monday night I only had two assistants. Leonardo, who was still badly hungover from the weekend, and Eric who was full of gut and humour as usual. Waiting on, waiting game. My perfect Waiting Game was for a Mr Winner, a regular gourmet client who could never quite bring himself to emerge anywhere near on time from the restaurant of his choice. However, at a waiting time of thirty pence a minute, I was more than happy to wile away an hour of my valuable time reading a book for a very cool eighteen quid. Not so cool were my least favourite punters, namely the rude and abusive. The first five minutes waiting time are always free in the trade and these buggers specialized in coming out six or seven minutes later without a word of apology but plenty of words of abuse. 'What's wrong with your sense of humour mate?' could only be answered that mine was possibly a trifle different to theirs, and by subtle insinuation slightly more elevated. Or if I hadn't inhaled enough distress or destress smoke recently it might come out a trifle differently. 'You are seriously unfunny, espèce de connard,' which usually managed to bring the conversation to an abrupt conclusion, but alas no tip.

> There must be a reason for all this inaction
> Does it mean that everything must change
> Sometimes I'm looking for perfection
> When I'm waiting on, waiting game
> When I'm waiting on , waiting game.

Certainly Van must know a thing or two about this taxiing business as well as cleaning windows. Does this inaction mean that my life is leading onto greater things? Hold on, what does one mean by greater things? Surely The Road is an honourable and fulfilling way of life? I have a bit of self respect back and can even pay a few bills de temps en temps. No, not with the old chèque en bois but in cash, glorious cash. Not a bad payoff in life. So, not greater things but different things. What is this lunatic perfection I'm seeking? No wonder my confrères in the Hutch on the Hill think I'm strange. In their vernacular all I really need is a bird and a bonk. No, its all right editrice, already excised. But I'm still looking for some kind of perfection, whatever you sods say. They would counter that it wouldn't do any harm to come out of the clouds for a while. Not easy when you have just lit another joint.

In that case Tommy, would you possibly mind cruising down to The Bear at your convenience for the perfect pick-up? The reason I love Van, apart from the fact that his music reaches my soul and brings me solace, is that he can be a grumpy old bugger and apparently doesn't always appreciate punters. He's certainly the man. You can possibly have too much perfection. The clients of The Bear certainly didn't let me down and they were indeed seven minutes late, but their cunning excuse that there had been leaves on the line in the saloon bar certainly had me laughing. You couldn't possibly take umbrage with anyone with a Reggie sense of humour. That's the thing about this job. Just when you really get really hacked off with it, you get the most ridiculous laugh and then we all kiss and make up. And then get arrested. God or Copernicus got it badly wrong. Its laughter that makes the world go round. Again Georgie was on the button.

> I too must yield, that oft amid these woes
> Are gleams of transient mirth and hours of sweet repose.

Thin Lizzie once said that swearing didn't become me, and for once I found the perfect if rather rude retort. 'When did you last become, Lizzie?' A lot of blushing later, I had won yet another Pyrrhic victory. When will you ever learn, you supercilious shit for brains? No tips for you today Tommy.

Ah tips, there's another dodgy subject. I never seemed to do as well as the others, but as they quite reasonably pointed out, I gave off the aura that my need wasn't quite as great as theirs. Or as Elise put it so pithily and prettily.

'Tommy, with your posh car, posh fags and posh accent, you don't deserve any fucking tips. The punters probably think you should sodding well tip them instead.'

Nevertheless, I never ceased to be amazed by the little old ladies who still gave me a quid tip on top of the three quid basic, while much wealthier members of society are unbelievably mean.

'Well, its bleeding obvious Tommy,' intoned Eric, 'that's why they're so bleeding rich. You may have a fancy degree but you've got no effing common sense.' I couldn't fault his impeccable logic as ever.

Anyway in normal reverse order, here are my three selections for Meanie of the Millennium. In the bronze medal position, stand up and take a bow my good Dutch friends who successfully kept up their well deserved reputation of The Mean Men of Europe. This lot had apparently jetted in from Malaga that morning after a total eclipse of the sun. The occasion was Gloria Garcia's marriage, Suffolk's wedding of the year and a banker benefit for us taxi drivers, or so I naively thought. Having rolled up at The Abbey Hotel, I was more than happy for once to dawdle in the manicured drive. Having waited an age, a flamboyantly dressed Dutch quartet just managed to waddle the ten metres from the blocked up entrance foyer of the hotel to my car through the light drizzle. Having given my distinguished guests the full benefit of the ultra smooth Gainsborough charm on the twenty minute journey, I parked the car impeccably in front of the ancient village church. Eleven pounds twenty pence please, I announced confidently. The male member of the quartet pulled out a wallet bulging with crisp twenty pound notes and placed one in my eager mitt. In reality I was just as greedy as QC when we really got down to it. Bloody hypocrite

Tommy. However when he magnanimously requested that I take twelve there was a sharp intake of breath from Wells Fargo's self-proclaimed top dog. In fact, my collapse was so total that I immediately reversed into the bride's Rolls Royce just as it rolled up behind me completely unnoticed. I didn't get where I am today by just being a pretty face, but as The Petty Officer put it so nastily one day in The Hutch after I had quoted Reggie again.

'Yes, where exactly are you in the world at this moment in time Tommy?'

Countless hours on the road later, I rolled up at the sumptuous Warmeg Hall for a midnight pickup at the wedding reception. Here was my chance to make amends. Sandy in the six seater had smugly informed me the previous evening he had not only picked up the four best set of legs it had ever been his good fortune to witness, he had also had a munificent tip and two kisses. Attention. Take a look at the Drivers Code that man. Past the suspiciously large numbers of policemen at the entrance lodge, down the candlelit half a mile drive and then a protracted loop round to the inner sanctum by the grand entrance hall. Here I was haughtily informed by the Hungarian major-domo to 'park over there with the others' as he pointed to the serried ranks of Omega Cars parked menacingly in battle formation. There had been many taxi wars in the past but I had thought they were long gone. Equally menacing were the security guards surrounding my car. Again I icily pointed out that my pickup was booked for midnight precisely and, as I was a very busy man, could the major-domo get cracking and send one of his minions to fetch Miss Campbell at once. He continued to point to the parking spot like a football referee theatrically giving a penalty after a particularly dastardly professional foul. It was rapidly growing into a Belfast-like stand-off and I didn't exactly alleviate the atmosphere by mischievously apologising for the quality of my fractured English and that the major-domo possibly hadn't quite got my drift. He may have been mid-European in origin but he was shit hot on this brand of English sarcasm. The situation was getting seriously out of hand when we were all rescued by the sudden arrival of Miss Campbell. I drove off with my spoils and casually flicked a 'V' sign out of my window in mock triumph and then for good measure blew the major-domo a kiss. Anyway I swept Miss Campbell back to Sutton Market. Imagine my surprise when she asked to stop at a cashpoint. It wasn't exactly what I expected with a client from The Sutton Palace. Surprise turned to consternation when the machine swallowed up her card. It transpired she was a friend of a friend helping out with the drinks and not a guest at all. The fare and a half rate was now sixteen pounds eighty pence but I had to settle for a tenner after the night porter refused to offer her a loan. Sod society weddings.

After that Ronnie Corbett type diversion, onto the silver medal position. Come on up and collect your medal Mr Jimmy Hayloft, late of Ipswich Town Football Club and reputably on a modest ten thousand smackers a week and therefore not exactly a candidate for the poorhouse. I picked him up from The Copocana Beach very late one Saturday night and made a slight tactical mistake when I asked brightly, 'have you been moved to Derby on business' on being informed by him that he commuted to that fair city. However, I showed nifty footwork in turning the conversation around to safer pastures and, when I finally dropped him off at his highly desirable village residence, I fully expected a right result. The fare was eighteen pounds and I was rather disappointed when only a crisp twenty quid note appeared. Disappointment turned to fury when I realized he both expected and pocketed the two pounds change. Sod footballers.

But after a Booker type huddle, the jury had no option but to give the gold medal to a suitably anonymous business man for the following cheeky number. I picked up this immaculately attired Mr X from the railway station at six thirty one fine May evening and proceeded to allow him to share in the enjoyment of a pulsating cricket World Cup semi-final between Australia and South Africa. We just had time to drive to his palatial period property in the highly desirable village of Kersey before Alan Donald agonizingly ran himself out after it had looked for all the world that Herr Klusener had done it again. Mr X was obviously an avid cricket fan and as I smarmily asked for my nine pound pence eighty fare, I sensed there was going to be another big winner in a minute as he brought out the expected bulging wallet. What I didn't quite expect was to be given another crisp twenty pound note and a regal 'just give me ten'. Oh, the sheer audacity of the man to give me precisely a twenty pence tip. I couldn't possibly get angry with the guy. Beaten at my own game. What upper class. Up businessmen. Omar of course was ahead of the game.

> 'How sweet is mortal Sovranty'-think some:
> Others - 'How blest the Paradise to come !'
> Ah, take the cash and waive the Rest;
> Oh, the brave Music of a distant Drum !

In reality one of my best ever tips came from a most unexpected source. Comme d'habitude. I took a little old lady from the well-used railway station for the little run to the fossilized habitation of Lavenham. The fare was a fossilized seven pounds fifty. However the LOL gave me yet another £20 note and in a very meek voice said, 'keep the change please.' I think that I had better do this vocation for another three years hard because I still haven't got a clue how it works.

One of the most memorable happenings in the cab occurred one apparently ordinary Wednesday night late in February. I picked up a young couple from La Vieille Maison and this fine establishment had obviously worked its magic once more as they seemed un peu amoreux as they vacated the restaurant. In any event as they had got into the back of the car and self evidently weren't interested in the guided tour routine, I for once concentrated on the job in hand, namely getting them to RAF Wattisham safe and sound. I turned up the music and disappeared into the zone. Subconsciously I became aware of the odd nudge in the back of my seat. The nudges increased gradually in tempo until they became positively frenetic and even for a man of my limited sensitivity, it was almost obvious what was going off. I turned up the music louder and louder until they came magnificently just as Van was belting out Full Force Gale. They were certainly lifted up by something. When we arrived at Wattisham they were still locking horns as it were and I hadn't got the heart to disturb them. Who said I lacked soul? After several minutes they eventually disentangled themselves and, dishevelled and sheepish, stumbled out of the car. The gentleman's barely audible 'how much mate' was met by my hearty 'ten pounds for the fare, one pound waiting time, two pounds kissing time and twenty pounds tupping time.' As he recoiled at my cheek, I added helpfully that I would break a rule of a lifetime and take a cheque on this special occasion. Wordlessly he made out the cheque and off they jolly well went, hand in hand. What a pleasing sight. When I looked at the cheque it was made out for fifty pounds. I warned you at the beginning that you always have to be on your guard in this line of business.

PS And if that anonymous officer is still mystified as to why the said cheque was never cashed, the simple reason is that it was carefully framed and now has a place of honour on my study wall with his name neatly deleted.

'You have a major attitude problem Tommy,' lectured the unctuous QC, 'you have got to learn to treat your fares with tender loving care, not bulldoze them into submission.'

'For a start QC,' I replied promptly, 'you can't have an attitude problem, major or otherwise. It is not possible to put two nouns together like that. For example take the terrible modern invention of the Scotland and England teams. Where have all the good old adjectives gone, long time passing? One either has a good, bad or indifferent attitude, not a problem. You could have said don't give me that attitude, my boy. That would have been perfectly acceptable grammatically. So do I have a bad attitude to the fares or am I just a problem?

'Case proven Tommy,' concluded QC smugly.

There's the rub. Behind the inebriated verbosity and pomposity, I bleed. I hurt like hell inside. Brought up into the strict post war family values society and allied to a typical public school education, we were taught not to show any emotion at home and certainly never to show weakness at school. Like thousands of other unfortunates I learnt to bury my emotions at a prepubescent age. And old habits die very hard. Thus one learnt to disguise ones innermost weaknesses for fear of ridicule, and my defences were built on the sands of apparent self confidence and arrogance. Whenever I felt threatened I always struck back with naked verbal aggression to hide my insecurity. Of course I'm a fucking failure. From riches to rags. No wife, no children, no home. No method, no guru, no teacher. I certainly need a lot more help from Van.

> There is a presence deep within you
> Sometimes they call it higher flame
> And the leaves come tumbling down, remember
> I'll be waiting on, waiting game
> I'll be waiting on, waiting game.

The leaves were certainly tumbling down outside in the wind and rain but I badly needed that Presence as well. Where oh where could I find it?

'Wakey, wakey Car 13, get your elegant arse down to The Bear.' I dutifully rolled down to afore-mentioned hostelry where the landlady explained that my fare was 'a bit worse for wear but wouldn't be any trouble.' Ha, I had heard that one before and I replied primly that I didn't take drunks. What a hypocrite, you pisspot. Eventually we negotiated an agreement where I would take my unfortunate fare if one of the pub's regulars came along to give assistance if necessary. And it was more than necessary because by the time we arrived at the salubrious Bosmere Heights estate the guy wasn't just asleep, he was virtually unconscious. The regular slipped me a fiver but that wasn't nearly enough. After quarter of an hour of cajoling and persuading we eventually managed to haul the guy's fifteen stone frame out of the car. After further huffing and puffing, I left him out for the count on the canvas of the flat's car park with the poor regular to look after him. The point was I couldn't possibly have left him alone because I would be morally as well as legally responsible if he went into a coma or, even worse, passed on to that Great Brewery in the Sky. Waiting on, waiting on.

That reminds me of another embarrassing episode one Saturday night long ago. I had just left The Café Gascon after my usual large cappuccino, fag and sly observation of pretty waitresses, when I noticed with horror that I had a puncture in the near front tyre and it was flat as Twiggy used to be. It had just struck eleven o'clock on the old church clock and we were heading for the peak period. I radioed into The Scarecrow saying confidently 'that I would just be a few minutes' and he mumbled something inaudible plus a loud shit and bugger. Of course we weren't allowed to swear over the airwaves in case Big Brother was listening. If he hadn't got anything better to do on a Saturday night than monitoring taxi conversations, he must be the saddest person in Britain.

Back to my specific problem. Being parked on a steep slope, I had to take a big risk in damaging the punctured tyre by driving over a hundred yards in order to find a suitably flat surface to do the business. Some hope, because although I am multi-lingual and highly intelligent, these admirable skills were bloody useless to the job in hand. My hands were designed for driving, drinking and denuding, not for such menial tasks as changing a wheel. Thus by the time I had located the relevant tools and managed to get the wheel trim off, my hands were already filthy with oil. And by the time I had spent several minutes struggling ineffectually with the first wheel nut, or whatever the damn things are called,

I was soaked to the skin in the driving rain which had started again right on cue. I got back into the car for another few minutes cursing and sulking. I was getting increasingly twitchy for another reason. The area I had parked in was rather dimly lit and there was an increasing number of dodgy looking characters and drunks passing, and I felt suddenly very vulnerable. Thus it was that I nearly jumped a mile when there was a gentle tap on the driver's window. Oh, it's all right, its the cavalry, or rather a solitary footslogging policeman. While he sympathized with my dire situation, he said he wasn't allowed to assist me. However he did have the bright idea of phoning the AA who I had never used since joining yonks ago. Why not now for a starter? He also said he and his colleagues would keep a periodic eye on me. As my recent dealings with the police had all been unfortunate to say the least, this very helpful constable almost restored my earlier faith in them. Anyway I called the AA and they informed me that they would have someone round 'in an hour'. So far, so good. Not so good when they hadn't even given any confirmation over an hour later, although in fairness to them I suppose it was their rush hour as well. Well, who the hell wants to work on a Saturday night? The future definitely didn't look rosy as the hordes continued to go past on their way to their favourite fast food takeaway, Best in Suffolk, a blatant lie as this dubious kebab house has poisoned more people in our fair county than any other eating establishment. Or perhaps that's what they meant. This wasn't what I meant about The Waiting Game. And this certainly wasn't a game any more. It was now nearing one o'clock. The reader may perfectly reasonably ask why the hell didn't I make another effort to change the wheel myself? That's an excellent philosophical question. And the answer as well. Well, work it out for yourselves, you normal people.

Anyway the panic factor was rising rapidly after a couple of yobs whacked the back of my car in passing, although I had of course locked myself in. A joint was more than called for. Oh shit, I had left the stuff back at the flat. More panic.

Then salvation, or was it? Two young couples were going past and came up to the car and asked if I wanted assistance. One of the lads said he was a mechanic and he could change it in a jiffy if I gave them a freebie home. Home was the remote village of Rickinghall, all of fifteen miles away. I didn't hesitate and nor did they. The two lads combined to do a fair imitation of a Ferrari pit stop and in five minutes flat we were on the road again. I whizzed off to Rickinghall, dropped the fab four off with profuse thanks, and was back in town comfortably before the two o'clock throwing out from The Copocana Beach. Throwing out and throwing up being the operative expressions for many of the faithful that night.

By Monday morning news of my exploits (or rather lack of them) had seeped back to the rest of the Wells Fargo crew. I was met with derision and cat calls. Who had ever heard of a taxi driver who couldn't change a wheel? 'What a prat' was about the politest expression that greeted me. What made it even worse was that The Milky Bar Kid had had a puncture at approximately the same time as me and even he had been back on the road within quarter of an hour. Oh the shame of it. I was still blushing furiously when I gratefully returned to the car. The scornful buggers had rewarded me with yet another nickname. After Tommy the Toff and Posh Spice, I was in future to be known as the AA Man. Fair does. He who lives by the verbal sword fully deserves to be painfully impaled on it. But I still hated myself for blushing, another deadly weakness even at the ripe old age of fifty.

I was going to say mature but that isn't true either. And I still haven't had the nerve after all this time to tell the Wells Fargo crew that when I went to have the puncture repaired, I was informed by the Dial a Tyre man that the tyre was totally buggered as I had evidently driven for quite a while with a puncture because there were tell-tale filings of rubber at the bottom of the tyre. A taxi driver who not only couldn't change a wheel but didn't even realize he had a puncture. And to add financial insult to mental injury the tyre was only two days old. Keep writing Tommy and give up the day job. I had long wished for the following epitaph. 'He was a crap driver but not a bad writer.' Would my wish ever be fulfilled?

Talking of new tyres reminds me that I had punctured the other front one only two weeks earlier when I omitted to observe a dwarf brick wall when carrying out a delicate reversing manoeuvre. It has always been my proud boast that in over one hundred thousand and fifty miles on the road, I had never had an accident. That boast may be strictly true in that I had never hit any moving objects when moving in a forward direction, but I had had more than my fair share of problems with stationary objects when in the act of reversing. Take the little incident involving Gloria Garcia's wedding Rolls where I had to take out a second mortgage on a nonexistent property to pay for the repairs. Other offences to be taken into consideration before sentence involved a curiously non-static lamp post, a second dwarf brick wall (obviously my Achilles heel, those crafty sods), a badly parked Wells Fargo car, and finally a nasty little concrete coal bunker.

Back in the Hutch the Petty Officer was moaning about the world in general, The Milky Bar Kid was boring on about cars (surely the most boring subject in the world, after house prices of course), The Fat Controller was hungry and QC was counting his money.

> I am the observer who is observing
> I am the brother of this snake
> I am the serpent filled with venom
> A god of love and a god of hate.

I am certainly the observer who is observing all the time. In my twisted mind I am also the serpent filled with venom who is waiting to cut down anyone who either crosses me, is even vaguely successful or just has the nerve to do me wrong. I'm the god who would love to love but is filled with hate against this unjust world that has turned against me. Sometimes I think my only talent is to criticize or belittle. Hell I just despise myself. Georgie, sock it to me.

> What is your angry Satire worth,
> But to arouse the sleeping hive,
> And send the raging Passions forth,
> In bold, vindictive, angry flight,
> To sting wherever they alight.

Luckily Eric broke my self recriminatory reverie with his usual happy crappy.

'You look like a constipated con man, Tommy, perched on that stool like a Little Boy Blue.' He was always one to mix his metaphors well, our Eric. There I go again.

Elise waded in with a 'come on, pretty man, give our Elise a nice smile.' I was back in the loop and ready even to rock n roll with the best.

'Okey-dokey, what's next', I asked in my most solicitous way to TFC. Wally from The Bear to the Highpoint estate of course. Wally was one of our regular crapulent patients who tested your patience at the best of times. And this wasn't the best of times as I limped round the Market Hill. The Wuffa District Council had in its wisdom inaugurated a new set of traffic lights, presumably in lieu of early Christmas decorations. They had always suffered from premature illumination. These lights were obviously specifically designed to ensnare both wary and unwary motorists into their little web. After quarter of an hour crawling in and out of the awkward twentieth century cobble stones precisely laid out at great expense with the complexity of a maze, I was already fuming, both literally and in the approved French manner. Oh yes, the Wuffa District Council loved its authenticity. However when I wrote to them suggesting we return to the original horse-drawn Hackney Carriages in the interests of true authenticity, I was naturally met with a dusty response. I think they had a problem with their giant pooper-scoopers. But then I couldn't resist risking my future as a Private Hire driver by writing just one more letter to the council suggesting that 'in light of previous correspondence and a sense of humour bypass I now propose that they amend their name to the Hackneyed District Council forthwith'. Serve them right for selecting such a pretentious historical name. Surprisingly I never received a response to this little foray, but I suspect that Mr Smiley is lurking round the dustbins in the bus station trying to catch me in delicto flagrante, although the thought of him being caught in the inverse position doesn't bear thinking about.

By the end of this petit diversion, I had at last reached The Bear but there was no sign of Wally. After ten minutes of sustained irritation on my part, he teetered out. Teetered being the operative word because he first bounced off the bonnet of the car inadvertently stubbing his fag out at the same time. After three abortive attempts, he finally managed to achieve the delicate manoeuvre of opening the passenger door and fell in with aplomb.

'Howstgong Tommy, you old fart'.

'Fine thank you, Wally, you bacchic bugger,' I replied in kind.

However, this was nowhere near offensive enough to deter Wally and we had a pleasant five minute journey while he recounted the vicissitudes of the day. Profuse thanks, a quid tip, more fumblings and he finally weaved off into the ether or rather nether. I never minded benevolent drunks. Humility Thomas.

And now for something completely different, speed-bumps. There is the round top, the flat top, the speed cushion, the speed table, or the rumble strip. Take your pick. It was once calculated in The Hutch that we averaged one thousand bumps a week. One thousand bumps a week! Think of the damage to our shock absorbers and our bottoms. Also think about all that extra pollution being needlessly generated. And the cost. Around a thousand quid on average for a bump seems a bit excessive to me, especially when there must be at least five hundred of the damned things in Sutton Market. No wonder our Council Tax bill has gone not just through the roof but into bloody orbit. Calm down Tommy.

On to another hectic Saturday night starting with Jools, the proprietor of the Déja-Vous, one of those pretentious wine bars which seem to be mushrooming even in backward Sutton Market. Knowing his little ways I broke another habit of a lifetime by popping in to tell Jools that time was of the essence. He said six minutes (why not five, like any normal person). I said two and went round the block again. After precisely nine minutes he ambled out and then casually informed me that he had ordered an Indian takeaway from round the corner. Six minutes later we were finally off to the oh so twee village of Chelsworth. In quarter of an hour flat I had received a potted history of his success in rivalling Wetherspoons in building an inn empire. Which was why I now found myself bouncing down a rough track to a derelict hovel of a thatched cottage. I couldn't be bothered to charge him waiting time and roared gratefully away in search of better things. But no. I was almost back into Sutton Market when Thin Lizzie informed me that Jools had just phoned to say that he had left a bottle of red plonk in the back of my car and would I mind (her words) turning round and returning it. There was only one thing to say. What a plonker.

On to another gloomy November evening and I couldn't get in the mood. The fares were spasmodic and ordinary and I descended into depression. I needed a lift, or a shock to my system. As usual I got the latter. 'The Bear for Timmy to Kings Road post-haste'. Post-haste indeed. Twelve minutes after landing on the pub's forecourt, I was still waiting. And then I saw him. An emaciated midget with thick horn-rimmed glasses immaculately attired but with the drunkard's all too familiar rolling gait. He slid into the passenger's seat and fixed me with a gimlet stare.

'You're new,' he intoned expressionlessly, but in a very broad Geordie accent.

'I may be new to you but I assure you I'm not new to The
Waiting Game. Sir.'

My patently sarcastic sir never failed to stir up punters. He
grunted something inaudible while still fixing me with the stare.
Off we not so jolly well went with him murmuring a string of
soft Geordie garbage totally incomprehensible to me.

However I caught the end of the next not so sweet nothing.
'★★★★★★★★★★★★★★★★★ , you toffee-nosed southern shit.'

My golden maxim in the car was if the fares are polite, you are
equally polite. However if they are gratuitously rude or aggressive
the verbal gloves are off. In this case, recognizing the tell-tale
danger signals, I tried a bit of equivocation at first.

'I don't think that's very constructive sir,' I replied icily. The
trouble was that when dangerous or unpleasant situations
transferred from body to brain, I always became very stiff and
formal and this often exacerbated the problem. Also to be
perfectly honest (what a stupid expression) I had never used sir
since I left school over thirty years ago. However for the purposes
of this job I had resurrected the hated S word to be used exclusively
on my most unpleasant and displeasing clients. This nuance seemed
to transfer all too well to the beneficiaries of my politesse and
Timmy certainly picked up the vibes all right. The next two
minutes were filled with mutterings of which the only words I
deciphered were something to do with my lack of parentage, sexual
activity and a very intimate part of a female's anatomy. Oddly
enough the really offensive words were said that little bit louder and
clearer. Luckily the short joy-trip was almost over, or so I naively
thought. After he had asked in a minatorily civilized way for the

fare, he unfathomably gave me a two quid tip. 'Twenty quid, take five'. He then proceeded to harangue me unmercilessly for five minutes. Even after all my experience on the road I am still crap in this sort of situation. Frankly, below all the bluster, I just don't like any form of unpleasantness. I go all taut inside, my stomach knots and my breathing becomes shallow as my pathetic fear factor triggers in. Fortunately or unfortunately all the opposition sees is an aloof and toffee-nosed shit and this enrages them further. Timmy was no exception and he waded in enthusiastically. I took it all stoically and metaphorically on the chin until he cuffed me in the face, playfully or maliciously I didn't care.

'Don't you dare touch me, you northern piece of filth,' mixing haughty superiority with the language of the gutter, although anger and fear were about equal emotions. The next couple of minutes involved an angry stare in, with me trying to muster all the hatred I was capable of into my eyes. Eventually he unlocked visionary horns, got out of the car and slammed it with the utmost venom I had ever seen. Oh yes, I had 'won' again.

> There is a presence deep within you
> Some people call it higher power in flame
> When the leaves come tumbling down, remember
> I'll be waiting on, waiting game
> I'll be waiting on, waiting game.

Where oh where was that 'presence deep within you?' It must be lurking somewhere but I sure had a lot more of The Waiting Game to come before I found that singularly elusive Philosopher's Stone.

3.   BRIGHT SIDE OF THE ROAD

> From the dark end of the street
> To the bright side of the road
> We'll be lovers once again
> On the bright side of the road.

It had certainly been the dark end of the street when I got divorced what seemed like a lifetime ago. It had also been a psychotic roller coaster in the first year afterwards, as I not so gaily mixed unemployment with a perilous cocktail of alcohol, tranquillisers and self pity. Georgie was right on the button in his usual nitty gritty fashion.

> Ye, in the floods of limpid poison nurst,
> Where Bowl the second charms like Bowl the first;
> Say how and why the sparkling ill is shed,
> The Heart which hardens, and rules the Head.

Then I found work, or rather The Waiting Game found me. I was in my usual haunt at The Rising Sun one freezing Tuesday evening in March waxing lyrical about world affairs and rugby, when Graham the landlord suddenly interjected.

'Tommy, you are always driving round in that blessed

Morgan of yours doing bugger all. And you also conveniently ignore the fact that you're now too geriatric to pull your ageing carcass out of the saddle, let alone pull the birds. Get real. Why don't you sell the damned thing, get a nice new car, sign on as a taxi driver and earn a proper living for once.'

Naturally I wasn't at all appreciative of this Suffolk brand of tough love and told Graham to 'fuck off, you jobanowl,' which wasn't very constructive either. Me work, a self-confessed workshy dreamer and self-appointed pub philosopher? The City had seemed to suit me brilliantly with its bacchanalian lunches and relentless Lords and Twickers networking. However Graham's suggestion had sown a seed. But work would mean that I would be for the high jump, or much, much worse, back into the frightening Real World. But reality in the familiar form of the bailiff had again come knocking. I had to do something.

Once the insidious germ had been planted in the leftover pin hole of my brain, the inevitable followed. So it was that exactly one month later I found myself reporting for duty at the illustrious headquarters of Messrs Wells Fargo Private Hire after surprisingly surviving both my police check and medical examination. Even more surprising was the fact that I had actually followed Graham's advice and flogged the beloved Morgan. Well, I hadn't got a lot of choice, had I? I was now the proud possessor of a gleaming new silver Peugeot 406 Hdi (high density idiot), fully equipped with all the latest gadgets including air-conditioning, passenger ejector seats and a brilliant hi fi system from which Van could effortlessly blast out all those irritating mobile phones and their ludicrous ringing tones.

Anyway, on the road I not so jollily went and after a while I suddenly realized the pain had eased and that I was also drinking for pleasure, not oblivion. Omar was the man this time.

> Come, fill the Cup, and in the Fire of Spring
> The Winter Garment of Repentance fling;
> The Bird of Time has but a little way
> To fly – and Lo ! the Bird is on the Wing.

Indeed it was and, much to my amazement, I was soon actually enjoying The Road. I hadn't got to sell anything, the work was all given to me on a plate courtesy of Wells Fargo in return for the rent of the radio, or desk money as it was called. Neither was there any paperwork (The Inland Revenue missed that sentence). All I had to do was make an informed and objective approximation of my profits that proved a damned sight more accurate in percentage terms than any of our Cheerless Chancellor's estimates or Messrs Enrons errant accountants for that matter. Anyway I pay more than enough tax already via petrol and cigarette duties, the latter nonsmuggled I'm heartily ashamed to admit. And when I returned battered and bruised after a sixteen hour Saturday double shift, there were no useless reports to write or trifling telephone messages to return. Just a dull glow of satisfaction in a job well done, young girls returned safely, benevolent drunks likewise, and cash in grubby hand from honest work. Christ I was becoming a paradigm of virtue. They always say that work deadens the pain. What they didn't add is that it also gives you self-confidence and self-respect, precious commodities in which I had always been distinctly lacking. I could now look clearly at that ice blue–eyed bugger in the mirror in the morning and think he's not all bad after all.

And laughs. There was always something ludicrous happening in 'The Hutch on the Hill'. Today it was a seriously stupid discussion on the Wuffa District Council's draconian 'Dress Code'. Leonardo had recently been reprimanded by Mr Smiley for wearing jogging trousers. This had caused our backroom lawyers to consult the 'Code' in detail. Eventually we found the relevant section nestling comfortably between Drivers Conditions 43 and 45 which suitably covered lewd behaviour (unspecified) and smoking illegal (un-named) 'substances', the sentence for both heinous offences being the immediate removal of one's Private Hire Licence, plus your testicles, should you have any. That should *encourager les autres* nicely. Back to The Dress Code. Here we found that the following forms of clothing are not acceptable for a driver to wear.

1. Garments containing printing or wording which may be construed by the Authorizing Officer or any passenger as being offensive. (Plenty there for Mr Smiley and Mrs Whitehouse's progeny to get stuck into).

2. Sleeveless singlets. (No room for manoeuvre here but luckily The Fat Controller can't read).

3. Torn jeans or trousers. (This is an unequivocal statement from the Council that plain trousers are just as unacceptable as torn jeans which leaves most of us in limbo as it were).

4. Shell suits, tracksuits or jogging bottoms. (At least something is pretty clear cut).

5.   Stiletto heeled shoes or flip flops. (Obviously Mr Smiley has a serious problem here).

6.   Shorts, <u>other </u>than of a smart tailored design. (That's all right then, with Mr Armani Smiley to adjudicate).

Curiously enough the above was strictly a list of what we couldn't wear, nothing at all about what we could, which would seem rather more important to my uninitiated eyes.

Naturally after that little perusal the conversation turned to sex, and very shortly after that, to Elise. Tonker opined sagely (well of course he didn't but you know what I mean) that The Dress Code should really read the Undress Code as, according to a strict interpretation of the above, it was not acceptable for Elise to wear her usual sexy black trousers revealing her exact thong line (on reflection, to keep down the base devices and desires of fellow drivers that seems eminently sensible), but if she took them off, her thong would be quite permissible (if permissive), especially if her blouse covered the vital lower regions. Shades of trouser suits from the swinging sixties came pleasantly to mind. However, Elise as usual effortlessly outwitted us pathetically limited males by announcing that she was quite willing to abandon her trousers if us blokes met her halfway as it were. Naturally there were no takers amongst our midst.

'You men are all the same,' she sneered (a rather sexy sneer actually), 'all talk but no fucking action.' For once there was a deadly hush in The Hutch as several grown men found a sudden attraction to their navels. Elise forty, men love. You wish. Even Leonardo couldn't handle this sexual Mary Magdalene head to head.

This mélange of reprobates and renegades had miraculously transformed my life. Feeling good was easy peasy as The Fat Controller sang the blues and I reflected idly on the decidedly odd direction that life had taken me.

Let's enjoy it while we can
Won't you help me sing my song
From the dark end of the street
To the bright side of the road.

Another somnolent Monday and most of us were back in The Hutch. Sandy was nursing a hangover of Herculean proportions and still miles over the limit. The Boy Racer had just broken another lap record. Sixty miles in forty five minutes from Stansted Airport. You do the sums. I just don't know how he never gets caught, although of course he does have a camera detector. Stack had had a hard game on Saturday afternoon, an even harder Saturday night and was consequently more morose than ever. Elise was as pretty as a picture and Leonardo was smirking. Eric was doing deals on his mobile and Tonker was nicking the last chocolate biscuit. The Scarecrow was back on driving duty after his ham-voiced heroics at the weekend. The Petty Officer was off on one of his mysterious account jobs and the Milky Bar Kid was adjusting his carburettors or whatever Milky Bars do in their spare time. I had just been mugged by QC and all was decidedly not well on the cash flow front. Everything normal in other words. Today's topic was pets.

The great debate was to be or not to be. Or rather should we take the little and large blighters or not? Elise naturally inclined to softness. However there had been a recent notorious Court case concerning some nondescript celebrity which left the matter up in the air, as it were. I was of the opinion that we were licensed to carry at most four passengers (i.e. people). Ergo we were people carriers (to invoke that ghastly term in sheer desperation), not dog carriers. If we were meant to carry animals, the Wuffa District Council would certainly have given us a comprehensive manifest of our permitted cargo.

'Get off your legal high horse, Tommy,' chipped in QC. 'Where's your soul ?' Not a bad question actually from that little master of rules and regulations and certainly not one I was prepared to answer.

Suddenly The Fat Controller interrupted our learned discussion. 'Tommy, Mr Goldfinger wants to go to Stansted pronto.' Now Mr Goldfinger was Wells Fargo's most illustrious client and had to be treated with due reverence. A self-made millionaire who dabbled in commodity futures or such like, he lived in a palatial Georgian pile appropriately named Claret Hall in the unspoilt village of Drinkstone. Don't mind if I do, as Rumpole would have said. Back to Goldfinger. That was the problem. He was too near home to what I used to be and it was far more difficult being deferential to my own kind, as I perceived it, than for people I still deemed to be below me. Ah, the trials and tribulations of lingering snobbery.

> And you, ye Poor, who still lament your fate,
> Forbear to envy those you call the Great;
> And know, amidst those blessings they possess,
> They are, like you, the victims of distress;
> While Sloth with many a pang torments her slave,
> Fear waits on guilt, and Danger shakes the brave.

Anyway I duly rushed off to Claret Hall where I was informed that a VIM (very important meeting) was still going on. I docilely waited for the great man's appearance reading my latest piece of escapism, Samuel Pepys, The Unequalled Self. Very apt. Twenty pages later he arrived, a bustling little double-chinned Napoleon with outsized briefcase in hand.

'Hi Tommy, lets go for it.'

And off we went for it. Out came the obligatory mobile and calls were made to Cape Town, Caracas and Cairo in quick succession. Gold, oil and artefacts were obviously hot today. Then a peremptory call to some poor unfortunate who was brusquely told to look for employment elsewhere, apparently because he just wasn't up to it, whatever 'it' was. Christ I despised the guy but, craven as ever, I just bit my tongue and said nothing. The next thing I knew he had retuned the radio and put his seat back to the prostrate position. Within a few minutes he was snoring like a wounded buffalo, so I had to endure the rest of the journey listening to Sing Something fucking Simple at full blast. And I thought that nauseating little musical love-in had gone out with the ark. I reeled against this twin assault to my ear drums and almost drove into a the white van in front of me. Mr G woke up just as we were entering the environs of Stansted then took his leave with a studiously polite thank you, I'm loathe to admit. The last I saw of him that day was his unattractive backside as he strutted imperiously into the terminal. Who said women had a monopoly on bitchiness? Georgie had my measure again all right.

> 'While some, with feebler heads and fainter hearts,
>   Deplore their fortune, yet sustain their parts–

Then shall I dare these real ills to hide
In tinsel trappings of poetic pride ?'

However, it hadn't taken very long for me to find out that
there was a truly seamy side of The Road as well. In fact, the
following notorious incident occurred during my very first week
at Wells Fargo.

It was approximately ten forty five on a Friday evening when
I innocently picked up two boisterous couples from The Bear and
transported them for a last quick one at the seedy Crooked Vine
on the High Point estate. As we drove into the dimly lit car park
I was vaguely aware of some figures at the far end, but thought
no more about it at the time. It was only when I went for my
well-earned break in The Hutch a couple of hours later that I
found out there had been a stabbing outside the Crooked Vine
round about eleven. That made me a very material witness
indeed. Common consensus in The Hutch based on the
ubiquitous taxi grape vine was that the assailant was a well known
local thug called Digger McVeigh.

After that life carried on normally for some time and I wasn't
traced by the police till Monday morning. Apparently the young
victim had since died so they were now dealing with a murder
inquiry. However, despite my proximity in both time and
distance to the stabbing, I was to prove a singularly ineffective
witness. When you watch Morse or Dalgleish, you often think
that witnesses are pretty feeble. However, when you are suddenly
directly involved, it is a totally different matter. Beyond the fact
that I had two young male and two female passengers, I could
barely offer any description at all. Of course it was dark and three
of them were in the back of the car, but I had been concentrating

on my driving and literally hadn't give them a second glance. Neither could I offer any useful information from my brief pit stop at the pub. My observation in my subsequent formal statement that my fares were pleasantly pissed fell on stony ground.

'Oh, the magistrates wouldn't like that,' was the bizarre reaction of the detective sergeant. Hello there. Point one was that, naively, I thought that it was my statement, not his. The second point, and far more importantly, the police were dealing with a brutal murder but seemed more interested in verbal niceties than finding the killer. When I asked if they had caught McVeigh yet, the sergeant pompously replied that he couldn't possibly discuss the possible identity of the perpetrator with a member of the public but 'they were actively pursuing their enquiries.' Yes, and they are still pursuing their useless enquiries over three years later while McVeigh continues to sun himself on a Brazilian beach. What a fucking shambles.

Another early lesson in my apprenticeship to the dark end of the street at Wells Fargo was administered one Tuesday evening in a bungled midnight pickup at The Café Gascon. This seemed a harmless enough exercise for a man of my calibre and I duly arrived five minutes early and settled down to wait a bit. I had been vaguely aware of driving past two or three loud gentlemen at the top of the Market Hill but thought nothing more about them at the time. Five minutes after midnight I was getting twitchy, but only to get the last fare over with so I could get home. The next thing I knew was that the three gentlemen had got into the car and ordered me to take them post-haste to the High Point estate. Despite a piercing signal of fear sinking to my guts, I tried to keep my cool.

'That's not possible, I'm afraid,' I said too brightly but with unwitting accuracy. 'I'm already waiting for a fare.'

At first they prevaricated, or whatever thugs do when thwarted. 'Come on mate, it will only take five minutes.' I stuck reluctantly to my guns and they upped the ante. 'We haven't got all fucking night, you pompous shit.'

Just then my fare emerged from The Café Gascon. However, salvation wasn't at hand because he took one look at the situation and not unnaturally said that he had decided to walk home after all. This left one pompous shit in the shit. As usual when you wanted the so and sos there was no sign of the fuzz. The Fat Controller had gone home and I was totally on my own. What to do? Despite being scared witless I desperately tried to clear my clouded brain. Although the situation wasn't looking very rosy on the hill, it would be a bloody sight darker in the wastelands of the High Point estate where I would be even easier prey. I just had to try and sweat it out. Was my fear being conveyed to the hunters? I tried a change of tack.

'I still can't take you, I'm afraid.' How often do we use in vain that innocent expression? 'I would lose my licence if I took you without a prior booking.' You hypocrite. You're quite happy to invoke the law when it suits you while pretending to be an anarchist the rest of the time.

'He would lose his licence if he took us,' they mimicked. Another rapid change of direction. 'I'll tell you what mate,' said the quieter spoken but infinitely more scary one in the front seat next to me, 'you know that it is illegal to drive without headlights.' It took me just a nanosecond to get his drift. Despite my funk, I fell back on the old tried and trusty cliché from my city days.

'I don't think that would be very constructive, sir.' However instead of making them even angrier, this feeble little manoeuvre was enough to bring another change of tack. I can only think they had become bored with their wretched hostage. Whatever, they suddenly slobbered out of the car and that gave me my opportunity. I accelerated with an alacrity which would have impressed even Nigel, but not before the front thug had indeed kicked out one of the headlights with his hob-nailed boots. Not a good night at the office.

A few weeks after the above incident, I had a third spine-tingler. It was a wild Saturday evening around midnight when Thin Lizzie asked over the blower if anyone fancied a London wait and return, fixed fare one hundred and fifty pounds, for a gentleman ominously known as Old Nick. As there didn't seem to be any immediate takers I naively said that I would give it a go.

'OK, Tommy, round to the Déja Vous pronto and just ask for Old Nick'. I did as I was told as usual and soon my mysterious fare emerged out of the gloom of the DV. Old Nick turned out to be a surprisingly youthful Nick, although judging by the length of an old wound on his darkly handsome and aquiline face, he should have been called Old Scar. Nick was quietly charming in a disquietingly Sicilian sort of way but we comfortably covered a suitably catholic range of subjects all the way to Brixton which he informed me rather ominously was 'the end of the road'. The heavy rain had abated soon after we left Sutton Market and for some reason I felt compelled to gun it at a not so steady ninety miles an hour all the way. Nick seemed pleased by our rapid progress so I eased my no smoking ban when he requested oh so charmingly 'for a quick puff'. He had already informed me that he had to be at his 'music studio' before two o'clock. Apparently he was a music entrepreneur and a very busy man. Hence the reason for the rather unconventional visiting hours. Being a gullible sort of guy and needing the money badly I didn't give much thought to the matter. Anyway, at one fifty two precisely we turned into a dingy street of three storey period properties in Brixton and I was advised to wait in the car for a few minutes as Nick disappeared into the darkness. After quarter of an hour had elapsed, I started at last to give a modicum of thought to my situation. Where was the studio? Where was Nick? What the hell was I doing in this godforsaken place? I would at that moment have given any amount of money (no, money didn't come into this equation) to emerge from the dark end of this menacing street to the bright side of any damned road. Bad vibes were enveloping me as my breathing became shallow, my palms started sweating and the familiar tightness bore down inexorably on my chest. Dark figures were moving in the shadows and I felt no alleviation in my plight by slamming on the sophisticated self locking system of my car. Or should it now read coffin? Just as my heart felt ready to explode I noticed the distinctly sinister figure of Nick approaching the car. I slid back the locks and he slid in. I was too shaken to say anything and my companion seemed strangely detached. The return journey was eerily quiet but totally uneventful and I dropped him back at the DV just as the clock was striking four o'clock. Nick in turn wordlessly dropped a bulky envelope back onto the vacated passenger seat and was gone. I gingerly opened the envelope and pulled out five big ones. Shit, what a night. I had just become a hard drugs-runner. That would really learn me to make facetious comments.

Into this life we're born
Baby sometimes we don't know why
And time seems to go by so fast
In the twinkling of an eye.

Indeed it does. So many things to be done so before I had to confront that 'higher power in flame' and perhaps not so much time in hand as I thought.

Money, no insoluble problem at the moment. Work, I could survive. Emotion, mega problem. I had made huge strides in several directions since the distress of my divorce, but there was still a massive void to be filled. Since Megan had walked out on me I had been agonizingly alone. We had had what I considered was a good marriage for over nineteen years. But what is a good marriage? Not what other people see but what goes on behind closed doors. Unfortunately not enough went on. Megan was a sparky, pretty and intelligent Welsh lass whom I had adored since we first met at a London undergraduate ball all those years ago. We had both gone with different partners but by the end of that unforgettable evening we were an item to use the modern if crude vernacular.

I also missed the boys like hell. Jack was now eighteen and Viv sixteen. On our separation they had sided with their mother and Viv had sacrificed a brilliant cricket future by finishing his education in France with her.

Where had it all gone wrong? I realized now it wasn't just the money. It was the selfishness. I always had to win. I had to come first. Megan had given up a promising career in publishing to bring up the boys. I was only conspicuous by my eternal absences. Megan strived manfully to keep the family together, but the emotional dam broke with my financial demise. She could take financial disaster but not the self-obsessed introspection that went with it. What a pitiful fool.

Since Megan left I had been living like a monk, or should I say priest ? No sex and too much booze. I had switched off from life emotionally to save myself from taking further punishment. In my job I had all the dolly birds in the world to look at but all I really wanted to do was to look into the soul of a mature woman. Megan had fired me as ruthlessly as Mr Goldfinger had dealt with his hapless employee. So was it finally all over on the love front?

As providence would have it, a few days later I had to pick-up a Mrs Sharpestone from Plantagenet Street, a road naturally consisting solely of Victorian terraced houses. Number fourteen was unremarkable in every way, which made the sudden appearance of my fare even more surreal. With a frisson of excitement I recognised her immediately, even after an elapse of time of over thirty years. She still had that coltish figure I remembered so well, long blonde hair, endearingly quirky slow smile, and of course those wonderful long legs, even if presently obscured from view by tight blue jeans.

'Hello Tiff,' I just managed to blurt out, the problem being that after the thrill of seeing her again, I was immediately consumed by a burning embarrassment. The last time we had met, I was an up and coming banker. Now I was just a menial taxi driver. What a fall from grace it must appear to her as well.

'Tommy, it is Tommy, isn't it,' she offered hesitantly. 'What the hell are you doing here', she added sharply, but then fixed me with that soft smile which electrified my body as of old. 'Oh, Bosmere Garage please.' Think Tommy, think. But I only had two precious minutes.

'Research,' I improvised brilliantly, but then relapsed into an awkward silence. Out of the corner of my eye I noticed her hands twitching just like my mother's did when confronted with a 'difficult' situation. So she was nervous as well. Yes, but was she on fire? Even more important, was she available?

'I'm divorced,' I said crudely, before I had a chance to bite off my scabrous tongue. Where oh where was that silver-tongued smoothie when he was most needed? Raw emotion, raging self-doubt and sheer discomfort had reduced me to the verbal nadir of a monosyllabic moron. How I hated myself for my abject weakness.

Luckily Tiff came to my rescue.

'My husband died six months ago,' she replied with quiet dignity.

Then, changing the subject rapidly, she added that her car was being serviced in town today, hence this journey. Thus from banality came serendipity.

> Tis all a Chequer-board of Nights and Days
> Where Destiny with Men for Pieces plays:
> Hither and thither moves, and mates, and slays;
> And one by one back in the Closet lays.

My two minutes were up.

'Give me a ring sometime Tommy,' she said getting out of the car so, so elegantly and handing me a business card. 'Lovely to see you again.' And then she flashed me that enigmatic smile and was gone.

I was still in a state of shock and drove round to the Café Gascon toute de suite without even consulting TFC. Quelle horreur but I badly needed time to think. Over my usual large cappuccino and Dunhill I microscopically dissected every word she had said. She had started with a hell and ended with a lovely. What did the switch of those two deceptively innocuous words signify? That seemingly casual 'give me a ring sometime.' Did it mean what I fervently hoped it did? Did she wish to reignite that stormy relationship of our late teens? Hell, I felt like a bloody teenager again. At least I now knew my heart was still in good working order.

I drifted off into another reverie as I went back thirty years in time. Tiff had been my first proper girlfriend. We met in prosaic fashion at a Sutton Market Young Farmers Ball. However there was nothing prosaic about our relationship thereafter. I was studying for my bankers exams in London at the time but came back every weekend to see her for the best part of a year. And what a year. Because, behind the placid exterior, Tiff had a truly passionate and volatile nature as well as that penetrating intellect. How I loved that brilliant mind almost as much as that delicious body. This led to any number of blazing rows followed by tearful and passionate make ups. And I still had the scars to prove it. But that was the attraction. That deliciously anguished feeling of flirting with danger and disintegrating into obsession. Bliss was it that dawn to be alive and living on the edge of a cliff. Tiff was certainly my first true love. But was it possible that she could now be my last as well?

Little darlin come with me
Won't you help me share my load
From the dark end of the street
To the bright side of the road.

Please, please, please let it be so. I couldn't survive losing her a second time. First time round I had lost her by a combination of her going away to Sheffield University and my unaccountable lethargy on the literary front. Men!

Back to work after that extended time out and a deserved bollocking from The Fat Controller for my unscheduled disappearance. I was always moaning at some of the other drivers for their unexplained absences and now I had committed the selfsame felony. To placate the ire of TFC I resolved to put in a faultless shift. Unfortunately my first fare after the resumption was a querulous old lady called Victoria from the Saint Felix Nursing Home. On ringing the entrance buzzer I was instructed by Victoria to come up to her room on the first floor where she would require wheelchair assistance. Well, I had picked up this old battle-axe before and I didn't remember her being in a wheelchair. However, I well remembered that in stature and bearing she was identical to that other old queen.

'Good morning young man, you're late,' was her opening salvo. I muttered my apologies as I fiddled with the wheelchair by the entrance. 'Not that one,' she roared imperiously, 'go and fetch the one in the entrance foyer.'

Already rattled by these nasty verbal bouncers I'm sorry to say that having ducked the first two I couldn't resist hooking the third.

'First I am not a young man even if I must appear so to an ageing spinster of your decrepitude. Secondly neither am I deaf which you have obviously assumed judging by your ear-splitting instructions. Finally in case you are blind as well to go with all your other frailties, nor am I a canine taxi driver.'

However if I thought that Victoria would simply crumple under my withering broadside, I was well wrong to use modern parlance.

'So that's the way you want to play it, young man,' she replied acidly while fixing me with an icy stare.

I snarled back and off we not so jolly well went in the general direction of the lift. As I tried to ease her wizened body plus unwieldy wheelchair into that confined space, I inadvertently whacked her heavily bandaged feet against the lift wall.

'Ahhh, you clumsy fool. Young Leonardo wouldn't have done that.'

This time I took it on the chin, although I couldn't resist a subversive grimace behind her back. The truth was she had wounded me. I felt like that guilty little schoolboy again back at prep school, but of course I managed to maintain my ever present hostile exterior. On reaching the ground floor I managed to eventually manoeuvre my vast cargo through the double swing doors, but only after the help of two friendly cleaning ladies. However one of the latter compounded my acute embarrassment with an unwelcome adieu.

'Cor, you aren't very good at this, are you mate?'

Five minutes later I had managed to get Victoria into the car, but only after some singularly unpleasant grappling and a near hernia. As we set off she sharpened the verbal scalpel.

'Isn't that nice Leonardo on duty today? Now he really knows how to look after an old and infirm lady. And where are you going? All the other drivers go the other way.' Silence from me this time. A bit later, 'I really wish they had sent Leonardo.'

This was just too much. 'Bugger Leonardo,' I hissed under my breath but with as much venom as I could muster.

'Don't mumble young man. You really are an odd sort of fellow.'

Relief, we had arrived at our destination. Her friend's house. How she had any friends at all was a bloody miracle. More grunting and groaning and I finally had the old crow outside.

'Don't leave the wheelchair there,' she commanded. 'All the other drivers take it back to the nursing home.' That unwelcome further reference to the other drivers' talents finally broke this reluctant dromedary's back.

'I'll tell you what madam,' I said, subserviently summoning up my sweetest old ladies' smile. 'Why don't you stick your bloody wheelchair right up where the sun never shines,' and off I flounced to the sanctuary of my car.

I never gave her a chance to reply but to be sure I'm sure that 'you haven't heard the last of this sorry little episode, young man,' wouldn't have been a million miles away.

I would also no doubt be hearing from Mr Smiley ere long, but I soon recovered my old jaunty self when I reflected ruefully over a fag on the sheer absurdity of life. Who needs fiction?

To further illustrate the above musings, the following ridiculous event occurred only a few weeks later. The Fat Controller had sent me on a pick up at The Bear and I was carefully approaching one of those silly mini roundabouts that littered Sutton Market. Just as I was preparing to negotiate the piddling obstacle an elderly gentleman with a large walking stick walked most deliberately across my path. Still not having learnt any patience, I gave him a loud blast on my horn plus a moderately obscene guesture with my spare hand. Note well that I had picked my target carefully. If the bloke had been six foot six and sixty years younger I would have probably have given him a sycophantic salute. Pathetic. Unfortunately I had badly misjudged my soft target on this occasion. He marched round to my car window and demanded to know what the dickens I was up to and could I please provide my driver's badge number. I 'had to' give way to him. As usual I reacted badly to reciprocal bellicosity and informed him that he was a 'geriatric jay walker' and wasn't fit to be let out alone at his age. Who was in the judicial ascendancy? Unfortunately before we had a chance to discuss the legal niceties of the matter, a crescendo of horns and a distinctly discouraging 'get a fucking move on, you wanker' finally persuaded me to be on my way, but not before this amazing old buffer had suddenly launched a savage assault on the bonnet of my car. The car and me were both shaken and stirred. It was just about comprehensible if not in anyway excusable to be attacked by a drunken youngster at three in the morning, but to be taken out by a sober octogenarian at three in the afternoon was too much. The Fat Controller later informed me with a nasty soupçon of malice that this ancient delinquent was a former university professor and went by the name of Chutney, presumably because his brain was now pickled.

A couple of weary hours later, I bid farewell to TFC and repaired round to The Rising Sun for a couple of pints and some psychiatric consolation from Graham. As usual he let me down badly by laughing uproariously at my misadventures.

'You know Tommy, its you who's the one who shouldn't be let out outside without a minder. Pick on someone your own age next time. Ha ha.'

Despite his usual lack of sympathy, I felt distinctly better by the time I had downed my second pint of bitter. I ambled back to the flat in the pleasant evening sunshine and opened my usual bottle of Madiran to go with my brie and biscuit supper. Dalgleish would of course had a bit of left-over cassoulet in the fridge to reheat in order to do proper justice to the crimson nectar. And that's why he's alone as well. Was this the moment to give Tiff a buzz? No, I wasn't quite ready to act yet because then I would have to tell the truth, wouldn't I? Better by far just to indulge the dream.

> Lets enjoy it while we can
> Won't you help me sing my song
> We'll be lovers once again
> On the bright side of the road.

But would we?

4. CLEANING WINDOWS

What's my line?
I'm happy cleaning windows.
Take my time
I'll see you when my love grows
Baby don't let it slide
I'm a working man in my prime
Cleaning windows.

That was the problem. I was now a working man driving cars for a living. Though whether I was still in my prime was very much open to question. A long term career as a not so humble taxi driver was hardly going to impress Tiff, was it? But if I didn't see her again our love was hardly going to grow either. What to do? Better get down to The Rising Sun to see old Graham. The latter was busying himself with the usual early evening suspects, Barry the builder, Chris the window cleaner and Gee the plumber. No posers here. I nodded to them and plonked myself down at my usual place at the end of the bar with my Independent. Graham was on pleine forme as he held forth about the iniquities that would arise if we were stupid enough to join the Euro. When his diatribe had finally run out of steam I quietly buttonholed him for a chat. He listened seriously for once and even sympathised with my dilemma.

'You've got to face the real music of life, Tommy,' was his sage counsel. 'Just tell her the truth man.'

After my third pint of Mauldon's I was feeling confident enough to follow Graham's advice. Unfortunately after my fifth pint I was nowhere near coherent enough to make that critical call. Never mind, I promised myself I would definitely make that call tomorrow. I waddled back to the flat and finished a bottle of Madiran with my meagre sandwich. Through the haze Omar's words returned to haunt me.

> Indeed, indeed, Repentance oft before
> I swore –but was I sober when I swore?
> And then came spring, and Rose-in-hand
> My thread-bare Penitence apieces tore.

Come the morning and a thick head I was back on the road. After the habitual school run I was back in The Hutch. Already ensconced were the Scarecrow, Tonker and Leonardo, all moaning about the recent savage increase in the cost of both The Private Hire Car Licences and The Private Hire Vehicle Licences. The Wuffa District Council certainly didn't take any prisoners on the Private Hire front. Or Hackneys either, for that matter. Oh well, I suppose someone has to keep Mr Smiley in Veuve Cliquot. The problem with the conversation in hand was that The Scarecrow's false teeth were giving him gyp and Tonker was effing and blinding like a good'un. This had the effect of making Leonardo's passable remarks getting sandwiched between incoherence and a lot of fucking.

Talking of The Latin Lover. Yes, Leonardo was the man. He knew all about women. This was the moment, again. I tentatively explained to him my dilemma as well and asked whether he agreed with Graham's suggested course of action. Alas, as I was quietly filling Leonardo in on the current state of play (or rather bad light had prevented any play at all), a huge, evil smile evolved around Tonker's rubbery lips.

'Ho ho, The Toff's got a new bird. Have you fucked her yet or's it only us lower classes that do that sort of thing ?'

'You are so crude Tonker,' I replied pontifically as ever.

'And you're just a fucking snob, Tommy,' he snapped back as quickly as a Freddie Flintoff bouncer.

The Scarecrow was just as deadly for once.

'And you're a sodding prude as well,' he managed to enunciate reasonably clearly for once. Perhaps the false teeth were just a blind hiding an erudite mind? Looking at him again very carefully, perhaps not. I know brilliance is often well-disguised, but not that well. From that lank, greasy long hair down to his winkle-picker shoes hung over from the sixties, he was the epitome of bad taste. But he had got me in one on this issue.

But had Leonardo got a plan of action? He had. He concurred with Graham's advice but also made a vital contribution.

'I don't think you're really that much of a snob now Tommy,' he kindly observed. 'But your main problem is that you're ashamed of your job. Deep down, you don't really think you can hook Tiff without money or whatever you suppose is status. That's why you're crap with women. If you gave Tiff the chance she might just like you for your big ugly mug, or just fancy the oily mechanic look which you are so good at now.'

Sarcastic bugger but he had read me like a book. I thought it was meant to be me who did all the reading. My fear of failure hadn't lessened with all my failures. I was still very much afraid of rejection. But I was even more afraid of not being good enough. Despite my protestations to the contrary, deep down I still believed I was just a taxi driver.

Sadly, being a taxi driver also involved driving occasionally as well as philosophizing. The Fat Controller interrupted our little tête à tête and asked if I could possibly fit in a little job, if I had a moment? Tonker unhelpfully added,

'We all know what Tommy would like to fit in at the moment.'

Off I went to The Post House in high dudgeon. Another businessman in a hurry, but first he had to ring his wife on his mobile.

A man of business feels it as a crime
On calls domestic to consume his time.

I tried very hard not to consume any more of his valuable time and dropped him off at the Magistrates' Court. It transpired that he was a barrister down for the day to defend a Mrs Archer from a claim for unfair dismissal. Next a regular, the notorious Bill Bandit, from Rockingham Road to The Red Lion. He was sober but morose, even before inebriety. Being hungover myself, I for once had a modicum of sympathy for the old devil.

> See Inebriety! her wand she waves,
> And lo! her pale, and lo! her purple slaves;
> Sots in embroidery, and sots in crape,
> Of every order, station, rank, and shape.

Next a pensioner to pick up from the Gaol Lane surgery just off the Market Hill. As usual parking was very tight but I eventually managed to squeeze in fairly close, albeit on the omnipresent double yellow lines. No sooner had I parked when there was an aggressive knock on the my window. It was Miss Mussolini, the most infamous traffic warden in the whole of Suffolk. She threatened me with a parking ticket if I didn't move on that very second. I tried to explain that I would only be a couple of seconds while I loaded up my semi-invalid fare, but to no avail. Miss Mussolini booked me on the spot after I had somewhat imprudently added a witty but tactically unwise aside concerning her lack of pulchritude. And then as an automatic response to her having the temerity to book me, I launched a counter attack.

'In that case I demand your proper name, number and rank so I can make a formal complaint against you.'

'Miss Blunt,' she replied.

'I'm not surprised,' I riposted nastily. 'But if you scrutinize your family's ancestral name with a bit more vigour you will discover that it doesn't start with a Blur but with a Ka and a big one at that.'

Off I went like the clappers leaving my fare very much in the lurch. Oh well, I could just call in a no pick up as a cover up. It was obviously going to be one of those days.

This was quickly confirmed by my next fare, The Spam Man. The Spam Man was another of our clients with learning difficulties, but like most of them as good as gold. Unhappily I had a brainstorm and couldn't remember his address. Something to do with my hangover?

'Well, it is about time you pulled yourself together,' The Spam Man said witheringly.

Christ I must be losing it. Demolished by a retard.

The Spam Man was also an avid Ipswich Town football fan. They had thrashed their bitter East Anglian rivals Norwich City five nil the night before and for the rest of the journey he kept repeating 'we stuffed them like turkeys'. It was all right the first time but by the twenty first stuffing I felt like stuffing him myself. Tolerance, Tommy.

I was cruising down the High Street ten minutes later, still ruefully reflecting on my little contretemps with Miss Blunt, when I got held up by a sluggish lady driver perversely driving one of those sporty Japanese numbers. I gave her a gentle beep of encouragement but was ill-prepared for what was to follow. She stopped the car not nearly so sluggishly, got out, nay stormed out of the driver's seat, and I couldn't help but notice the sexy mini skirt she was nearly wearing. What followed was not nearly so sexy as a torrent of filth emanated from her lovely lips. This was certainly no lady as she questioned my parentage and sexual prowess and with a few more choice terms of abuse thrown in. Before I had a chance to respond she flounced off to her car, but not before she had carried out a very elegant kick onto the side of my car with her very expensive but lethal stilettos. This time the rubber scorched the tarmac as she shot off into the ether. I had obviously awoken the sleeping giant in her, or rather the sleeping bitch. I was rather shell-shocked after this further attack on my morale, not to say morals, and decided a little break at the Café Gascon was more than called for and accordingly got prompt permission for once for my exeat from The Fat Controller.

One of Sabine's most ravishing smiles quickly restored my battered equilibrium, together with my usual Cappuccino and a smoke. This gave me the opportunity to relax further while appreciating the splendid architecture surrounding me. From the magnificent heights of the over-decorated ceiling to the delicate depths of the imported yellow wood flooring, this magnificent Art Deco room always brought me solace. So did the staff. Luc the manager came over and commiserated over my driving travails of the morning, although of course I couldn't let him into the inner sanctum of my love life, or rather lack of it. He had just had two really obnoxious customers in the café as well, he confided, and we had a pleasant five minute chat on the vicissitudes of life.

I was now ready to face those vicissitudes again. In fact the rest of the day went very smoothly for once, until the very end of the evening. Yes another double shift had been called for to pay for recent problems on the carburettor front. Ironically the pick up was back at the Café Gascon, and I just had time to observe some frantic hand signals from Luc before my two male punters both got into the back of the car. They were father and son it transpired, evidently out for a bit of filial bonding.

'No we had a crap meal,' was the father's caustic response to my solicitous enquiry. He was evidently the original Surly Scotsman, so I thought I would go into mute mode adopted for contingencies such as this one. Fat chance. I had been informed by Thin Lizzie that our destination was Lavenham but hadn't been given the exact address. Therefore on the outskirts of town I naturally turned onto the Lavenham Road. Suddenly SS barked.

'This isn't the road to Lavenham.' This rattled me so much that I replied in kind.

'What the hell are you talking about? Of course it is.'

Or was it? The events of the morning came back uncomfortably to mind. Had I really lost it? Perhaps I had made another stupid mistake. No of course I hadn't, I reassured myself, but not before another not so brief mental check. What was SS on about?

'Of course I know where I live, you stupid idiot. I've lived there over for over two years,' he resumed in superior fashion. But I wasn't to be put off that easily.

'This is the road to Lavenham' I replied stolidly. And then not so stolidly I added, 'at least it was the last time I looked at the map.'

The son tried to give me a bit of support.

'There is another way to Lavenham, Dad,' he chipped in hesitantly before being flattened by SS.

'I'm not having any more of this crap,' he snarled. 'Take me back to the town centre at once.'

With relief I turned round and headed back to the Market Hill as instructed. But SS wasn't going to let me off that easily.

'The least you can do is to apologise and give me a reduction on the fare. So I mumbled an apology and SS seized on this apparent sign of weakness. 'OK, you can take me home after all. I will give you precise instructions as you are obviously not very experienced at this sort of thing.'

Now although I didn't of course consider myself just a taxi driver, perversely nothing incensed me more than a fare questioning my lack of The Knowledge. After all my time on The Road, in addition to my youthful geographical explorations, I considered myself shit hot on knowing my patch. Yes, SS had struck a nerve all right.

Of course I had twigged exactly where he lived by now. It was in a select area called Lavenham Lakes, right on the boundary with Cockfield and the quickest route (just) was via Cockfield. Naturally it was a very quiet journey indeed after our little contretemps but it gave me the time to devise a plan of campaign.

When we arrived at his naturally sumptuous residence, SS barked.

'How much ?'

'No charge,' I replied smoothly.

'What do you mean, no charge ?'

Then I slowly turned towards him and looked at him directly in the eye. 'I don't want any of your fucking Scottish money,' with as much contempt as I could muster.

Oh yes, he got the message all right and realized his pathetic protestations were not going to cut any ice with me now. Finally he got out and threw a bank note carelessly down on the back seat.

'Well, give the bloody money to charity then, if that's how you feel.'

He stormed off into the welcoming bosom of his mansion, if not his wife. The fare had in fact been nine pounds twenty but I didn't want any of the arrogant bastard's money. Christ I felt good. He must have now forced his way into a medal position. I hoped he realized what a prat he had made of himself in front of his son. So much for bonding. To round off an interesting evening, when I got home I retrieved a very crumpled twenty pound note on the back seat. He obviously hadn't got a clue what the fare was. Caveat emptor as the saying used to go.

Not so, my little flock ! your preacher flie,
Nor waste the time no worldly wealth can buy.
And while the bad they threaten and control,
Will to the humble and pious say,
Yours is the right, the safe, the certain way,
'Tis wisdom to be good, 'tis virtue to obey.

Unfortunately, unlike Georgie, I was neither humble or pious.
Ah well.

Next day after the usual school run, I had another of our odd-
ball runs. The Fat Controller's instructions were first to buy
two hundred Marlboro Lights from a newsagent together with
The Guardian and The Sutton Market Express. Then Dewhursts
butchers (it had to be Dewhursts apparently). There I had to
purchase two pounds of their special sausages, a three pound
beef joint and some bones for their dogs. Next a dozen red
roses. Finally believe it or not, I had to buy five packs of
Virgin Mates condoms. I never did get my head around that
anomaly. Why would a virgin wish to buy her mate condoms?
Then I had to take my purchases to a property improbably
entitled Spout Cottage in an obscure hamlet called Workhouse
Green. Surely TFC was taking the piss. But no, I soon found
the hamlet using the invaluable Cyclists Guide to Suffolk. It was
only some dozen miles out of town but what kind of nutters was
I going to meet ? They were obviously chain-smoking, dog-
loving sex maniacs having a passionate affair in their little love
nest. I must admit my trepidation was mixed with intrigue.
Anyway my purchases came to eighty one pounds and forty
pence in all and I had to pay using a variety of my numerous
dodgy credit cards. Us taxi drivers certainly have to be flexible.
But would I ever get paid? I found Spout Cottage easily enough.

It was one of those typical detached Suffolk thatched cottages that I heartily disliked, obviously formerly a pair of labourers' cottages knocked into one with interleading bedrooms and a lot of ducking and diving, plus the obligatory ground floor damp bathroom off the kitchen. How twee, overrated and overpriced. When I was a kid you couldn't give them away. Thatched cottages I mean, not rubber johnnies as they were then known.

I knocked on the door. No reply except for a dog's fierce barking. They obviously couldn't wait for the condoms. I had already noticed a brand new Mercedes and the obligatory Four plus Four replete with evil buzz bars in the drive. Perhaps my wild thoughts weren't so far from the mark after all. These thoughts were interrupted by a Halle Berry lookalike opening the door at that precise moment in a delicious negligée but with less than precise make up and hair do. Just as I thought all my Christmases had come at once John Shaft appeared and asked in a not so delicious cockney accent.

'How much mate ?'

I duly informed him and he handed over five crisp twenties. But then the door was firmly shut with an equally final 'thanks mate,' thus satisfying my financial honour, but not my curiosity.

After that little deviation TFC sent me on a nice simple sounding wait and return from Bosmere Heights to town and back. I arrived outside number twenty seven, Royal Sandwich Drive, precisely at midday as commanded, but then waited impatiently for five minutes for someone to appear. Finally a smartly dressed lady of pensioner age appeared but then spent a further two or three minutes apparently fiddling with the lock. Eventually as I was beginning to get seriously agitato she turned away and limped to the car. It was then that I noticed one of the most macabre sightings in all my time on this bizarre road called life. There was a pathetic little hand flapping through the letter box. This was Hitchcock in the flesh. Real flesh. Madam pensioner noticed my startled expression and turned round to see the apparition herself. But of course it wasn't a ghost, sadly.

'Oh bugger,' she exclaimed in a very unladylike way, and limped back to the house. She unlocked the door and there followed an animated conversation with an unseen adversary. Eventually she appeared to double lock the door and limped slower than ever to the car. It was then I noticed the large bandages round her swollen legs. This was getting more bizarre than ever.

'Sorry about that,' she explained as soon as she had got into the car. 'My husband has Alzheimer's disease and I have to lock him in to prevent him doing something loco.'

That dreaded disease again. It's going to be one of the great medical problems of the Western world in the twenty first century. Madam Pensioner continued.

'I also had to placate him by saying that I would be back in quarter of an hour. But if I didn't get out alone occasionally I would go bloody mad myself.' What a bloody life. An elderly cripple living with a tormented husk of a husband. Who wants to get old on The Welfare State? Whose life is it anyway?

As I drove away from that mental and physical nonperambulating disaster, I reflected sadly that old age, like life itself, wasn't fair. But before I had the chance to get too altruistic about the world in general, I was confronted by a very different, more intense and much more personal feeling. TFC had sent me on my next assignment, namely to pick up a Mrs Sharpestone from Rattlesden. Mrs Sharpestone was of course Tiff. Oh bugger, I wasn't mentally (or physically) ready to meet her again yet. I would have to tell her the truth about my 'research.' I had only a quarter of an hour's drive to compose my story, and myself. It was no good. I would just have to take Leonardo's advice and come clean and fall upon Tiff's tender mercies. Damn, I was there already. But when I knocked on the door Tiff didn't come out alone. She was with another man.

He was a fair bit younger than me and immaculately attired, if you like that sort of gear. Expensive navy blue Armani jacket, open-necked check shirt, beautifully cut trousers with creases that you could shave on, and of course fashionable loafers. And he was vaguely good-looking, if you like that rugged Michael Douglas cleft chin sort of bloke.

Yes, you've got it in one. I was stomach-churning fucking jealous.

> What's my line?
> I'm happy cleaning windows.
> Take my time
> I'll see you when my love grows.

Fat chance now. And of course I wasn't happy driving taxis. What gave me that stupid idea. And neither was I happy with

Tiff's far too casual greeting.

'Oh hello Tommy.' Not much love growing there.

Anyway Tiff and Michael Douglas got cosily into the back of the car together and then proceeded to have a cosy conversation all the way back to Sutton Market.

> Baby don't let it slide
> I'm a working man in my prime
> Cleaning windows.

I must have been completely deluded to think that I ever had a chance with Tiff. A middle aged, reluctantly working man driving bloody taxis.

And of course, as luck would have it, I had to drop them off at the Café Gascon for a nice little intimate lunch for two. After Michael Douglas had paid me off literally with a huge tip, all I was left with from Tiff was a little flip of her hand.

'Bye Tommy, nice to see you again.'

Not lovely this time, I grimly noted.

To deepen my gloom my next fare proved to be another old acquaintance, this time from my cricketing days, also of long ago when I was in my prime. The pick up point this time was from the august offices of Chance and Chance. Despite their discouraging name, Chance and Chance were the premier firm of accountants in Sutton Market and I was to pick up the senior partner, one Gerald Long. How I hated picking up old acquaintances.

Since my return to Sutton Market and subsequent cab career, I had spurned my earlier haunts outside the closed circle of The Rising Sun. The latter was sufficiently shabby and non trendy to keep out all my successful friends of an earlier vintage. Now, Gerald was a genuine guy and well bred enough not to express open surprise to find his old banking and cricket chum at the wheel of a taxi. Instead we reminisced about all the good old days. We remembered that brilliant team-mate, the incomparable Roger Prior, he of the classic cover drive and scorching bouncer. The gregarious Roger had been just as dominating in the bar. In Georgie's words.

> For he was one in all their idle sport,
> And like a monarch ruled their little court;
> The pliant bow he form'd, the flying ball,
> The bat, the wicket, were his labours all.

Gerald was off to Silford Hall, a luxury hotel complex with conference facilities, spa and championship golf course about six miles away. Cricket was therefore a comfortable subject to cover the journey and kept us off unmentionables such as failure and future. Gerald was kind enough to give me a generous tip and said we must get together soon, but I knew we wouldn't. The tip felt like charity and I would continue to shun my earlier haunts and former friends until my fortunes had improved. Gerald was attending a one day conference for prominent businessmen in the area. A few years and tears ago, I might have been the guest speaker, not merely a bringer of guests.

As Omar put it so sombrely.

> The Ball no Question makes of Ayes and Noes,
> But Right or Left as strikes the Player goes;
> And He that toss'd you down into the Field,
> He knows about it all – HE knows – **HE** knows !

Someone certainly knew I had been out for a not so golden duck in the first knock. Could I make a ton in the second innings of my life?

But in this game you are never allowed to stay down for too long as I should have learnt by now. Circumstances just don't permit it. Take my very next fare.

Ted was an old favourite with older habits. Habit number one. He was always exactly seven minutes late after the appointed time for his appearance from pub. Habit number two, he always stopped at an off-licence on his way home. Habit number three was a little homily on arrival at destination. We always had to allow at least twenty minutes for these little diversions which we called 'The Ted Run'. However, he was always good company and a good tipper to boot so I never minded.

Ted worked at the local brewery and was an occasional frequenter at The Rising Sun. Today he had a problem. Or two, it transpired. On our way to The Red Lion he confided that he was very nervous at the prospect of meeting his daughter with her Spanish boyfriend for the first time. His daughter was only eighteen and he had a natural paternal concern for his only daughter's safety at the marauding hands of a dastardly foreigner. In fact he was in such a tizz that at the end of his little homily he found he had left his wallet behind. No pounds and no plastic. What to do? Pas de problème. I asked him if he would like a little loan, and presuming the answer was yes, would twenty quid be enough? Yes and yes. The look of gratitude and effusive thanks made the pleasure all mine. Christ what a generous and noble bugger you are Tommy. No wonder I'm not a bleeding millionaire. Instead of four quid for the fare I found myself twenty quid down. You've got to laugh. At least The Fat Controller might appreciate now what I mean by 'caressing the punters metaphorically'. Last time I had used the phrase he looked at me very strangely. In his little piggy eyes I was obviously either a sex fiend or had been using those funny substances again. TFC in the sky with diamonds. I can see it now.

But Ted had lifted my slough of depression. I had meant to the bottom of my heart what I had said about the pleasure being all mine. In fact I was more than ready for more laughter.

PS One small thing Ted, I wouldn't mind that twenty quid back now.

'Planet earth to planet pot.' TFC was calling me again. 'Pick up Connie from The Bear immediately and transport her back to Seckford Street. At your convenience, of course.' Connie was another old favourite. A delightful Irish widow (that's still politically permissible isn't it?), old, infirm and a bit tipsy as usual. She struggled into the car with her meagre shopping and we negotiated the two minute drive to Seckford Street agreeably as usual. I helped her with her shopping and even unlocked the front door for her as her eyesight was also rather sketchy. 'You're a fine broth of a man Sir.'

I can last a hell of a long time on a compliment, presuming

that 'broth' is a compliment.

Back to The Bear for yet another old favourite. It was certainly proving to be a vintage day after all. Favourite was also a very appropriate word as Willy, my fare, was a true punter in the traditional use of the word. We would always discuss his latest coups in great detail. Willy was a little old widower, always dressed in the same old but respectable jacket and fading grey trousers, plus some sort of regimental tie of course that was never unknotted. He invariably had a wicked twinkle in his eye, and he had obviously been quite a ladies man in his day. He once said to me that there are only three things in life, wine, women and the gee gees. And he'd only just given up the women. No wonder he was called Willy. Today he had been celebrating a nice little yankee touch at York and was pleasantly pissed, as they say in the trade. I always left his company in better humour.

Back in The Hutch an hour later, I was disappointed to see that only The Milky Bar Kid and The Boy Racer were in for a cuppa. I badly wanted another chat with Leonardo concerning my calamitous meeting with Tiff earlier in the day. The Kid and Nigel were wittering on about cars as usual so I nestled into a gentle perusal of The Independent.

About ten minutes later Tonker and Elise came in together conspiratorially. I didn't have long to wait long before I found out the subject. Me. Or rather me and 'The Toff's new bird'. Elise asked me sarcastically if I had needed a few tips ('on any subject, luv') as I was obviously out of my depth. Tonker increased my squirming embarrassment by making further enquiries of an overtly sexual nature. The Kid obviously caught their drift immediately, taking great pleasure in my discomfiture, although he didn't dare to chip in for fear of reprisals. Nigel merely smiled and added unhelpfully that he would be pleased to help Tiff with an oil change any time she wanted. I declined his offer in as haughty a manner as possible, but they were all well amused by my lack of verbosity for once, or any words at all for that matter.

From a highly unlikely source came my saviour. The Fat Controller wanted me to go to Percy Pocock Drive on the classy Thedwastre Estate asap. For the one and only time in my illustrious driving career, I accepted his kind offer with alacrity. I shot out of The Hutch like Nigel at a Le Mans start, but still not quite quick enough to escape the cruel cackles. I was still blushing when I arrived at Percy Pocock Drive. The distinguished Percy had been a prominent Councillor for over thirty years, and the Wuffa District Council were always very keen to reward their own. The residents were naturally not quite so keen on the idea, but the Council had high-handedly overruled their eminently reasonable objections. But then none of the current crop of Councillors had to live there of course. In the taxi trade it was known, a touch disrespectfully, as Pokers Hill on account of the nefarious events that went on in the wee small hours at the end of the drive. My fare naturally proved to be a prim matron with not such a trim figure. Or I presumed she was prim till I caught a salacious smile on her face when I glanced in the rear mirror. Was nowhere safe?

Talking of trim figures I used to get childish pleasure out of beleaguering girls with fuller figures, shall we say, who had the temerity to jaywalk in front of me in town. I responded by flicking down my electric window and bellowing, 'your legs aren't good enough for that sort of manoeuvre.' I in return naturally received plenty of verbal abuse and hand signals for my uncalled for troubles, and one day ere long I would get my come uppance or knockdownance no doubt. But I still thrilled to the risk.

After I had dropped off the prim matron in town I soon had another chance to show off further my risky skills. My next pick up was at a house called The Warren on the exclusive Mayfair Drive, although us drivers unimaginatively referred to it as Nobs Hill. Oh dear, I seem to be bogged down rather a lot lately by Pokers and Nobs. Obviously I was beginning to get artificially inseminated by the very basic conversations in The Hutch. This would only prove Tonker's assertion that I was just like the others, despite my unconvincing denial to the contrary. When I was careless enough to describe a seminal moment in my career, Tonker retorted.

'Yea, I told you. You Toffs are all the bleedin same. All you can think about is effin semen all the time.'

Another total collapse of The Hutch.

Back at The Warren a languid, elegant lady in her early thirties appeared and asked me if I would mind waiting a couple of minutes, but of course it was a rhetorical question and a travesty of an estimate. Fully ten minutes later the same lady and her Dinner Jacketed dressed partner came out simpering sweet nothings to each other, and indicated to me with a regal wave that the others were just coming. A further five minutes later, another glamorous and immaculate couple with champagne glasses in hand condescended to make an appearance. Obviously they were going to a bit of a posh do.

Off I went at a speed which again even The Boy Racer would have been proud. The least I could do was to make them spill their precious champagne.

Aha, a bit envious are we Tommy?

Our destination proved to be a property called Gobblecock Manor (yes really) only about three miles away. However in that time the two couples had managed to wind me up even further with their affected and over-affectionate chatter. I felt like Lizzie's father in Pride and Prejudice, but bit my tongue for the time being. However by the time we had arrived at The Manor, I was overheating as badly as Eric's crappy old Cavalier. As I would say in court later, I was severely provoked, my lud. This led to my slightly intemperate observation concerning the property as it hove into view for the first time.

'I see. A pretentious tree-lined drive leading to a house only outstanding in its mediocrity.'

Tactically unwise but so, so satisfying. Estate agents everywhere would have been proud of me.

My fares were too flabbergasted by my bare-voiced cheek to respond at all verbally, but the disapproving response was in the meticulously counting of the five pounds, sixty pence fare. Funnily enough, I didn't get the return journey.

I went home and read my Christmas Humphrey's book on Zen
Curiosity killed the cat
Kerouac's 'Dharma Bums' and 'On The Road'.

However at the end of my shift I wasn't still laughing.

I went round to see my counsellor at The Rising Sun. Graham was chatting with a couple of locals so I made steady inroads into the Mauldon's while considering my options, which was usually a euphemistic precursor to getting smashed. Graham didn't like it when I continued to morosely study my glass of ale. In a foul mood himself, he came over to see what my latest problem was.

'You're bloody bad for business Tommy. What's your problem this time?'

I brought him up to speed and awaited his words of wisdom. By the serious set of his mouth more tough love was in the offing.

'Look here Tommy, I'm getting seriously pissed off with you. I gave you some sound advice the other day and you totally ignored it. Now listen hard and listen good this time. No more beer today, and no wine at home either. Or at least till you have made that phone call. The worst that can happen is that she is actually going to marry this Michael Douglas fellow. That at least will put you out of your misery, and the rest of us won't have to put up with your juvenile moping any longer.'

Tough love indeed but before I could respond he continued in softer vein.

'On the other hand if she isn't going out with him seriously, ask her out. And not for one of your inebriated sessions either. A meal at La Vieille Maison is called for. Soon. I know you can't bloody well afford it but desperate situations call for desperate measures. Now bugger off and keep me posted, you old fool.' And off I jolly well buggered, shell-shocked but sober with his

Cockney tones ringing in my ear.

Back at the flat I procrastinated for an eternity and then lit a fag. At least Graham hadn't banned that little source of solace as well. But a few minutes later I reluctantly stubbed it out and, even more reluctantly, picked up the phone. I had always been a coward, both physically and emotionally. Perhaps she was out? No such luck. Tiff answered on the third ring. She had obviously been waiting for that youthful Michael Douglas to ring and coo sweet millions in her ear.

I had naturally mentally prepared my little speech beforehand. However I had only just started my hesitant spiel when she brusquely interrupted. Oh no, it was all over before it had begun. What was she saying? No, it appeared that my luck might be about to change as she hastened to explain that the cleft chinned wonder was only her solicitor down from London for the day to try and sort out some complicated details of her late husband's estate. I'd been stopped in full fumbling flow. She fell silent but still I hesitated.

'Well Tommy, what did you ring up for?' I had nowhere to run to now so I blurted out my invitation.

'That sounds great Tommy. How about Thursday week at seven thirty? Meet you there and we'll go Dutch.'

'Great. See you then. Bye for now.'

I put the phone down and found my hands were trembling. Love certainly does funny things to you. But Graham and Leonardo would both have been proud of me, I'm sure. I think

I will have that little glass of Madiran now after all.

What's my line?
I'm happy cleaning windows
Take my time
I'll see you when my love grows
Baby don't let it slide
I'm a working man in my prime
Cleaning windows.

I'm even happy driving taxis again. And not feeling so old either. A middle aged man in his prime perhaps?

5.   DARING NIGHT

> In the daring night when all the stars are shining bright
> Squeeze me don't leave me in the daring night
> Galactic swirl in the firmament tonight
> Oh with the lord of the dance
> With the lord of the dance in the daring night.

Well I had eight days to think about that celestial Lord of the Dance. Would Tiff squeeze me and not leave me in the Daring Night? Some hope.

From the initial feeling of great elation when I heard Tiff's voice agreeing to our date, I eventually came back to earth when I rationally assessed what she had actually said. 'We'll go Dutch.' So had she already guessed my real situation? In any event I had to earn a fair bit of extra dosh just to pay my half of the deal if my dodgy plastic wasn't to take a mortal hit.

Today my luck was in as I had a private Heathrow Airport run. Walter had become a friend of mine through innumerable runs all round the country. His secretary had phoned up at the last moment as usual to see if I could pick him up from his New York flight at midday at Terminal 4. Of course I could. The pick up time was a bit of a bonus as most of the flights from the States seemed to come in the wee hours. Crap journey to Heathrow. Twenty nine minutes late due to lorry fire on the road at Potters Bar. You seem to hear about lorry fires every day on the M25. I know this cursed motorway has always been seriously irritating but lately it seems to be seriously combustible as well. That's why I had all but given up the Heathrow and Gatwick rat runs. It was hardly worth getting out of bed for when you considered the hassles of getting to either of these two architectural disaster zones. For a pick up you always had to allow acres of time in case of traffic delays. When you had taken into consideration the exorbitant parking fees and an emaciated fare, it didn't take an Einstein to work out that it was more lucrative and restful just to potter round Sutton Market instead. I also had a hang up about having to dangle a sign round my neck announcing I was not a good old convict but a bad old taxi driver. It made me feel so conspicuous. Me who would always prefer to merge into the shadows. 'The observer who is observing.' I found Terminal 2 especially depressing with its claustrophobic low ceilings. What the hell tourists coming to Britain for the first time thought about it I tremble to think. Give me brave new Stansted any day with its dashing lines and lofty light ceilings or intimate Toulouse, Shaggers (Sharm-El-Sheik to the uninitiated) or Aggers (Agadir) to those of us with a more exotic bent.

Walter gave me a buzz and explained that he had arrived a bit early. This was a huge plus as it meant I didn't have to penetrate the bowels of the catacombs. This was also the one great advantage about mobile phones when they could be used as a sophisticated homing device. Otherwise President Tommy would have them banned in public places, just like us outlawed smokers. I had heard enough about other people's problematic love lives to last me a lifetime. It is as if we taxi drivers don't exist as we are compelled to listen to all the painful details of another love hitting the rocks. Speaking of which, a little pang homed into my stomach to remind me uncomfortably of my own little sally to come on the love front.

I arranged to meet Walter at the entrance to the put down area for departures. Five minutes later I had battled through the nether regions of Ali G territory and there he was looking like a grinning tourist (Walter, not Ali G) in his wrapround shades and his smartly casual gear. Walter was a self made guy who had spotted a niche and need in the market for the translation of specialized commercial documents. He was both intelligent and witty and the perfect antidote from my usual dross. He also paid a business premium for the privilege of me coming to pick him up. Class costs, and so it should. Anyway two hundred pounds was my price for his privilege, a healthy fifty per cent plus premium on the basic fare. But Walter put it down to his client's account so we both were winners.

The traffic was much easier on the M25 on the way back, even at those notorious junctions which narrow down to two lanes. Whatever were the Department of Transport thinking about when they allowed that to happen? In fact it may have been all part of a cunning plan on their behalf to build the M25 by stealth.

Anyway Walter and I soon polished off transport problems and moved onto a far weightier subject, namely breasts. Plus of course the necessary, or unnecessary depending on your point or angle of view, appendages attached to such delicious objects, brassières. From my point of view, I just couldn't handle them as it were. Since the catastrophic introduction of the Wonderbra, it was downhill all the way on the brassière front as far as I was concerned. However it did give me the chance to show off my masterly knowledge of the French language and its subtle nuances. The French as usual had a far more accurate description of this curious object of male desire. They called it le soutien gorge, literally supporting the throat, and but of course masculine to show also their rather cavalier approach to underwear (men's briefs are naturally la culotte; both feminine and singular). British boobs were now pushed up so far they certainly were right up the throat. We British inaccurately borrowed comme d'habitude another ancient French word, bracier, a protector for the arm. No wonder the bi-lingual French contemptuously remark that les rosbifs can't tell their retentive arses from their inadequate elbows. Walter was seriously impressed, at least I thought he was, by my eruditeness on such an obscure subject although he did tentatively suggest that I shouldn't let it become an obsession. No chance of that. And then he beat The Poet-Laureate at his own game by quoting Georgie right back at me.

> Know, thow art all that my delighted eyes,
> My fondest thoughts, my proudest wishes prize;
> And is that bosom – (what on earth so fair?)
> To cradle some coarse peasant's sprawling heir,
> To be that pillow which some surly swain
> May treat with scorn and agonize with pain?

After I got over my amazement at Walter's outright forehand winner down the line and Georgie's unsuspected knowledge of breasts, I recovered a bit of street cred. 'Oh yes, old Wordsworth was always keen on plagiarism.' It also opens up unlimited conjecture on what the old boy actually saw on Westminster Bridge. He wouldn't have lasted long in the law courts these days.

We had just begun a potentially acrimonious argument about the Middle East when we were saved by our arrival at Walter's rather plush stable conversion offices a couple of miles outside Sutton Market. I said my farewells to Walter and moved back into the real and less hospitable world. What was next on the agenda?

Not a great deal after eight o'clock, being a typical Wednesday evening. A few Wattisham lads and a bit of this and a bit of that. Mentioning the latter reminded me I had sometimes thought about popping over to Northern Ireland to start Tommy's Atheist Taxis or just TAT. If Reggie could make such a success of Grot, Belfast should be a doddle. Could even be a big hit.

But all this agreeable reverie wasn't actually earning me any money and I still needed an extra hundred quid over the next week if I was going to convincingly avoid the humiliation of going Dutch.

The evening continued to drift quietly which didn't suit my financial purpose at all. In keeping with the lethargy of the evening, I had a long and lingering pit stop at the Café Gascon. Mario had a stirring tale to tell of some Italian derring do and Luc also had a few pithy remarks about some obnoxious earlier punters that evening. Eventually I ambled out of the Café and parked up at the top of the market hill as I was informed by The Scarecrow that it was still 'very, very clear' which was more than could be said for his diction. Some half an hour later, we were still clear and I was dozing contentedly with thoughts of Tiff aided by a touch of Van on that singularly elusive Daring Night.

Suddenly there was a firm knock on my window. Startled, I twiddled down my window to observe a scruffy looking little bugger with more of a scruffy goatee than proper designer stubble. 'Owmuchulmate?,' was his totally incomprehensible question uttered in some broad northern dialect. My secular public school upbringing had rendered me incompetent at identifying this weird species. However, after asking the gentleman thrice to repeat his question, I elucidated that he wished to go to the fair city of Hull on Humberside. Or is it now back in South Yorkshire?

My geographical inexpertness matched my accent deficiency of anywhere north of The Wash. However it still didn't stop me doing my best Professor Higgins impersonation.

'Are you sure that you don't really want to go to Hertford, Hereford or Hampshire, my man?'

I honestly thought he was going to belt me but then his face broke into a rueful grin. 'You fancy southern bastards always like to take the piss, don't you?'

After a quick burst of the Ascot Gavotte from me we called a truce and shook hands on it. I then radioed in to The Scarecrow and after a quite understandable delay, a figure of two hundred pounds was tentatively mentioned. Messrs Wells Fargo naturally didn't stoop to computers or satellite navigation. In fact we didn't stoop to using anything technical that might actually have aided the efficiency of our operation. I reckon that QC thought it would be cheating to take advantage of any modern systems. It might have taken away the challenge. After all, we weren't named Wells Fargo for nothing. We were full of pioneering spirit (and other rather stronger spirits in the case of some of us) in the frontier town of Sutton Market. If it wasn't for the fact that we were all owner drivers, I'm sure it would be horse and carriages all round. Except QC would be too mean to pay the blacksmith's undoubtedly outrageous farriers fees.

Back to the future, I quizzed The Man from Hull about his reasons for the journey. He had already been round to The Hole in the Wall and extracted his two hundred quid. He duly handed over the ten crisp twenties and said we had a deal. However it was no good taking him up to Hull if he was going to relieve me of the fare (and the rest) on the way or on arrival. A lot could happen between here and Hull dearie, as the actress said to the bishop. Anyway it transpired that Robert (as the taciturn Yorkshireman had cagily revealed his Christian name) had just written off his Peugeot hot hatch on the A14 and had managed to hitch a lift into town. He had been on his way from Felixstowe docks, where he worked as a welder, back to his home town of Hull and the loving arms of his girlfriend. The story seemed plausible so I decided to take the gamble. After we had stopped for a fill up and a sandwich for Robert, I studied the map and realized what I had let myself into. As I drove off into the drizzle and the darkness I reflected gloomily that I wasn't at my freshest and I didn't know which was going to prove the greater physical risk, tiredness or my passenger. But shit, I needed the money, didn't I?

The first hour didn't go badly at all as I powered along the A14 past Cambridge and Huntingdon and onto the A1(M). Robert was quite chatty about his work at the docks and I even learnt a thing or two about welding, a subject that hitherto hadn't been too close to my heart, apart from when Jennifer Beals was wielding her weapon so sexily in Flashdance. What a feeling!

Forbidden thoughts of Tiff came unbidden to mind again.

> In the firmament we move, we move and we live
> And we have our being
> Squeeze me don't leave, leave me in the daring night.

On the road I was even making a bit of progress on the accent front and could now understand at least fifty per cent of Robert's guttural utterances. I was even getting quietly confident that I wouldn't be mugged on arrival. This comforting feeling was reinforced when Robert fell soundly asleep at Peterborough.

But then I had a different sort of problem. It was now well past midnight as I passed the Newark turn off and the rain had started to come down in earnest. There were still plenty of heavy goods lorries about and the spray on overtaking was horrendous. I slowed right down to about sixty miles an hour as I really had to concentrate on the job in hand. No time for any more daydreaming. I once did a journey from Sutton Market to Stansted Airport and realized with horror afterwards that I couldn't remember a thing at all about the drive. I'm sure that too many people have had that similar scary experience when they have been lost in their own world of thought, music or conversation and suddenly haven't got a bloody clue where they are, even on a road you know intimately.

'How dangerous is that ?,' as Graham Taylor might have said if he was Minister of Transport. On reflection, he couldn't possibly do any worse than the present incumbent, and we might even get a joined-up Crossrail sooner rather than posthumously after the Olympics. The only trouble would be is that Graham probably thinks it's a new sort of midfield system.

Talking of systems I was now having real trouble with the current road system. I hadn't been on this piece of road since a memorable drive in the Morgan with Tiff three decades ago. I told you that I didn't venture north much. Oh hell and damnation, I couldn't get her out of my mind. It was July 1972. I was young, footloose and in love of course. Tiff was still a teenager and coltishly attractive. The mini skirt, those young, long limbed bronzed legs and that crooked smile. To die for. My flame red Morgan surged down the same road in the setting sun. We were off to Blyth, the Riviera of the North East apparently, to see Tiff's cousin who was working in this godforsaken place for the summer season. No matter. With her red dress dangling and the hood down, God was in his heaven. The sheer electricity of living made my spine tingle. We stopped off at Richmond for a bite and a pint or two. From that magical square we looked up to the castle and then at each other. This was the real thing. And then a lorry overtook me, breaking the spell and spraying me once again and shaking me back to the present. No more thoughts now of unrequited love.

Back on the A1 (no M now) the road was getting tougher. This was getting really serious. It seemed to be all twists and turns and adverse camber. I much prefer the straight and narrow. And the A1 was narrow all right, a tight and measly two lanes. But then again I suppose successive Ministers of Transport over the years have suffered from the same prejudice as me.

By now though, it wasn't quickly on at all. We had passed Doncaster and I was looking for the turn off to Hull. I had now dropped my speed to barely fifty miles an hour, as tiredness combined with the filthy conditions was making this a real marathon. Why the shit did I take on this mad venture? If the next wall of water turned out to be the side of an artic, there wouldn't be any dinner with Tiff, or anyone else for that matter. Robert was still snoring placidly beside me and some bore on Radio 5 Live was droning on about drains. Did anyone really care, especially at this unearthly hour? And it wasn't doing anything to keep my already drooping lids apart either. I couldn't even indulge in a quick blast of Van either that was certain to wake up Robert, and I certainly preferred to let sleeping dogs lie in this case. It was coming up to one o'clock and the miles seemed to be ticking off slower and slower and I certainly needed a shock or an alarm to keep me going. Don't ask or you might receive.

Suddenly the lorry in front which I had been following rather aimlessly and too closely for miles and miles did a sudden lurch to the right. I immediately braked hard in anticipation of some sort of obstacle or animal in the inside lane. Unfortunately this only had the effect of provoking a vicious skid. I may have had an ABS whatever that was, but it certainly didn't assist me in this case. I was also a taxi driver by profession and 'a very experienced driver' but I had always been absolute crap on the thankfully rare occasions when my car had been involved in a skid. I always panicked and wrestled with the wheel like a demented dervish, instead of keeping my cool and turning into the direction of the skid or whatever you are meant to do. The car swung from one side of the carriageway to the other for what seemed like an eternity. I really thought it was Curtainsville Arizona this time and we would smash into the unseen obstruction. I just closed my eyes and waited for the end.

But an age later I realized we were both stationary and alive. I opened my eyes again and saw no sign of any obstruction or destruction. The errant lorry driver had disappeared into the darkness. No, I was undoubtedly the guilty party for being too bloody close. Doubly luckily there was no vehicle behind. I started off again shaken and stirred to the marrow. But at least we were alive and unhurt. Robert had had his second miraculous escape of the evening. Perhaps I really did have God beside me. The one plus was that I was wide awake now which was more than could be said for my deified passenger. Miraculously again he had slept through the whole drama and was still snoring like a baby. In my heightened sense of awareness the rest of the journey passed off relatively smoothly, except for a minor confusion on the motorway front. Just before Doncaster I had safely negotiated the turn off on to the M18. I hadn't noticed on my earlier perusal of the map that there was another motorway numbered confusedly the M180. When we came to this junction there was no mention of Hull in either direction. Not knowing which route to take and not being able to stop, I decided to plug on up the M18 and hope for the best. Happily my luck was well and truly in now and I soon arrived at the M62 with a gloriously clear choice of Leeds or Hull. Thankfully I turned eastwards and stormed along the M62 and then the dualled A63 and arrived triumphantly at the Welcome to Hull sign at precisely quarter to two. At least the sign didn't have the nerve to call itself A Fine City as it has recently been voted the Crappiest Town in Britain. I could also now see why it was situated on the eastern fag end of England. The miracle was that someone had thought it necessary to build some mouldy old bridge to connect it to the south. It was probably that bugger Hadrian. Or perhaps it was to facilitate rapid egress for discontented natives? That seemed far more likely.

I awoke my holy companion and found out with dismay that

'we still had a problem.' At least Houston and Hull had got something in common. Robert didn't know exactly where his girlfriend lived. This was both annoying and ominous. Naturally I was very impatient to be on my way down south for the return two hundred plus miles and I didn't take kindly to any unnecessary delay. However far more worrying were the bad vibes emanating from Robert's apparent ignorance of his destination. I had been in this job long enough to know when something didn't feel right. I had also learnt to trust my gut instinct and here my guts were distinctly queasy. Shit I had come all this way, survived a near fatality, battled on just to be taken out when the end was in sight. But was it the end? I glanced over surreptitiously at Robert and he seemed pretty normal. But what is normal and what choice did I have? I decided to humour him for the moment while at the same time find out all I could about this elusive girlfriend of his. They had apparently only been going out for a while and on their few meetings he had always approached her house from the town centre. Accordingly I drove into the town while Robert rather too ostentatiously for my liking searched his memory. After a fruitless and increasingly alarming ten minutes, I had a belated brainwave. I'd often noticed my brain never functioned very well when my bowels were rumbling.

'Why don't you just give her a ring Robert?'

I had already noticed he didn't have a mobile with him so I produced mine with alacrity. He accepted my offer with limited enthusiasm and there followed a long and muffled telephone conversation between Robert and his mysterious girlfriend. On concluding it he ordered me peremptorily to take the first right, then first left and second right.

'This is it,' he murmured and indeed it was. The moment of truth. 'Stop here,' With that he ambled out, muttered a muted thank you, and then he was gone. Long, long gone. Phew.

A quick peep at the map revealed that an alternative route would take me over the aforementioned bridge and then down on to the M180. It was too dark to see anything going over the bridge but that was probably just as well. By the time I reached the welcoming shores of the southern side it was gone two thirty. However I was still flying on adrenaline from the earlier incident and I roared on into the night. Now there was no need for reserve at all and I let Van vent out my frustration full blast over the air waves. The sky was now clear after the rain and Van's words were perfect for the moment.

> I see Orion and the Hunters
> Standing by the light of the moon
> In the daring night, in the daring night
> And the heart and the soul
> As we look up in awe at the wonder of the heavens
> Oh and we go with the lord of the dance
> With the lord of the dance, the lord of the dance
> In the daring night.

Unfortunately, by the time I passed Doncaster again the adrenaline surge had almost totally worn off. I battled on but by the time I got to Newark I was absolutely buggered. By the time I got to Newark. It just doesn't quite have the same romantic ring as by the time I got to Woodstock, does it?

But what was painfully true had been that it was near Newark all those years ago, that I had let Tiff slip away on the return journey. Searching for what? Well I was going to find out very soon, wasn't I?

Suddenly I saw a sign for one of those Butlers Cabin places. Forty nine pounds ninety nine pence wasn't a bad price to pay for salvation. But how badly did I need the money? How badly did I need to stop? Sleep won.

But no, salvation would have to wait a while. The place had seemed deserted at first but eventually I found an asylum seeker working in the kitchen. In very hesitant English she nevertheless informed me rather precisely that there was no room in the inn. I collapsed into one of the less than comfy armchairs and muttered an oh shit. The girl also understood this piece of vernacular English and my knackeredness would have been obvious in any event to all but the most myopic migrant. She very kindly made me a pot of tea, my first sustenance for almost five hours. She also dug up some mouldy digestive biscuits but I wasn't in the mood to be fussy. After this much needed fuel stop and a ciggie, I was ready as I would ever be for the remaining road.

Off I went again into the Daring Night. My pin holes for eyes peered into the dark. By now I was down to a pathetic forty miles an hour despite the near perfect driving conditions and almost complete absence of any other road users. In the next two hours I barely covered seventy five miles, such was my exhaustion and pitiful speed. What the fuck was I doing still driving and what would Health and Safety make of it all? This was pure madness but some inner voice wouldn't let me pull over and have some sensible sleep. It was as if I was in some madcap marathon driving contest but of course the only competition was inside me. I still had to prove to the other buggers in The Hutch that I wasn't a poser, or a posh wanker as Tonker so delicately put it. I still had to flagellate myself, both mentally and physically. Who was I really trying to beat or prove myself to? My failure as a banker, a cricketer or, worse, as a husband and lover. I was just a failure, a loser. I had been dealt all the aces in life but had trumped myself effortlessly. Drive on, rave on. Oblivion beckons.

Come on Tommy, you've got Tiff to live for. Destiny was offering me another chance. But what if destiny lets me down yet again? I just couldn't face it. But I needed somewhere to stop again, even if it was only one of those ghastly Little Chef neon lit shacks which mar our trunk road landscape. Again the French do it better linguistically. Petit gives just the right contemptuous nuance for this abomination of a cuisine. So when I take over Granada, or whoever owns this chronic enterprise, I would immediately rename them all Le Petit Chef which would give a similar in your face warning as Smoking Kills on a fag packet. Or worse still, Can Make You Impotent. I'm really pleased about that actually. Otherwise there would be little Tommies all over the western world.

Then I saw it. The welcoming sign of an all night truckers café. I nervously opened the door but inside there was merely a sprinkling of normal people doing normal things. The attractive thirtyish waitress gave me a sparkling smile as she served up a large mug of strong tea. With lots of sugar as energy and a fag this should see me all the way back to Sutton Market. Contentedly day dreaming with my tea and Dunhill, I glanced out of the window and saw the first streaks of daylight. Or as Omar put it so memorably.

AWAKE! for Morning in the Bowl of Night
Has flung the Stone that puts the Stars to Flight:
And Lo! the Hunter of the East has caught
The Sultan's Turret in a Noose of Light.

I was going to make it. The dramatic sunrise gave me my third wind and I pinged towards Sutton Market with the force behind me once again. At seven thirteen precisely I arrived back in town.

'Car Thirteen to base.'

'Come in Car Thirteen.' came the surprised voice of QC himself. What the hell was he doing about at this hour?

'Clear and going home to bed.'

'Yes, I suppose I can find someone else for the school run this morning just for once Tommy,' was QC's magnanimous response. 'Oh, and well done Tommy.' I puffed with pride after praise from such an unlikely source. I felt like that nine year old prep schoolboy again after I had taken my six for thirteen in a needle match against Saint Joseph's College and my worshipped cricket master Ted Dawe had uttered the self same words. I looked down at my mileage clock. Six hundred and ninety two miles. Yes, well done indeed Tommy. I would be able to afford Tiff after all. Bring on that Daring Night.

By the time I had struggled back to work in the late afternoon, news of my exploits had spread and I was a temporary hero. Temporary being the operative word. Back in The Hutch after I had enjoyed my fifteen minutes of fame, I was brought down to earth from a most unlikely source.

'Now that you've won Le Mans Tommy, do you think you are ready for Everest? I mean bien sur your rendezvous with this bird at la maison d'amour.'

'You're French is crap Stack. I would stick to rugby if I was you. That's all you're fucking good at,' I snarled back. But of course he had hit a raw nerve as well he knew despite my angry protestations. For once there was silence in The Hutch until Elise eased the tension in her own inimitable fashion.

'Come over here Tommy and I will give you a few more tips.' But she couldn't help herself and added wickedly, 'But it will cost you.'

From there we went on to discuss the government's new road proposals. I think we all reached agreement that 'they hadn't got a fucking clue.' I thought that this government should at last grasp the nettle that an Englishman hasn't got an inalienable right to drive a car whenever and whenever he wishes. Christ he thinks like an Ulsterman with all talk of rights and none of responsibilities and look where that has got us. Someone has got to grasp the bloodied nettle and restrict, tax and toll to stop us disappearing into the polluted and congested nether. Eric more succinctly thought that it would be preferable to take all private cars off the road altogether and leave only buses and taxis. 'Then we'd all be bleeding millionaires wouldn't we?,' and as usual I couldn't fault his logic. Another example of joined up thinking perhaps?

But I couldn't procrastinate with my inebriated verbosity anymore because the Daring Night was fast approaching. It worried me shitless. I didn't dare to get too inebriated and Tiff would be equally unimpressed by verbosity. Then an alarming thought hit me, fuelled by alcohol and nervosity. We wouldn't have to talk dirty would we? Talk about real feelings. Crikey.

Well just one drink, one for the nerves. Or perhaps two, to improve my philosophising ability. And a final one to discover the meaning of life.

> Then to this earthen Bowl did I adjourn
> My Lip the secret well of Life to learn :
> And Lip to Lip it murmur'd – 'while you live
> Drink ! – for once dead you will never return.'

With this little bit of wisdom of Omar in mind I felt justified in taking a little detour on the way to La Vieille Maison via The Rising Sun. However after a couple of Mauldon snifters I was eased on my way by mine host.

'Bugger off Tommy, before you get pissed and totally fuck up,' was Graham's constructive Anglo Saxon advice as he ushered me out of The Rising Sun into the Daring Night.

Thus fortified for the off with wit and wisdom I ambled round to La Vieille Maison. I was still a few minutes early so I tarried awhile at the bridge over the River Bosmere and the romantic lights shining bright on the river. My time was up but I didn't know whether I was going to a celebration or an execution. I entered the hallowed premises and was warmly greeted by Madam Corbière, the proprietoress. She was so typically French, petite and chic, and probably in her early forties. I had only been able afford this exclusive establishment a couple of times over the years, but Wells Fargo always

111

recommended it to discerning clients and we were always bumping into her when picking up fares. It also gave me a chance to keep up my French which she seemed to appreciate. I had already tipped her off for tonight and she carefully led me to a romantic table for two tucked away in the corner. Naturally Tiff hadn't arrived yet so I ordered a bottle of the House White (a light and nifty Vin de Pays du Gers) to wile away the minutes. I only had the chance for half a glass of this little slider before I saw Eric's crappy Cavalier splutter up. Not a propitious start. It was too much to hope that The Crafty Cockney had kept that great orifice shut for once and he would have had ample time to regale Tiff of all my foibles and failings. He saw me through the window and gave a big thumbs up. At least Eric was ever the optimist. On verra.

Tiff got out of the car. Her informal jeans of our previous meeting had been replaced by a pencil thin black skirt of a non-committal length but which also served to proved that age had not withered those magnificent legs. I was positive that a bit more custom would not stale their infinite variety either, but would I get the chance to find out? To complete the ensemble she was wearing a silk black shirtwaister with one button carefully undone to reveal a wisp of black lacy bra. A careful sip of cold water to cool my ardour. Come on Tommy, you have got to get through that scintillating mind first, and then that simmering soul. But was it just geriatric lust or did I still have true feelings for her? Oh dear, it was back to those bloody feelings again. I knew I couldn't cope with those insidious little buggers.

'Hello Tiff. You look great.' That was pretty neutral but pretty true.

'You don't look too bad yourself Tommy, for an ageing reprobate that is.' Eric had been talking.

'A glass of white OK?'

'Fine.'

The pleasantries settled, we took time to assess each other while pretending to study the menu with enormous concentration. It took just two seconds for me to make my choice, ballantine of foie gras with toast followed by that equally succulent south west delicacy, magret de canard, served with a succulent cranberry sauce. It took Tiff over ten minutes to make exactly the same choice. At least we still had one thing in common. A half a bottle of 1999 sweet white Jurançon to wash down the foie gras and of course a bottle of 1998 Frederic Laplace Madiran for the magret and lavish cheese board to follow. I knew that if there was one thing I had enjoyed about being a banker, it was the trappings of life as a champagne socialist. Now I feared that I had been reduced to the ranks of an Old Labour beer bore.

The essentials over we got back to basics.

'OK Tiff, you go first.' I had always been frightened of facing the first ball of the match.

'Not much to tell Tommy. William and I met in Sheffield, as you remember?' I didn't but wished I had. 'That must have been in 1975.'

'What did he do?'

'He was a lecturer in law at the University when I was also working there as a history researcher. 'It all seemed to suit so well,' she added dreamily. 'We married and settled there.'

'Any children?'

'No children.' Silence followed. I wasn't doing very well. Christ she wasn't giving much away.

I tried again. 'What brought you back to Suffolk?'

'Oh, after William died I decided to return to my roots and try again. I have been trying to qualify as a counsellor since I came back.' Silence followed again.

The arrival of the foie gras briefly relieved the tension until the first mouthful of culinary bliss. Then she hit me where it hurts most.

'You have children, don't you? Where are they? What are they up to?'

This certainly wasn't the road I wanted the conversation to go. My response was monosyllabic and uninformative in the extreme. Luckily, after a little procrastinating on my behalf and a lot of looking into space, our minute entrée was cleared away in the knickers of time.

But then she hit me again. 'What about Megan? Where is she now?' So she knew about my divorce. What else did she know?

I was saved by the bell, or rather by the arrival of the magret.

I didn't want my dubious past and even more uncertain future to be scrutinized too carefully, but of course I knew her of old. She could wheedle far more out of me than she would disclose about herself.

She waited until the main course had been served and then she hit me again. For the first time she fixed her eyes directly on mine and smiled that crooked smile. Crikey.

'Well Tommy, you seem to have had a far more eventful life than me. Wouldn't you like to tell me a bit more all about it? We have all the time in the world. And I'm just fascinated by this research into the taxi world. It sounds far more interesting than my boring research in the academic world.' She had always more than matched me on the sarcasm front, but was she being sarcastic this time?

Well I too of course had plenty of time to work out my line of defence. However, as usual I prevaricated and went into a long and detailed description of my bankruptcy and broken marriage, interspersed of course with some witty anecdotes. Or at least I thought they were witty. This took most of the main course which was as usual delectable and she appeared to be listening intently if not perhaps with glazed rapture. But as I mopped up the last of the magret sauce and reached yet again for the comforting arm of Monsieur Laplace she grabbed my arm fiercely. I wimpishly yelped with the sudden pain.

'OK. Stop bullshitting Tommy,' she snapped. 'And put that bloody glass down for a moment. That's not going to rescue you now. And that's what I want to know about. The now.'

I had forgotten quite how piercingly direct she could be when she put her steely purpose to it.

'And just to make it a tiny bit easier for you, drop the stupid research act. I never bought it for a moment.'

All that agonizing for nothing, but of course she had always read me like a book. A book that seemed about to be consigned to the dustbin of life in the very near future unless I came up with something very quickly. Unless, of course the truth. I had nothing to lose now. And out it came like a rush of verbal diarrhoea. And what a relief. I groaned and lit a cigarette, ignoring the vicious tutting from two stolid matrons at the next table.

'OK. You win. I've been doing this bloody job for over three years now. I've paid a few bills in that time, regained my self respect and even the occasional respect of others. I've stuck at it for over one hundred and fifty bleeding thousand miles and I'm proud of it. But all that time I have avoided my original haunts, still humiliated by my financial downfall. I'm still afraid to meet people I used to know. Then the sheer horror when I met you again, driving a bloody taxi. All along I've been searching for that fucking elusive Philosopher's Stone but recently I've let it slip away. Oh shit, I'm never going to find it now.'

'You certainly swear more than you used to.'

'So,' I said defensively.

'Come on Tommy, it was an observation, not a criticism. I see you are as touchy as ever. Why shouldn't you still find it?'

I ground out my cigarette furiously. Tiff had never smoked but had never seem to mind a bit of passive smoking herself, but not in the middle of a meal and her disapproval showed itself with that little purse of the lips.

'I've had enough of The Road, Tiff. It's totally ground me down.'

'There you go again. You sure are an angry old man.' But then she smiled that mischievous smile and I was in heaven again.

'I still fancy you like hell Tiff.' There, I'd said it. She had certainly dragged me out of my shell. Shit I had been trying so hard to be Mr Cool and had failed pathetically yet again.

That smile again. 'My mind or my body? It's all right, don't look so alarmed. You needn't answer that one.' But then she grew serious. 'Look Tommy, I came back to Suffolk to regroup. I'm still trying to come to terms with William's death. It wasn't easy, you know. I don't know if I can ever take on another serious relationship again.'

Where had I heard that before I wonder? My disappointment was patently all too apparent.

'There's no need to put on that pathetic puppy dog face. You are far too old for that.'

I squirmed at that but then she took pity on me.

'Look, it's been a lovely evening Tommy and great to see you again, and looking so well despite yourself. I like your idea of searching for that fucking Philosopher's Stone, to use your own inimitable words. Who knows one day you may even find it. As you are so keen on saying, on verra.'

At that stage Madam Corbière instinctively brought us two expressos. I had gone off the idea of cheese and Tiff had never been a sweet woman if I could put it that way.

'Am I allowed an armagnac?' I asked tentatively.

Tiff smiled again. Perhaps I wasn't doing so badly after all. 'Look Tommy, I'm not an ogre. Just go easy on the hard stuff that's all I'm saying. In fact I'll have one as well this time and keep you company. I'll pay for them.' She really knew how to hit me where it hurts most. Cue Omar.

> Lo! some we loved, the loveliest and the best
> That Time and Fate of all their Vintage prest,
> Have drunk their Cup a Round or two before,
> And one by one crept silently to Rest.

Was Tiff simply going to join the others and creep silently away to rest? She was certainly the loveliest and the best. Hell, I loved her so and always had.

'What about your sons?' she suddenly asked startlingly me out of my reverie. 'You didn't say much about them earlier?' She hadn't elaborated why she hadn't had children herself but again showed her unerring knack of homing in on my Achilles heels.

'I just feel so much guilt about them. I didn't support them at all, either spiritually, physically or financially. Now Megan is doing so well with her landscape paintings, I can't even help them on the latter front. Even worse, they don't even seem to miss me at all. I had never been there for their formative days. Always too busy, the successful businessman's traditional lament. I left it there. After I had lost my business and had more time to spend with the family, I found out far too late that I no longer had a family to spend it with. I just hadn't the heart or spirit to elaborate on that to Tiff.

'Poor Tommy, not so good,' but of course I didn't want her pity. Far better a little bit more self pity. Oh, forget about yourself for once Tommy. Tiff had lost a husband at a very premature age and had no chance to even lose any children but she wasn't complaining, just 'regrouping'. I loved her composure, her compassion, her complexion and complexity. In fact, her everything. However there would be no chance of that sort of thing in this particular Daring Night.

'Thanks for a lovely evening Tiff. You make me feel good about myself again. And we haven't even talked about the good old times that we thought would never end. Another time, another place perhaps?'

'No Tommy. Same time, same place next month.' With that she picked up the bill that had mysteriously arrived at the snap of her long fingers. 'I'll deal with this one. You pay next time. Please ring Wells Fargo for my taxi.' I do so like a masterful woman.

Ten minutes later Eric's crappy Cavalier appeared on the scene again. 'All right Tommy,' he leered as I gave Tiff the traditional two chaste kisses on her not so chaste cheeks.

And then off alone into the Daring Night with the dream still alive.

Don't ever leave me in the daring night
When all the stars are shining bright
And don't let go, and don't let go
Don't let go don't let go in the daring night.

6.   IVORY TOWER

When you come down
From your Ivory Tower
You will see how it really must be
To be like me to see like me
To feel like me.

Three months passed by. Three long hard winter months interspersed with three more little dindins with Tiff at La Vieille Maison. However both females were beginning to lose a little of their allure. Tiff had been enchanting as ever at first during these tête à têtes. However, despite pinning me with those wide blue eyes of hers for long periods of time, something didn't feel right. I couldn't put my finger on it at first but then with a flash of unusual insight I realized she was treating me as if I was her first 'client'. While she appeared to be hanging on my every word like a starry-eyed lover, she was really examining me. She didn't let me see her at all between our rendezvous', and seemed to be keeping me at bay apart from our monthly meetings. She had become obsessed with her counselling diploma and it was as if I was on the metaphorical counsellor's couch for the whole of our sessions at Madame Corbière's. Whereas me as a typically, naive, blue-blooded male only wanted to get down on a real couch with Tiff, or coucher with her as the French put it so seductively. But

121

all she really wanted to do with me apparently was to heal me for Christ's sake.

'Look Tommy, you are still very hurt and angry inside from your bankruptcy. You feel that as you are a failure in business, you are a failure in life. You are also still traumatized from your divorce with Megan and separation from the boys. And of course we haven't yet addressed the problems associated with your parents banishing you to boarding school at the tender age of eight.'

'Bollocks. Get with it Tiff. Look at yourself, a wealthy widow living alone in her luxury ivory tower wittering on about healing. I'm only interested in the present, unlike you are still buried in the past.' Oh shit. How could I have committed such an unforgivable faux pas? At that moment I wished the ground could have risen up and buried me as well.

The immediate flash of anger in her eyes was quickly subsumed by tears.

'OK, Mr Taxi Driver. So that's the way you want to play it,' she said icily. 'Why don't you just carry on playing at being a pathetic little taxi driver and leave me to my apparently meaningless studies. Let me pick up the tab this time as I'm sure you can't really afford to eat in such flash restaurants on your meagre income. Why don't you just bugger off, to use your own crude vernacular, and leave me to deal with all the boring details of life which appear to be beyond your understanding.'

And off I buggered to bed, too shell-shocked even to get pissed.

The next day I had no time to dwell on my catastrophic rendezvous with Tiff as it was straight in to a double shift on the weekend grindstone. It was a quarter past eleven on a typically frantic Friday night when Thin Lizzie sent me to one of the no-go areas on the Highpoint Estate. It was with the usual trepidation that I entered this insalubrious area and arrived at the designated street number. Naturally I never got out of the car at night on this estate and waited nervously with my right index finger on the automatic lock button and my right foot resting on the accelerator. After five minutes I was about to utter a relieved no show to Thin Lizzie when two fuzzy figures emerged out of the gloom of the side porch. It appeared as if they were in the middle of a heated argument and carried on beside my car as if I wasn't there. One was a long haired blond girl dressed like a leftover hippy from the sixties and not unlike Joni Mitchell, while the other figure was a dead ringer for Jim Morrison of The Doors. Unfortunately the latter was behaving just like Jim but, unlike Jim, was very much alive. However, as I slid the car into gear ready for a very rapid getaway, Jim suddenly launched himself into the front passenger seat. Ominously it was soon apparent that Joni wasn't coming with us. 'Bildeston mate, and sharp.'

With a last vicious 'fuck off bitch', we were on our way. Jim didn't say much at first as we drove out of Sutton Market and seemed to be marshalling the last of his mangled dandelion thought processes. However, as we left the comforting lights of the town behind he suddenly dropped something hard and metallic on my lap.

'What do you think this is mate,' he demanded harshly. 'I haven't got a fucking clue, mate,' I replied in kind, but my difficulty in swallowing told its own tale.

123

'Its a gun.'

'Oh.'

'Don't you believe me?' he harshly stepped up a gear.

'Oh yes, I believe you all right.' Did Jim detect the tremor in my voice or had he got enough tremors of his own to occupy him fully?

He grabbed the 'gun' off my lap. 'Do you know what I'm going to do with it?'

'Again, I haven't got a fucking clue. Mate.'

I don't know what the hell had got into me. I should have been trying to placate this bloody madman but just couldn't curb that errant tongue. Was it Tonker who said I would get my come uppance one day? No, of course what he actually said was as ever a bit more upfront and personal.

'Tommy, someone is going to knock the shit out of you one day, you toffee-tongued prick,' beautifully mixing his metaphors again. In the circumstances I would have settled for that less than permanent fate like a shot. Shit.

'I'm going to waste that bastard who tried to steal my girl friend.'

'That sounds an excellent idea, Jim.' Fear does funny things to you, especially your tongue.

He went silent for what seemed like an eternity. At last he spoke again.

'Are you taking the mick, Mr Fancy Taxi Driver? Perhaps I should take you out instead.'

Oh God, was I going to meet that GUT? Christ, not yet please. Someone once said that imminent death makes Christians of all atheists. But surely I wasn't going to die for a measly nine pounds fifty, was I? I thought I had known fear before but this was just blind terror. My heart rate went off the Richter scale and I thought it would explode. My hands were shaking so much I could barely hold the wheel. I desperately tried to concentrate only on the road ahead.

'Lost your voice have we, you little shit-scared wanker?'

Weirdly enough, this accurate and deserved insult somehow stirred me into some sort of verbal and physical coherence.

'I don't think that would be very good idea,' I heard myself say. 'My controller has got both the pick up point and your address in Bildeston. I have just pressed my emergency call button and the police would already have been alerted. You wouldn't get five yards.' Where that inspiration came from I haven't got a clue even to this day. I went on quickly as I sensed I was winning this deadly battle of wits. 'Why don't I just drop you off on the outskirts of Bildeston and then I will call my controller to say that it was a false alarm?'

'How do I know that you won't double-cross me?' I was winning.

'Look chum, I just want a quiet life. In fact any sort of life.'

He snorted with approval at my confessed cowardice.

'But I'm still going to kill that other bastard.'

'Sounds like he deserves it,' I murmured sympathetically. Christ, were there no depths to which I wouldn't sink to?

I felt him looking at me carefully to detect any more hint of irony. There was none of course.

'OK drop me off right here.' We were just reaching the parish boundary of the village. I didn't need a second invitation and braked sharply. As he climbed out of the car I could see the gun clearly in his hand. It looked big, ugly and lethal. 'I'm off.'

And then I went and spoiled it all.

'No charge of course this time. Sir.' I must have had a death wish.

But he only muttered darkly that 'there won't be another time,' and then miraculously he was gone. I had survived.

Of course I didn't report the incident to anyone but made a feeble excuse to Thin Lizzie that I wasn't feeling very well and went straight home. I know that she didn't believe me but frankly, I didn't care a damn. I was still alive and very glad of the fact. I wasn't ready to die yet. There were things still to do. First a drink was called for. And another and another. Go for it Omar.

One moment in Annihilation's Waste,
One Moment, of the Well of Life to taste –
The Stars are setting, and the Caravan
Draws to the Dawn of Nothing – Oh make haste !

I had often wondered where Van had got the inspiration for Caravan. Now I knew. I also knew that I had had a very narrow escape and was indeed going to make haste for the 'Well of Life to taste', and then a touch more of 'Annihilation's Waste'. I also had a little joint to assist those Setting Stars. By the time I had consumed my second bottle of Madiran I was getting there. But I was also getting seriously angry with Tiff, however unfairly.

Don't you know the
price that I have to pay
Just to do everything I
have to do ?

I had almost paid the ultimate price just to try and find that fucking Philosopher's Stone she had so casually encouraged. Time for another confrontation. And a conflagration, if I had my way.

I was having a really bad trot on all fronts. Somehow I had managed to keep a clean driving licence for over thirty years before embarking on The Waiting Game, and then out of the blue I got done twice for speeding in under one month. Six points on my licence and almost two hundred quid in fines. That hurt but luckily I could put them down as deductible expenses against tax. One thing you could never say about me was that I lacked creativity, even if I lacked understanding. Perhaps I should have been an accountant. After all I was shit hot at those elusive black holes.

Then I got done again, this time in very dubious circumstances, or so I thought. Of course being a natural appealer, I immediately appealed against the decision. Unfortunately after the case had originally been earmarked for Sutton Market, it was then deferred and relisted for Peasenhall. As British wheels of justice move slowly this happened to be another six months after the 'offence' had taken place. Equally ominously, the case was now listed to be heard the week after my tiff with Tiff and my showdown with Jim. Not a good few days at all.

As luck or rather fate would have it, Eric had been up before the beak as well a fortnight before on an almost identical charge as mine. He had returned to The Hutch in triumph after his case. He might have said veni, vidi, vici. In fact his words were Anglo-Saxon and thus all the more effective.

'I effing well stuffed them. I tied up those fuzz buggers in knots. Their evidence was crap. The Clerk virtually told the Mags to throw out the case.'

Eric beamed with pleasure as we showered our congratulations on him. It also augured well for me. If the crafty but ill-educated Cockney could win his case so effortlessly, it should be a piece of piss for a man of my learning. Unfortunately I had of course forgotten Omar's ominous warning.

> And strange to tell, among that Earthen Lot
> Some could articulate, whilst others not.

Much, much later, I found out from Nigel who had witnessed the whole event that Eric had in fact been very crafty indeed. He had apparently been the model of politeness and reasonableness.

The police were 'mistaken', not 'bloody liars'. His seat of the pants mental dexterity was remarkable as he smilingly demolished the prosecution's case. And he never lost his cool, even under severe provocation from the Crown Prosecutor. Even more vitally, unlike the erudite but temperamentally fragile Tommy, neither did he crack under pressure. Discussing Court cases in general with Eric long after these events, the latter revealed his secret.

'You see Tommy,' he revealed with a twinkle in his eye, 'I have had rather more experience than you at this sort of thing and have learnt to learn from my mistakes. Such as not leaving fingerprints on a beer glass in the local pub before you carry out a break-in. I did two years for that little mistake.'

I looked at him sharply to see if he was taking the piss. He wasn't. Back to the present, it was now my turn to shine or shit myself.

Thus it was at ten past nine on a suitably funereal grey Friday morning that I found myself arriving with trepidation and surreal tiredness at the legendarily unforgiving Peasenhall Magistrates Court. I was already completely knackered after arriving home well after three the same morning and then spending a panic struck hour looking for my driving licence. Then up at the crack of dawn to finish preparing my case and driving the twenty extra miles The East Suffolk Magistrates' Courts had so thoughtfully made necessary for me to travel to try and secure justice. Justice, what a utopian hope. I parked my car in the convenient and spacious car park immediately behind the Court and then watched with amusement as an infirm elderly gentleman and an officious looking middle aged woman fiddled in vain with a nest of keys in a futile attempt to enter the fortress.

I just hoped they weren't two of the magistrates. I left them to it and ambled round to the front where I spent a pleasant quarter of an hour chatting to an elegant foreign lady. She was apparently acting as an interpreter for two Portuguese gentleman who were also going to have the pleasure of being up in front of the beak that morning. Apart from them there was no obvious sign of life. Five minutes later the doors were eased open by a harassed looking middle aged lady who transpired to be The Usher. I didn't know I had come to a sodding wedding.

Mrs Usher asked me to identify myself. I had already elucidated from an earlier phone call to the Court that my case was definitely due to be second on, so I was very surprised to be informed that the order of play was solely at the Clerk to the Court's discretion. I then asked to speak to the Duty Solicitor as helpfully advised by the Citizens Advice Bureau. Unfortunately there was no solicitor available as Peasenhall apparently ranked very low on the totem pole. To make matters worse Mrs Usher then advised me that the Clerk to the Court (henceforth to be referred to CTTC) was not at all happy with the presence of my car in the official car park. When I protested vociferously that there were several vacant parking spaces she told me to take it up with the CTTC. I retorted that she could take it up with me if she still wanted me to move it. Not a propitious beginning.

Back to the Court and more waiting. Ten minutes later Mrs Usher informed me that, as mine was a very straightforward case and wouldn't take long, we were first on. No time to compose myself or control those damned nerves. I had been hoping that I could watch the first case to get the hang of the proceedings and size up the opposition. Fat chance. Into the legal eagles den. I was ushered into the dock by Mrs Usher (so that was her job) and it really did feel as if I was heading for the gallows. Looking round I observed the three magistrates on their raised podium and my heart sank. The chairwoman was a lady of a certain age with dyed blond hair and a rat trap mouth and looked suspiciously like Lady Thatcher. Oh shit, she hadn't come out of retirement just for this, had she? On Lady T's right was the elderly gentleman I had comically observed earlier and on her left was a Miss Marple lookalike, but it unfortunately transpired without the latter's sharp brain or even any power of speech at all. Worse still, in the middle below the dais was the earlier observed officious looking lady who turned out not unnaturally to be the CTTC herself. Why oh why couldn't she have waddled over earlier in the car park and gently asked me to transpose my vehicle? Opposite the dock was evidently the witness stand and in the middle further back from the CTTC was Mr Blair, the Crown Prosecutor, an unassuming and pleasant-looking gentleman. At the far end of the room by the entrance door was my bête noire, PC Hacker himself. No-one else was present. The local press obviously deemed this to be a nonevent and they were dead right.

I was asked to stand as the charge was read. I felt like I was a real criminal at the Old Bailey. Luckily, or unluckily depending on your point of view, Rumpole wasn't there to defend me. The charge was that on Friday the thirteenth of November the previous year I had committed the heinous crime of breaking Section 36 (1) of the Road Traffic Act 1988 (i.e. jumping a red light). How did I plead? Not guilty, milady.

Mr Blair then opened the batting by calling PC Hacker to the witness stand. The latter had a pleasantly open and honest-looking face. Looks can be deceptive though as I had already painfully found out during our earlier brief encounter and his later witness statement. Mr Blair competently and smoothly ran him through his evidence which mainly confirmed that he had seen me drive through a red light. Time for cross examination. Shit, I wish Rumpole was here after all.

In fact I had just two simple questions to put to the PC. First, how far would he estimate was he positioned from the junction? He answered confidently about one hundred metres. I then asked him how many passengers were in my car? He answered not so confidently that there were two. I then turned triumphantly to the bench in true Perry Mason fashion (I knew my TV lawyers if nothing else). 'As a matter of fact the distance from PC Hacker to the junction was in fact only fifty metres and I had three passengers, not two. So if the PC is one hundred per cent out on one simple fact and fifty per cent on another, I would just like the Court to consider how much credibility can be given to the rest of his testimony. I have no further questions to put to this witness,' I finished pompously as ever. However as I looked to the Bench again they seemed singularly underwhelmed by my revelations. Perhaps it was the pony tail they didn't like. Anyway it was patently obvious they weren't impressed and the urbane Mr Blair slipped the PC a couple of half volleys to get back on track.

It was now my turn to present my case.

However as I was reading my beautifully crafted statement in my best legal voice, each time I looked up there appeared to be a glazed expression on the three beaks' faces. Didn't they understand what I was saying or were they deliberately ignoring the daggers aimed specifically at a delicate part of PC Hacker's anatomy? Anyway who were these guys sitting in judgement over me?

> You've got opinions and
> judgements about
> All kinds of things
> That you don't know
> anything about.

Well they wouldn't know anything about Van either, would they?

Who appointed them and why? What were their mental qualifications? What were their legal qualifications? How impartial were they? Not very it would appear, as Mrs Thatcher was looking at me as if I was something the cat brought in. I shuddered to think how she would regard some poor unfortunate girl or boy with rings all over their anatomy and up on a shock horror drugs charge.

Anyway back to the case in hand, mine. I had started my oratory strongly as I thought I had got a sound a defence as England's rugby team but, as I got the gist of the referee's decisions, I finished lamely in a weak whimper. My main point that I had only very fractionally gone over a red light as opposed to PC Hacker's blatant lie that I had jumped it by a country mile seemed to be totally lost. After my feeble presentation, Mr Blair had only one apparently innocuous question for me and delivered with a sweet smile.

'Did I see the signals changing from green to orange to red ?'

'Yes' I replied naively.

He turned triumphantly to the bench. 'No further questions,' he smirked. I had just shot myself in the head without even realizing it.

That was the end of the proceedings and we now had to wait for the judgement of the magistrates. First I must reluctantly admit that I had done Mrs T a teeny-weeny injustice. She had indeed picked up my mention of the Section 151 of the Highway Code although, naturally, she hadn't got a clue what it was all about. For all you backroom lawyers itching to know all its subtle complexities, I quote it in full.

Junctions controlled by traffic lights.

151. You MUST stop behind the white 'Stop' sign across your side of the road unless the light is green. If the amber light appears you may only go on if you have already crossed the stop line or are so close to it that to stop might cause an accident (my italics).

Oh god, what a prat. Why hadn't I read out the Section in full and given maximum emphasis to the last italized part? I had also fallen comprehensively into the innocuous looking Mr Blair's trap. Of course I hadn't seen the lights change from green to orange which I had just admitted to doing as I had been side-tracked for a split second after glimpsing PC Hacker's police car. Anyway, why was I being so honest when PC Hacker was lying through his teeth? And why was he so desperate for a conviction?

Anyway Mrs T asked CTTC to rustle up a copy of the aforementioned booklet and then they all shuffled out together to discuss its full ramifications, or so I hoped with a sudden onrush of optimism. But after less than a quarter of an hour (just time to leisurely imbibe a cup of coffee, although two of them looked liked they needed a double expresso to explode them into life), they returned and hope left as quickly as it had arrived as I could see the metaphorical black cap already placed above Mrs T's grim mouth. This insight was quickly confirmed when Mrs T said that, although they had looked carefully at Section 151, they had no option but to find me guilty as charged. Before passing sentence had I anything to say in mitigation? But I had already put all my eggs into one basket during my evidence statement, hadn't I? I could therefore only mumble unconvincingly that this was my only source of income, but I could see on Mrs T's face that my personal attack on PC Hacker had counted heavily against me. Of course the police never tell lies, do they? As Georgie put it so brutally,

> Whose murd'rous hand a drowsy Bench protect,
> And whose most tender mercy is neglect.

It was only left for Mrs T to insult me further by asking the CTTC to read out my record. Oh dear, I had driven at sixty two miles an hour on a dead straight piece of dual carriageway in perfect driving conditions on the A14 just outside Sutton Market and ditto forty three miles an hour in a thirty mile speed limit on a main road near Woodbridge, thus incurring an accumulated six points on my licence. CTTC read out my offences with unconcealed relish and made me sound like a hardened criminal. This time it was another three points and a further savage two hundred quid fine plus costs. Here endeth my first direct experience of English law in the raw and I trudged out of the court in deep depression. For the time being I had completely forgotten the ever enlightened words of Omar.

But leave the Wise to wrangle, and with me
The quarrel of the Universe let be :
And, in some corner of the Hubbub coucht,
Make Game of that which makes as much of Thee.

As I drove back morosely to Sutton Market, I reflected that I would need to again utilize that lamentable football cliché and keep a clean sheet not just for a measly ninety minutes but for an awesome eighteen months.

Where is the logic in rescinding points solely on a time scale? Taxi drivers and salesmen do upwards of fifty thousand miles a year while the average driver does little more than twelve and a half thousand miles. More important it wasn't just either, which I jejunely thought was the idea of justice. So Tommy the taxi driver has an amendment to the Road Traffic Act to be implemented immediately. Penalty points on a driving licence should be deducted either every three years (as at present), or every fifty thousand miles driven, whichever is the lesser period. In the latter case the onus of proof would obviously be on the driver, but with careful logging and the assistance of the records of the DTA that shouldn't prove to be an insurmountable problem in this computer driven age. Should it?

Back at The Hutch I received only mild sympathy from Elise and Leonardo for my swingeing fine and three point penalty, while some of the others were openly contemptuous.

The Boy Racer naturally led the attack.

'You shouldn't drive like a sodding maniac Tommy,' he chortled. 'And anyone who is stupid enough to jump a red light right in front of a police station deserves to get done.

I bridled immediately and launched into a predictable counter attack.

'Ah, there speaks the paradigm of virtue. I've never known you stick to any bloody speed limits Nigel.'

'Its no good trying to confuse me with your fancy words Tommy just because I drive with my eyes wide open on the road while all you can think about is other things wide open.'

This obscene reference to Tiff really got me going.

'You're the fucking nutter Nigel.'

'And your language has gone downhill badly Tommy. That's the trouble with slumming it, isn't it?'

Just as we were about to come to blows Tonker chipped it in his customary diplomatic fashion.

'You two are both effing stupid. Actually, Tommy's problem is that he drives with his nose in the air and his head in the clouds. That's why he sees nothing. And Nigel is effing clever enough to spot all the effing hairdryers because his brain is in his bollocks.'

That last bit of Tonker's convoluted logic eluded us all but he had broken the tension as usual with his good-humoured intervention.

'Its getting bloody stupid with all these cameras everywhere,' chipped in Stack.

'And all those buggery breathalysers,' breathed Sandy suspiciously.

'And all these thirty mile limits in the middle of the bloody country,' Nigel came back strongly. 'Plus those sodding crossings at East Bergholt and Haughly. They should be bloody banned.'

Tonker naturally had the last word.

'They want more effing fuzz cars on the road and less effing cameras. That would stuff the buggers.'

That seemed to cover buggers in general but The Hutch got the point all right.

I had to get to the point in another direction as well. By some major miracle I had been allowed back on the metaphorical couch again at Madam Corbière's for our monthly meeting. Tiff's forgiving nature apparently knew no bounds. Her philosophy of life was obviously much more effective than mine. As usual, she was perfectly dressed in another black silk blouse, but this time matched with an impeccable black midi skirt. Christ, she was beautiful. Don't lose her this time Tommy. Tonight we had been allowed an extra bottle of Frederic Laplace's special 1998 nectar to make up for the last encounter but, unfortunately, this only served to stir my repressed bellicosity. After another meaningful sigh from Tiff following another too quickly refilled glass, I suddenly snapped.

'Do you want to treat me for alcoholism as well as all my other problems ?' I snarled.

'Oh Tommy.' Only two words but so much pregnant meaning. 'I want to help you because I still care about you. Despite everything.'

'Do you? I thought you still wanted to heal me. And talking of you, which we weren't of course, is there any chance in the not too distant future that Mrs Sharpestone will be ready for another relationship?' I wasn't going to let her off that lightly even now.

'Dear Tommy, please give me just a little more time.' And then she smiled so seductively like in the good old days and I was lost again. 'What about your next court case? Could you cool it for once, just for me?' Of course I could.

As luck would have it, only a month after my disastrous appearance in front of the beak at Peasenhall, I had been invited to prostrate myself again before the Magistrate Courts. Tiff had tactfully restrained herself from mentioning the earlier debacle during our meal. However this time the hearing was in Sutton Market itself, and the magistrates here had a much fairer reputation than those zealots at Peasenhall. Well I just hope my informants were well informed or this time it would be my Private Hire licence that would be suspended or even revoked. I had appealed to the Magistrates Court under Section 61 (3) of the notorious Local Government (Miscellaneous Provisions) Act 1976 against a decision of the Wuffa District Council to suspend my licence for three months for foul, offensive and blasphemous language to a fare. They had got me under the self-same Section 61 of the above Act, this time under sub-section (1) b. This

139

covered 'any other reasonable cause' which must be the biggest and most unreasonable catch-all ever. My 'crime' was to mutter within the tender hearing of a fastidious fare who just happened to want me to transport her and what seemed like half of the contents of B&Q to her precious Edwardian villa.

'Jesus Christ, I'm a taxi driver not a fucking removal man.'

Unfortunately my fare happened to be a prim female member of the Wuffa District Council and a strict Catholic to boot. She was to strict and prim that I had also been goaded to tell her the joke about when the lamb of God descended into Hell, the Devil swore because there was no mint sauce with the roast lamb. She had subsequently lodged a complaint against me, hence the current state of affairs. There had already been a hearing before twelve so called upright citizens of the Wuffa District Council where I was found guilty in absentia, not deigning it worth my time and hence loss of income to appear before such a non-august body. Hence the current situation.

This time I was up against the mighty Tony Braithwaite, esteemed Head of Wuffa District Council's Legal Services. TB didn't belong to the other TB school of oily smoothness. He was more of the Prescott bruiser type and I fancied my chances a lot more against this sort of upfront opposition. My legal case was also much stronger (or should I say more intangible) than last time and I had learnt a lot from my earlier debacle. You will also observe that I was still arrogant and mean enough to dispense with both the experience and expense of learned counsel. Would I be up for it this time? On verra.

The momentous day started dry and sunny and I felt the

omens were good. But of course that was my trouble. I had always been stronger on omens than reality. Strange for an atheist or should I say pantheist. The Magistrates Court at Sutton Market was also much friendlier. We had been allotted Room 3 which was a bit smaller and intimate than the others and, with its fine oak panelling and embossed ceiling, was very agreeable visually. There we were. The feng shui, architecture and the omens were good but would I be any good?

My case was but of course listed first again. We couldn't waste any of the Council officials valuable time could we? The Usher was again female, agreeable but agitated. Perhaps these characteristics were compulsory. However in the Courtroom itself all the participants were totally different. Mrs T had been replaced by a kindly looking, smart bloke of about my own age, Father Time had miraculously metamorphosed into a young cool looking coloured gentleman and Miss Marple was now a middle aged lady with not so prim horn-rimmed glasses. Everything was going to be all right.

TB opened proceedings predictably with a simple recitation of the facts and then called his star witness. Mrs Batty was a dowdy middle aged woman with little sex appeal. Not even my roughest fares would want to give her one, to utilize Sutton Market vernacular. She also had that old style permanently turned down mouth which indicated she had stepped on or in something distinctly unpleasant. She had of course, me and my car. TB started cautiously on the foul and offensive bit of the case. But here he had a problem. He just couldn't get Mrs B to actually say the word fucking. The mouth turned down further and further but she just couldn't utter the filthy word. She didn't look as if she had ever done the act either. In the end the chairman asked her to write the word down. TB then read it out aloud and asked her if that was the terrible word Mr Gainsborough had used so gratuitously. She gritted her teeth and with a pure look of hatred at me for inflicting this ordeal on her, came out with a loud and clear yes. With a look of triumph TB turned to the bench but then unwisely didn't pursue the matter. He obviously thought it enough just to prove that I had used the 'f' word.

More sensibly he went easier on the blasphemous bit but this was where Mrs B became distinctly animated about Mr Gainsborough contemptuous taking of the Lord's name in vain. I certainly wouldn't be getting a Christmas card from her this year. TB then returned to my 'grossly offensive and foul language' to an inoffensive fare and wanted it known that the Council wouldn't tolerate this sort of behaviour from any of the two hundred and fifty four licensed Hackney or Private Hire drivers under its omnipotent jurisdiction.

Did I have any questions to put the witness? No, but another look of pure hatred was hurled in my direction from Mrs B as she left the witness box.

Now it was my turn. Determined to learn from my earlier humbling experience, I was resolved not to alienate the Bench this time. Originally I had planned a full frontal assault on the Bench. I was firmly of the opinion that they were only competent to judge on legal matters. Their competence didn't extend to mastery of the English language, did it? And then for once sanity prevailed in that oversized ego of a brain and I realized that it wouldn't be a very constructive approach, although it would no doubt give me a very short bout of vicarious pleasure. Thus I resolved to use only cold-blooded logic this time.

I started with the blasphemous side of things as I didn't think that would take very long to demolish.

I patiently explained to the Court that, as a non-believer in Christianity, I didn't believe in a GUT. Moreover, although I had no problem with the actual historical existence of Jesus of Nazareth, I didn't subscribe to any of that Resurrection or Son of God nonsense. Hence if I didn't believe, there couldn't be any such offence as blasphemy. I looked up to see Cool Hand Luke and Middle-Aged Lady nodding while the Chairman looked neutral. No offence so far. I consolidated by saying that as far as English common law was concerned, only the Church of England could bring a charge of blasphemy. As the lady in question was a Roman Catholic, I was completely innocent in legal terms as well. I also pointed out to the Court that the last blasphemy trials in this country were the Gay News one in 1977-79 and the Satanic Verses case in 1988-89, and look what a nest of vipers they unearthed. Surely the most desirable single thing to do with the common law of blasphemy would be to abolish it, together with the obsolete ecclesiastical laws against heresy, schism and atheism. However, returning to the present case, I could provided full details of the above two trials to support my legal point if necessary. I looked up again at the Bench and saw that it wouldn't be necessary. As clearly as the last Bench was antagonistic, this one was clearly sympathetic. Perhaps they were impressed by my legal expertise, or perhaps just my restraint. Don't blow it now Tommy.

Moving on to the obscenity charge, I referred the Court to the Collins English Dictionary, Millennium Edition. The definition of the word obscene to be found there was as follows:- 'offensive or outrageous to accepted standards of decency or modesty'. I said that I didn't think that any reasonable person would have any problem with that definition. I looked round to see everyone nodding, even TB. To me the key words were accepted standards. But what were accepted standards? The average fare in Sutton Market where every other word was a fucker or a wanker? Or that little old lady on the Clapham Omnibus? Or somewhere in the middle, say the legal profession? I know for a fact that a lot of their language outside the courts is none too chaste. Or take one of the most popular family films of recent years, Four Weddings and a Funeral which even my mother enjoyed. In that film I think the very first five or six words were fuck but nobody seemed to be offended by them. It is very easy to pontificate in the cosy atmosphere of the Court room. If the Bench would care to join me outside The Copocana Beach on a Saturday night, they would soon see what were 'accepted standards'. And if anyone here has to ask what The Copocana Beach is, they are not in the real world by any accepted standards. Taxi drivers have to put up not only with all the verbal crap, we also have to put up with the physical danger that embodies the 'accepted standards' of behaviour of the general public. As the legendary singer Van Morrison put it so devastatingly.

> Don't you know the price
> that I have to pay
> Just to do everything
> I have to do
> Do you think that there's
> nothing to it
> You should try it
> sometime.

'In conclusion, I wouldn't say that I swear an inordinate

amount but do avail myself of these rustic words in times of need for emphasis or to release frustration. After all, fuck is merely an adaptation of a good old Germanic word from the sixteenth century. And I don't direct my swearing at people, only objects. You see the subtle difference? In my opinion contemporary jargon like double whammy or spin doctor are the real verbal obscenities. Or far, far worse such euphemisms as 'collateral damage' or 'friendly fire' which must be the two most obscene phrases in the English language and offensive to accepted standards of decency in anyone's book.'

As last time I asked the Court to dismiss the case, but this time I was truly confident I would win. Confident enough to end with the words of Georgie.

> Yet why, you ask, these humble crimes relate,
> Why make the Poor as guilty as the Great ?
> To show the great, those mightier sons of pride,
> How near in the lowest are allied.

Indeed the end came quicker than I expected when TB said he now wished to withdraw from the case and even came over and shook my hand. Christ I had bloody pissed it.

But now came my true moment of triumph as I asked the Bench to award me financial compensation 'for loss of time in attending to answer complaints not substantiated' under that cheeky Section 65 of the Town Police Clauses Act 1847. My cup truly ranneth over (to borrow the Bible for a minute with a touch of side) when the Bench returned after a brief adjournment and awarded me one hundred pounds damages against Mrs B. Even I hadn't got the heart to point out to the sad old bag that if she defaulted on the payment the Justices could imprison her for a period not exceeding one month. Before my head got too big I remembered just in time the wise old words of Omar.

> Myself when young did eagerly frequent
> Doctor and Saint, and heard great Argument
> About it and about; but evermore
> Came out the same Door as in I went.

However to bring the chapter to a close on a lighter note I have a real cracker. The history of absurdity reached truly Monty Pythonesque heights recently when good old progressive Wuffa District Council turned down an application for a Hackney Licence in Sutton Market for a real horse-drawn Hackney Carriage. Their reasoning that it would take business away from motorized Hackneys must be the excuse of the Millennium if we hadn't just passed it. Words fail me for once but Van will sock it to them once again.

> When you come down from your Ivory Tower
> You will see how it really must be.

Which just left me with the modest task of scaling the mighty ramparts of that other Ivory Tower at nearby Rattlesden. Was I still in with a chance?

7. ALL WORK AND NO PLAY

> All work and no play
> Makes Jack a dull chap
> When it comes to the crunch
> It's too much I've got to stop
> No pain and no gain it's driving me insane.

Yep, you've got it. I was getting pissed off with The Road and there would be no more tiffing with Tiff in the near future. The above clichéd lyrics had certainly caught Van in a singularly uninspired mood, but there was no mistaking the gist of his message. More bills to pay and more thousands of miles to drive. The future was a gigantic bore, as I was in grave danger of becoming. Me, the Oscar Wilde of Sutton Market. The inarticulate buggers had got to me.

But all was not totally lost on the fare front. Just when one was in deepest despair came a flash of inspiration from Omar.

> And suddenly one more impatient cried –
> 'Who is the Potter, pray, and who the Pot ?'

Now that is a truly philosophical question.

Quickly on to other philosophers. Being a Monday we were back in The Hutch mid morning waiting to be mugged again by that great philosopher of greed, Quid Carpenter himself. The little man was positively quivering with excitement at the thought of all that dosh. Also in The Hutch was the Socrates of Sutton Market, aka Tonker Townsend.

'Not so hot on the love front, eh Tommy? No tonking with Tiff at the weekend?' he leered. It was obviously going to be a crude love in this morning, not an elevated discussion on Eros.

'The subject is not for discussion Tonker,' I replied haughtily.

'The toffs aren't very good at it, are they,' chipped in Stack impassively but unhelpfully.

'You can always cry on my shoulder Tommy,' came in Elise. 'I'm sorry, I forgot, big toffs don't cry, ha ha.' Christ, they were all at me this morning.

Before any other comedian could have a pop at me, an ecstatic QC put his little head round the battered door of The Hutch.

'Technology, that's the key. Computerisation is the way ahead if we are going to beat those buggers from Omega and Lone Star.'

'Have you been drinking already QC,' was Sandy's rather unhelpful response. Talk about the kettle and the pot. Or rather 'who is the Potter, pray, and who the Pot?'

'Shut up and go back to your whiskey bottle Sandy,' rejoined QC We sure were one big happy family at Wells Fargo. Or were we soon to be renamed Microcarpenter Cars?

'Computerisation for all bookings and prices with Data Heads in each car instead of mikes. That's the future,' continued QC with all the messianic passion of one of the privileged few who have finally seen the light.

'Don't we have enough dickheads in the cars already QC?,' yawned a soporific Stack.

'Shit, you rugger buggers are all the same. Thick as two short planks. Go back to your silly little scrum Stack, and leave the thinking to visionaries like myself.' Christ, he had got it bad.

'Excellent idea QC,' smarmed the Milky Bar Kid. 'I'm all for progress and even our thickest drivers can't go wrong with the address in front of them on the screen. And that also means none of us will have to struggle with the indecipherable utterances of The Scarecrow any more.'

Bloody hell, I didn't know that the odious little Kid could be so coherent if not positively eloquent.

'I'm with the Kid and you QC' The Petty Officer naturally took the side of the officers if not the gentlemen.

Then a terrible wail emanated from round the corner. QC in all his new found fervour had forgotten The Fat Controller.

'I've never ever used a computer and I'm too old and too fat to learn now', he sobbed. Equally sadly, nobody demurred. After a prolonged and poignant silence, The Crafty Cockney typically came to the rescue with a masterly intervention.

'Look QC why don't you get hold of another portacabin first. I'm really pissed off with this crapheap. In the meantime you can send TFC on one of those PVC courses or whatever they're called.' Eric may have been quite naturally confused with these ludicrous modern acronyms but he was also a born diplomat. He was totally wasting his talents with Wells Fargo. If The Messiah was truly listening, Eric could have crooned sweet common sense into his tender ears from Washington to Harare with great effect.

The thought of actually spending some of our hard earned money on a new Hutch quickly stopped QC in his tracks.

'Excellent idea Eric. I will look into it.' That meant Eric had very neatly put the white heat of the technological era at Wells Fargo back by at least a couple of years. Pity it wasn't so easy with GWB.

However, all this little conversation didn't help the immediate cause one iota. I had tweaked my back over the weekend, not how Leonardo had lewdly suggested, but by just getting out of my shoddy shower. I must be getting old. Therefore I had backache to add to heartache and financial ache.

But just when work and life is getting you down along comes another humorous rainbow. It was perversely lashing with rain that same Monday a few hours on from QC's attempt to move from the nineteenth century to the twenty first in one giant leap for Wellskind. I picked up a funny little old lady from Kings Road and as it was only a two minute drive to her house in Crimea

Street it seemed like easy money. Or so I thought. But as I dropped her off at number sixty four she had a strange request. 'Could you just check my front path for snails ?'

'Snails,' I spluttered.

'Yes, I'm terrified of the little buggers. Have been since I was eleven.'

'I can't. I'll get soaked.'

'But you must.' And must I did.

'And don't kill them.'

So I shot out of the car, had a quick peer for nonexistent snails, and then scuttled back to the dry sanctuary of my car. But it was not quick enough and I was already soaked.

'You were quick,' said The Snail Lady accusingly.

'Oh yes I'm bloody quick when I need to be, as the Australian said to the bar maid.'

'Well thank you ever so much young man, despite your risqué remarks. Are you sure you really are a taxi driver? Never mind you've saved my life.' Isn't the English language full of irony? With that she handed me a crisp fiver and ventured cautiously out into the deluge. Young man indeed, and a two quid tip. I felt twenty years younger straightaway.

Humorous rainbows are like London buses. You wait ages for

151

one and then two or three come along at once. At five minutes to six that evening as I was about to knock off, The Fat Controller had two intriguing questions. First did I have plenty of money on me and second, could I squeeze in just one more? It sounded promising (i.e. lucrative) so I said 'why not?' Why not indeed as I heard this evil cackle over the radio.

'Right Tommy,' spluttered TFC still trying to control his laughter. 'Round to Fishy Tales to collect some fish and chips and then take them round to The Seckford Nursing Home. Ha, ha.'

I still didn't see what was so funny about a few portions of fish and chips so I innocently ambled round to Fishy Tales and presented myself to Mr Fishy himself. Forty three portions later I had well and truly found out the source of TFC's mirth. What a stitch up or should I say fry up. Quarter of an hour later I tottered out of Fishy Tales with my one hundred and seventy two pounds worth of purchases piled up in a great big cardboard box and drove round in a massive sulk to the above-mentioned nursing home. There I was greeted by the female warden of a certain age, not with open arms as I had naturally expected, but with a huge scowl.

'What kept you?', she snapped.

'Well, there was quite a lot to pick up,' I stuttered, put out of my stride as usual by other people's aggression.

Thus it was that I found myself meekly following this iron warden into the dining room where I suffered the ultimate indignity of being slow hand-clapped by a clutch of decrepit old age pensioners. To add financial injury to injured pride I was paid precisely one hundred and seventy five pounds and sixty pence by the old battle-axe after she had suspiciously inspected Mr Fishy's scruffy bill. A three pound sixty pence delivery charge. I would have said she was taking the piss but of course female wardens don't do that dirty masculine sort of thing.

Straight round to The Rising Sun to complain about my treatment at the hands of these innocent old dears. Instead of the expected sympathy Graham roared with laughter and said from now on I would be known as The Fish and Chip Man in his establishment or FAC Man for short.

The next day it was out of the frying pan into the fire, or rather should I say curry house. A curry takeaway with me as the takeaway man. How I hated takeaways, either to takeaway or worse to actually eat. How people gorge down such crap food I really don't know. Anyway round to The Bombay Duck. The nearest connection the occupiers of Sutton Market's finest Indian cuisine (their words I hasten to add, not mine) had with Bombay was Sunil Tendulkar on the telly and the ducks came from The Croft or so I had been unreliably informed by my mole (code name Alistair Campbell). Having waited impatiently for over ten minutes for my special cargo we then had another little contretemps over money. Apparently I had to pay them twenty five pounds sixty pence for the takeaway, refundable by the client of course. Makes me sound like a proper business man, doesn't it? Mr Bombay then asked me the cost of the fare. I didn't see the relevance of the question. He then had the temerity to ask me 'didn't I understand English very well?' That was when I rather lost it and the atmosphere became as heated as a vindaloo. Of course I am not a racist as Enoch Powell once memorably said, but for an Indian (or an Irishman or even worse a Yorkshireman) to question my knowledge or use of English was the deadliest insult possible. And then the penny dropped. It was just me being thick. The restaurant was encouraging the takeaway trade by offering to pay for the cost of taxiing the food to the home themselves. Bygones.

Of course by the end of the day I could see the funny side of it. The whole event was too preposterous for words. You certainly couldn't make it up. You certainly didn't get these sort of belly laughs in the dreary world of merchant wanking, sorry banking.

Talking of the former I had four girls in my car the other day. No, not like that, certainly now that I have been reliably informed on my packet of fags that smoking might affect my sperm count. If that sounds bad, you want to read the warning in French. Crikeys, perhaps it is only Dunhill cigarettes that have this castrating effect. Or is it just a cunning plan of the government to implement an insidious form of birth control on the toffs? Come back George Orwell.

I found it equally disconcerting when girls said they had had me last week and I couldn't even remember. Anyway back to the four young ladies in question. One of them was apparently a student at the University of East Anglia about to start her final year in a philosophy course. She had been working at Matalan during the long hols and there had been Ugly Rumours of a young man 'pleasuring himself' in the changing cubicles (no, that's not where they came from). I hadn't realized that Matalan was Top of the Pops in the aphrodisiacal stakes. It must be all those dreadful shoes. Anyone would need a little light relief after a trying session of trying them all on. Anyway when the young

154

man returned the next day the young student was more than ready for him. Matalan had the same singularly homoerotic effect on him as before and he was soon up to his old tricks again in the cubicle. The prescient young lady waited till she heard him finish his ablutions and then ripped open the curtain.

'Is that it then?', she asked witheringly, looking directly at his rapidly diminishing manhood.

The unhappy bloke looked up startled, adjusted his kit and scuttled out of the shop, never to be seen again in the hallowed malls of Matalan. The young lady had just earned her retail spurs as it were.

Not to be outdone by her fellow student, one of the other girls apparently worked in Marks and Spencer and had more tales of derring-do or whatever you call it these days. A couple of days ago, a middle aged man overdressed in an obligatory dirty raincoat had been observed on the security cameras persistently putting down a suspicious bag immediately next to a number of young ladies in the lingerie department. After he was seen repeating this trick next to a particularly attractive oriental lady with no tights (the last observation I hasten to add helpfully inserted by the student), he was apprehended by the security guards who found a video camera in his bag. He had been filming up girls' skirts. I think that these large chain clothes stores should deroticise their shops forthwith or there will be mayhem or something far worse happening out there in the retail sector. Perhaps analysts should rename it the rectitude sector to really get the message across to all these errant shoppers.

But the smile was back. Van was wrong for once. One can

both work and play at the same time. I didn't feel so dull either. And my backache was miraculously better. Omar knew the score.

> Dreaming when Dawn's Left Hand was in the Sky
> I heard a voice within the Tavern cry,
> 'Awake, my Little ones, and fill the Cup
> Before Life's Liquor in its Cup be dry.'

The next morning I shot out of bed and was rewarded with a gleaming sun. There was still a tinge of mist in the meadows and GUT was in his or her heaven. I had by now detached myself from the dreaded school run. They were more hassle than they were worth. And more important, I could properly enjoy my days off and my lie ins. I never had been an early morning person. I read a bit of Omar, had a joint, and then ambled off to do the business.

TFC was in business mood as well.

'Tommy, get your arse down to Hair Incorporated pronto and pick up Vintage Violet for Borley.' Oh no, it sounded like another God's waiting room pickup. I pottered round to Hair Incorporated for the allotted fare. Unfortunately this establishment was trickily positioned adjoining a complicated traffic light system and I had to go round the block again when there was no sign the first time of my elderly fare. Second time round a new Mercedes was blocking my rightful path so, with an elegant flick of my fingers, I indicated that a little retreat might be in order. Mercedes Man didn't react very co-operatively to my digital instructions and came back with his own variation of rather rude hand signals. Nevertheless he had got the message and essayed the required reversal. Unfortunately his colourful language through the open window wouldn't have been endorsed by Mrs Whitehouse. With one obstacle out of the way, I made a second attempt to locate the elusive Violet. Ah, there she must be with her back obdurately to the window of Hair Incorporated. I made frantic hand signals to the staff that there were several cars up my backside and time was of the essence. This made no difference at all as the staff responded with some rather more unsavoury hand signals of their own. Eventually, and in her own time, Violet emerged with her zimmer frame and chassied towards me at a snails pace, oblivious to the fact that behind me the motorists were now in uproar. I hurried her into the car with horns hooting all around me and with an embarrassed wave at the sea of aggression behind me. I hated being the focus of unwanted attention.

'Shut the window young man.' No feel good factor this time about the term young man. 'And shut my door.' She peered at me suspiciously. 'You're not Omega Cars are you? I always have Omega Cars. Am I in the right cab?'

'Well, you're not going with Omega Cars this morning so tough cookies,' I responded through very gritted teeth. 'Look, you are going to Borley aren't you? Where exactly by the way? The office didn't tell me.'

'I don't know. Surely that is your job.' This was getting surreal and uncomfortably close to the retard who, when I asked 'where are we going', replied in kind 'I'll tell you when we get there.'

Belatedly I twigged. Our destination must be Borley House, one of Sutton Market's most infamous old people's homes. Hell,

I was extra slow this morning. Too many fares like Violet. Having established our destination, we shuffled round to Borley House where I was commanded to escort Violet inside.

'How much young man?'

'That will be five pounds exactly ma'am indeed.' What was wrong with me? I was treating her like the late Queen Mother, and me a fervent republican.

'That is the second time you have used that phrase. What is wrong with you young man?'

'Nothing,' I muttered and retired in some disarray with my exact fare, but not without carefully noticing the row of ancient vegetables looking into space and lined up in their armchairs with zimmer frames up front. Shit, who wants to live that long if all quality of life is long gone? What a bummer.

> I'd like to be somewhere else
> Like to be all by myself
> Like to be down at the beach
> Relaxing at the sugar shack.

Now you're talking Van, but unfortunately circumstance just won't allow it for the moment. Work must go on. And on.

First a quick pit stop at The Hutch for a reviving cuppa where The Fat Controller informed me that I was to be rewarded after my not so gallant efforts with Violet with a stimulating journey to the coast of Suffolk with the exotic sounding Miss de Winter. Shades of Rebecca began to close on the growing boy.

158

'I hope she is pretty TFC. I have very exacting standards.'

'At your age Thomas? Stick to the old ladies with their zimmer frames if I was you.' Trust The Milky Bar Kid to put the knife in.

'Luckily, I'm not you. Kid.' I responded with what I hoped was icy contempt. But the truth was that The Hutch had brought me down to earth again with a big bang. What hope had I with the super elegant Tiff if everyone regarded me as a geriatric fart at best, or an old perv at worst?

Back to the mysterious Miss de Winter. Promisingly I was to pick her up at The Abbey Hotel. I asked the snooty receptionist to call up Miss de Winter, which she did unwillingly after first giving me the look that indicated I was a particularly nasty smell. Luckily my fare proved much friendlier as well as being much more attractive. She had long black hair and was probably in her mid thirties, striking looking rather than conventionally attractive, and beautifully turned out in black polo neck, black midi dress and black boots. With a hundred watt smile she asked me if I could possibly take her as far as Aldeburgh. With a smile like that I would have gone as far as Land's End or even beyond.

She got demurely in the back seat immediately behind me and settled into easy conversation. Before I knew it I was telling her how I started as a taxi driver after my divorce and bankruptcy. She seemed genuinely interested and drew me out effortlessly to talk about all the sordid details of my chequered career and my unhappy descent to my present position. Before I realized it we had reached the delightful little village of Earl Soham and I had told this glamorous stranger more about my sad life than anyone, even Tiff. Perhaps it was the fact that she was a complete stranger that made it easier to talk about it. She was not involved with any of the characters and was totally nonjudgmental. Hell, it was Miss de Winter who should have been the counsellor. With difficulty I eventually managed to turn the conversation round to her. In a quiet understated way she explained she was a model and that she was going to a chilly shoot by the Martello Tower and The Brudenell Hotel. Again, almost posthumously, in fact by the time we got to Saxmundham, I realized the identity of my mysterious passenger. She was only one of the most famous models in the country and had been using a pseudonym at The Abbey Hotel for anonymity. The tactic had worked only too well from my point of view.

'I'm sorry', I spluttered, 'I'm afraid I didn't recognize you.' But she didn't seem the least put out, rather amused if anything. We passed the rest of the journey talking agreeably about the county which she didn't know at all, and I tried to explain inarticulately and inadequately about some of the rugged delights of the Suffolk coast. Georgie does it so much better.

> No; cast by Fortune on a frowning coast,
> Which neither groves nor happy valleys boast.
> Where other cares than those the Muse relates,
> And other shepherds dwell with other mates;
> By such examples taught, I paint the Cot,
> As Truth will paint it, and other bards will not.

Eventually we arrived in the delightful old seaside town of Aldeburgh, former home of Georgie and Benji, and I won the contest by seeing the North Sea first. The fare was exactly twenty five pounds twenty pence. Miss de Winter graciously gave me three tenners and told me to keep the change. She said that I deserved it, whatever that meant. She also gave me the benefit of her hundred watt smile for the last time and wished me good luck in the future. What a lady.

I drove back to Sutton Market, via Wickham Market this time, almost as high as Neil Young in The Last Waltz.

It was certainly proving to be a weird week, even by the bizarre standards of Wells Fargo. The next day Thin Lizzie asked me if I would mind going to number six Plough Lane, wait and return to Monks Eleigh for Yvonne. On account by the way. As you know by now I was getting pretty experienced at The Waiting Game, so when I am asked by the Controller if I minded going somewhere and the job was on a non existent account the alarm bells rang twice. Therefore it was with more than a soupçon of trepidation I drove round to Plough Lane where I found a blowsy lady of a certain age in a state of considerable agitation. On the pleasant journey to this typically attractive Suffolk village, Yvonne gave me a potted version of her life history. And what an unhappy tale it was. Married to a cruel wife-beater for fifteen years, they had now been divorced for over five years and were still fighting over the custody of their only son. When I asked who had got the court's custody of him on their divorce, she was suspiciously evasive so I didn't pursue the matter. But that didn't stop the bad vibes resurfacing. Yvonne went on to explain that her ex-husband had just kicked Liam out again and she needed to go over to the 'bastard's filthy house' to pick up a few essential clothes for him. She reassured me it wouldn't take more than a couple of minutes. But I wasn't reassured, not by a long way.

We arrived in Monks Eleigh where Yvonne directed me to a little dilapidated hovel of a thatched cottage with a seriously unkempt garden. Or rather as Rottweiler and Sons, Sutton Market's self proclaimed leading estate agents would have put it given a mere quarter of a chance to exercise their flowery hyperbole, 'a unique opportunity to renovate an enchanting love nest deep in the bowels of darkest Suffolk'. They never did have any sense of shame or irony. Anyway the bastard's car wasn't in the drive so it looked unexpectedly as if I was going to be let off the hook. But not so fast Tommy.

The next thing I knew Yvonne had got out of the car to 'have a little look.' But I had subconsciously relaxed and returned to my latest Robert Goddard where I could retire into his fantastic world of cross and double cross. However after ten minutes of engrossed reading I suddenly realized that Yvonne hadn't returned. A trifle perturbed, I looked up to find no sign of her. I got out of the car and walked over to the cottage. There I could see her inside through the leaded windows of the front room rifling through some clothes. Alarmed now, I called out and asked what she was doing. She replied that she would only be 'a couple of minutes' and I was to go back to the car. How often had I heard that expression used so casually and inaccurately in this job?

I returned to the car in a state of uncertainty. What to do? Call the office? What could they do? So as usual when I had a problem I did nothing, except to retreat back into my Goddard. However after a further fifteen minutes of blissful ignorance even Walter Mitty realized he must do something. So off I trooped again to the front door of the cottage and called out to Yvonne. As before she said she would just be a couple of minutes. I said this wasn't good enough and if she wasn't out in two minutes precisely I was off. Her response was to come to the door and hand me a television.

'Take this,' she commanded. And then she relented. 'It's all right, don't look so worried. I'm not doing anything illegal. I'm only taking things belonging to Liam.'

'How did you get in?'

'Through the back door. It was open.'

'OK.' But it didn't feel OK. Not by a long chalk.

So I reluctantly helped with three or four bags of clothes, the play station, TV and various other appendages. We had just loaded up the last bits and pieces when there was a loud bellow from behind.

'What the fuck are you doing?' I turned round and saw a thick set man in his forties with an angry scar across his forehead. And the guy was certainly angry.

'Oh Jim, hello. I was collecting a few of Liam's things,' replied Yvonne a shade too casually. I could see the whites of her eyes and I saw fear. I could feel the wall of aggression emanating from Jim and didn't feel too good myself. Shit again, this was going to get nasty.

'How did you get in?'

'Through the back door. It was open.'

'No it bloody wasn't.'

'OK. Liam told me how to open it.'

'Did he fuck?'

'Actually he did.'

The hard blue eyes did a pretty good impression of Clint Eastwood at his best (or rather his nastiest) and I was again ready for a rapid if puscillanimous exit. The eyes appeared to be considering the matter interminably. Finally, when I could hardly bear the suspense any longer, he appeared to have made up his mind and nodded.

'All right, fuck off and take your fancy man with you. But if I ever catch either of you snooping round hear again, I will knock off both your fucking heads.'

We didn't need a second invitation and again I did a fair imitation of The Boy Racer.

'Shit, that was close,' breathed Yvonne. 'Did you know that Jim has just done four years inside for armed robbery?'

I did now.

Still shaking from our mutually close escape, I dropped off Yvonne back at Plough Lane and retired rapidly to The Rising Sun.

'A pint of Mauldon's Best and pronto please, Graham.'

'Another bad day at the office Tommy ? I'm beginning to feel guilty for getting you started in the taxi business.'

'It's not your fault Graham. I just feel I'm a magnet for disaster, that's all. The other drivers never seem to have my sort of problems.'

'Another one Tommy? That was quick.'

'Cheers Graham.' The Mauldon's was beginning to work its magic. 'No,' I sighed, 'I've had enough of The Road. I have done well over one hundred and fifty thousand miles now. Don't you think that I have done my penance yet? And the omens don't feel good,' I added. Too many incidents, as our esteemed police force are overfond of saying. Oh, fuck it.'

'Stick at it Tommy.'

Where oh where had I heard those words before? Oh yes, her. Bugger it, it was time to break her rigid self-imposed rules.

> I'm just a wild and crazy guy
> But I'm tearing at the seams
> Before you can say Jack Robinson
> I'll be seeing you in my dreams
> She's on a blanket with a book.
> In the shade, white suit.

'OK, I'm off Graham.'

If he was surprised by my premature exit, Graham wasn't showing it.

'Good luck Tommy.' He did understand after all.

'Hello Tiff.' I wasn't hanging around tonight.

'Why are you calling tonight Tommy?' Her voice sounded uncertain down the phone as if I'd caught her off balance.

'We're going on a picnic tomorrow Tiff.'

'We are?'

'Yes, we are. Tomorrow at ten. Be ready.'

'I'll be ready Tommy,' came the stifled response. Hell, I had cracked it.

'See you Tiff.' Perhaps I should have tried to be masterful before. Or perhaps the timing was right. Who knows and who bloody cares?

> I think the Vessel, that with fugitive
> Articulation answer'd, once did live,
> And merry make ; and the cold Lip I kiss'd
> How many Kisses might it take – and give!

Could I reach Tiff's cold lips and how many kisses might she give, or take?

> There's no crack double back

Moving on down the track
Moving on down the line
Got to chill out in style
Got to ease my troubled mind
Thinking just might be a crime.

A couple of glasses of Madiran 'to chill out in style and ease my troubled mind.' A couple more glasses and I was beyond thinking.

No pain no gain it's all going
Down the drain.

But was it?

8.   DAYS LIKE THIS

When it's not always raining there'll be days like this
When there's no one complaining there'll be days like this
When everything falls into place like the flick of a switch
Well my mama told me there'll be days like this.

Dead on ten o'clock, I hammered on the front door of Tiff's heavenly cottage at Rattlesden, which was appropriately situated adjoining the imposing church of Saint Nicholas in the middle of the village. I didn't want to waste a moment of this potentially perfect day. And there she was, as radiant as ever. And dressed in an impossibly chic white cotton suit. I knew Van's music was inspirational but I had never suspected the old bugger was psychic as well.

'Hi Tommy, you look smart.' I had naturally dressed in my best gear, or rather my one and only smart piece of gear. Powder blue casual non-Armani jacket, button down navy blue denim shirt, plain black slacks and serviceable black shiny shoes. Black and blue and boring as usual.

'You look OK yourself Tiff.' Never overcook the poached egg as CJ might have said to Reggie on a good day. 'On y va?'

'Avec plaisir Tommy.' The omens were indeed looking promising. The sun was shining and I was in my own heaven. Tiff seemed strangely different as if she had decided on a new course of action. She was, dare I consider the thought, the old Tiff. Something had happened in the interim. But what? Had she at last decided to cast off her widow's shackles and why? As a feeble male I hadn't got an inkling at what was going on in that delicious brain of hers, but I was all for giving it a go. Hope springs eternal from the male breast to the female breast.

I had picked my route and destination oh so carefully that morning over a powderpuff breakfast at an unseemly Tommy hour. Eventually I decided that our target would be the Elysian Fields of Ickworth Park adjoining the small West Suffolk village of Horringer. I didn't want to take the direct route on the boring A14 on such an auspicious day, so I had worked out a circuitous route along minor B roads and through a variety of pretty villages. But first we had to have a little recce round Rattlesden itself. As it was well off even my beaten track, I hadn't been aware before of its subtle charms. This consisted of circular sweep of the Upper and Lower Streets which revealed nothing remarkable. Then a quick peep at the seventeenth century Clopton Hall, a timber-framed and plastered extravaganza that might induce another spontaneous overflow of powerful feeling from sex-starved estate agents, and we were more than ready for the road. The quaint villages tripped off the tongue. First feisty Felsham with its unique square brick mausoleum, the huge Great Green at Cockfield Green, and then Cockfield itself with its classy barn conversions and thatched gems. Then down and across the main A134 road and a little hiccup. We had reached the sububurbanesque sprawl of Lawshall where the central core of ancient properties had been more than overwhelmed by indifferent twentieth century expansion. To compensate for this aesthetic disappointment we did a little detour to Ms Schiffer's immodest pad at Coldham Hall nearby. We took advantage of the adjoining public footpath from the road to have a cheeky look at this richly renovated sixteenth century mansion. It was all a bit formal for my austere taste, but Tiff seemed to quite like it.

We then twisted in and out of more quiet country lanes through to Whepstead with its sublime view to the north west over rolling farmland to woodland in the distance where the tip of the mighty Rotunda could be glimpsed protruding out of the treeline. Not so sublime to the north west was the sight of the top of the sugar beet factory. Finally we reached Horringer itself with its rather too quaint main road cottages.

The countryside hardly changed an iota throughout our journey. It remained defiantly and modestly undulating, heavily arable, but with intermittent bursts of woodland relief. However, the overall effect was one of a timeless tranquillity. Suffolk doesn't ever reach out and grab you, it just absorbs you into its web.

We passed virtually the whole journey in agreeable silence. The beauty of the drive was matched by the beauty of my companion and Van crooned gently in the background. It took me back thirty years to the days of long hair and long nights. To escorting Tiff in the Morgan with the hood down to various out of the way Suffolk hostelries, whatever the vagaries of the pernicious British weather. I glanced across at Tiff and she smiled back mischievously.

> When you don't need to worry there'll be days like this
> When no one's in a hurry ther'll be days like this'

When you don't get betrayed by that old Judas kiss
Oh my mama told me there'll be days like this.

Oh crikeys. I was dead in the water.

We turned in past the charming little village church of Saint Leonard, whoever that old fraud was when he was at home and in his pomp. Oh Christ, he wasn't one of Leonardo's ancestors was he? That would explain a lot. On through the narrow gates and the little lodge, then over the cattle grid we eased into the park itself. In front of us was half a mile of angled metalled road with the flat eighteenth century parkland stretched out on either side. There were some magnificent oaks and chestnuts to complement the scene with obligatory lambs gambolling around their sedate mothers. Truly a proper pastoral scene. Cue Georgie, ever the cynic.

I grant indeed that fields and flocks have charms
For him that grazes or him that farms;
But when amid such pleasing scenes I trace
The poor laborious natives of the place,
And see the mid-day sun, with fervid ray,
On their bare heads and dewy temples play.

He would have been delighted that the poor laborious natives of the place have long gone, but not nearly so pleased to see their nouveau riche replacements walking their aristocratic dogs.

Just before the T junction at the end of the road there was a new left turn off to the Ickworth Hotel which had been recently converted at great expense from the old East wing of the Earl of Bristol's magnificent folly. The hotel had a fantastic setting overlooking the southern part of the park set below in a natural amphitheatre. Unfortunately not only was it miles out of my modest price bracket but it was also sadly devoid of charm. Sterility reigned absolute from the forbidding front elevation, to the inhospitable entrance foyer and continued on to the over the top grandiosity of the public rooms. Expense hadn't been spared originally by the seventh Earl of Bristol but taste had a surgical modern bypass. The exotic Rotunda luckily still remained in the eminently safe keeping of The National Trust. However, it wasn't primarily old buildings I had on my mind that day, however uplifting architecturally. Rather trimmer structures were far more dear to my heart at that precise moment.

> So must the Lover find his way
> To move the heart he hopes to win –
> Must not in distant forms delay
> Must not in rude assaults begin.

Georgie certainly understood this love business far better than me. But could I learn from him?

I found a parking space in the large National Trust car park and unpacked my gourmand picnic basket. All the goodies were there. Duck paté, saucisson, ham, brie, rolls and salad. And of course the inevitable bottle of Madiran. Plus mineral water your honour.

We strolled past the Rotunda through the open gates into the lower park. The first part of the lower park was flat alongside the brick walls of the formal Italianate garden. Down the hill past the family church and the old walled kitchen garden, and then finally down to the little stream that snaked through the park. I vividly remember my mother bringing me here as a very young boy and playing Pooh sticks by the old stone bridge and building ineffective dams for hours. That was over forty years ago but I still could remember it like yesterday. Happy memories indeed.

However, although a perfect spot for little boys to play, I immediately realized with a wave of chagrin that it was a totally useless place for big boys to picnic. The stream had completely dried up in the summer drought and the whole area was far too exposed and public. Not the place for an intimate picnic at all. Oh bugger, I had ruined the day before it had barely begun. And after all my so called meticulous planning. What a pathetic failure I was, even at something so elementary as the siting of a simple picnic.

As usual it was Tiff who came to the rescue. Having noticed my transparent despondency she suggested a little sojourn might be in order back up the hill.

'Let's investigate a bit behind the walled garden area Tommy. It looks intriguing.'

I was still sulky and only grudgingly agreed. What a curmudgeon. What did Tiff see in me? Perhaps she saw that little boy as well by the stream all those years ago and just felt sorry for him. Or perhaps she just wanted to mother him. Crikeys, I hope not. That's not what I had in mind at all.

'It might even be fun Tommy, you funny old sulker. You haven't changed in that respect either, have you?'

Our luck was in. Or rather I should say that Tiff was right. When we reached a quaint cottage built right into the massive wall of the garden, we espied with delight the edge of a lake at the bottom of a well-worn footpath. I had read about a lake in the blurb about Ickworth but I had never worked out exactly where it was. The church completely obscured it from the main house and the huge wall did the rest. From our privileged position at the Hole in the Wall we also noticed that the inside of the garden was filled with rows and rows of mature and ripe looking vines. Again I had heard vague talk about Bristol Wines, but I'm afraid I had written it off as a dubious joke.

With an immediate lift in my spirits, I eagerly escorted Tiff down the footpath to the lake itself. There we found a truly idyllic location, to borrow again from the old estate agents book of clichés. And even better, we were alone. At weekends and special vineyard open days I am sure that the area would be veritably humming with curious people, but today there wasn't another person in sight. A number of ducks were shuffling round the lake but there were only three of those messy Canada geese marring the shore. These dirty buggers get everywhere don't they? However, having found the Elysian Fields, so to speak, I wasn't going to let a few fowls spoil our day.

The lake was relatively narrow but must have been over a furlong long and formed an almost perfect oval. Looking back across to the other side of the sparkling water with the sun directly behind us there beckoned an enclosed grassy area adjoining an elegant brick summerhouse. Yes, the perfect place for a picnic after all. Blimey, I rather think I believe in miracles after all.

Having walked round the lake and entered through solid wrought iron gates to our secret garden, I carefully unpacked our sophisticated picnic. Out came the waterproof rug and the corkscrew and I reverently opened the Madiran. As this was such a special occasion I left it to breathe a while and poured the Badoit instead.

'Cheers Tiff, here's to you.' I looked straight into those wide blue eyes and saw a welcoming warmth in them.

'And you Tommy. It is lovely here isn't it ? Many thanks for inviting me.'

We looked across the glistening canal to the peace of the parkland beyond. It was truly a magical place. But keep it light Tommy, keep it simple.

'No sweat. Oh, look at those fat pheasants over there.'

A couple of these beautiful (well the males were) but totally stupid birds were making a bird line for us. They had obviously become park trained by too many classy snacks.

'Sod off, you greedy sods.' A bit churlish I know, but I didn't want to share Tiff with anyone on this special day, even with birds of the feathered kind. They retreated only to a rather disrespectful distance but that was sufficient for her apparently.

'Do you remember those summer evenings at the Groton Fox? All primitive scampi and chips on the front patio, washed down with that funny beer.'

Tiff had never been a great beer drinker. In fact in those days the Fox sold the very fine Newcastle Exhibition Bitter, another little nectar I had discovered on that earlier memorable northern trip with her. Memories. More golden memories. How had I ever let this gorgeous creature go? Even in her late forties, she was still entrancing. The sun was catching the totally natural ash blonde strands of hair on that wonderful head and her face was equally unlined. No young bimbo could compete with such mature beauty and anyway, why do the young think they have a monopoly on love? But could an ancient roué still compete in the love stakes and more important, could he get his timing right? In my incurious youth I had always thought that timing was all about stroking a cricket ball through the covers, which helped greatly to explain my current dilemma.

> For such attractive power has Love,
> We justly each extreme may fear:
> 'Tis lost when we too distant prove,
> And when we rashly press too near.

It was evidently time to pour the Madiran.

'A toast. To the beauty of the days gone by.' Stick in the past for the moment. It was safer that way.

'To the beauty of the days gone by. And the beauty of the days to come Tommy.' And a singularly direct smile that reached down to her very bosom as she made her own toast.

> The beauty of the days gone by
> The music that we used to play
> So lift your glass and raise it high

To the beauty of the days gone by.

And the future?

We settled into our intimate little feast, feeding greedily on the beauty and tranquillity of the setting.

'Tommy, I've been thinking. You really aren't a bad old bugger, to borrow your own inimitable vernacular. Perhaps we could see a bit more of each other now after all.' She saw my eyes light up. 'No, don't get too excited. You will still have to go gently with me. I've got set in my bachelor girl ways and I am still very fragile. But I must reluctantly admit I'm still vaguely attracted to you and your silly little ways for some unfathomable reason.' At least she had refound her sense of humour. 'Or rather despite your incorrigibly dissolute ways.' She could still put the knife in, but in such a delicious way. 'I haven't felt so relaxed since...Well you know when.' My heart and soul rocketed up through the non-existent clouds. I was also speechless as a giant lump came to my throat.

'Oh Tiff,' was all I could manage. Only the mighty Omar could adequately summarize my true feelings at that momentous moment.

> Here with a Loaf of Bread beneath the Bough,
> A Flask of Wine, a Book of Verse - and Thou
> Beside me singing in the Wilderness -
> And Wilderness is Paradise enow.

I rather think that old Omar would have approved of the vineyard setting as well, and my touch of poetic licence with the actualité.

A quick peck on the lips was called for. Her eyes immediately closed demurely and I made delicious contact with the immediate objects of my desire. Electric shocks reverberated through my whole body. Hell and damnation Tommy, excise that sort of desire forthwith.

She looked so soft and vulnerable as I retreated in disarray. She opened her eyes, grasped my hands and eased me down to lay next to her on the rug. The Madiran, the park, the occasion must have waved their combined magic because I suddenly woke up with a start with the raucous double cry of those jolly pheasants again. I looked at my watch. It was almost five o'clock. We had been asleep for over two hours. Tiff had also been woken by the pheasants. We looked at each other and just burst out laughing. Blimey, laughing had never felt so good.

We gathered up our things and rushed up the hill to the classy new restaurant in the West Wing. The tea ladies were just shutting up but relented under Tiff's persuasive pleas to make us a quick pot of Earl Grey. Old habits, and standards, die hard.

The bonus of our little slumber meant that most of the alcohol must have drained out of my recalcitrant body and Tiff pronounced herself satisfied that I was now under the limit. Anyway I couldn't afford to throw away my licence so casually, even if the combined efforts of the Magistrates and the Police Force seemed determined to rip it off my body, dead or alive.

But our little day of paradise was far from over. It was still a glorious day and cried out for a little change of direction. Then I remembered just in time a little tavern from the past. The Weary Sportsman public house was situated in another little gem of a village at Hawkedon only a few miles due south. So off we tootled again back through Whepstead, then rheumy Rede and finally onto Hawkedon itself. The latter was a tiny one street village leading down to the imposing if forbidding church of Saint Mary's almost at the bottom of the hill, with the reassuring Hawkedon Hall providing an agreeable backcloth behind. Next to the pub was a fascinating blue tile hung property and opposite were the usual old thatched cottages. The Weary Sportsman itself was situated atop the colline, as some other poet might have said in another era. It was a rugged half timbered property plastered in correct Suffolk white stucco and heavily black beamed inside. Nothing much seemed to have changed over the years. There was still the same wood burning stove in the ancient fireplace, and the old dog sofa adjoining was still in situ, plus the big pine tables and, most important of all, no irritating music. There was a good range of guest beers as befitting a quality freehouse and a friendly landlord. But best of all the latter had Wadworths 6X from Devizes in his cellar, and in my immodest opinion one of the finest bitters ever brewed in England. I couldn't persuade Tiff to join me in a bitter-in. Instead she asked brightly if she could have a glass of Chardonnay (well nobody's perfect).

After a further two and half pints of 6X consumed by me and surprisingly copious amounts of Chardonnay downed by Tiff (I really had found her Achilles' heels), I realized that we had a wee problem with the old breathalyser. Never mind, what are taxi firms for if not to assist a colleague in his moment of distress? So I got on the blower and summoned up one of Wells Fargo's finest, to wit the mighty Tonker. Thin Lizzie assured me that he would be with us in under half an hour.

I still had time with a now tipsy Tiff for further hilarious reminisces about the good old days. Like dining at the now defunct Stinking Fanny's, a tiny gourmet restaurant in a culinary desert in Sutton Market. To the repeated playing of the theme tune from M.A.S.H where 'suicide is painless, brings on many changes,' we used to get thoroughly pissed and then I had the cheek to drive Tiff home afterwards. Home for her in those days when she was still just plain Miss Tiffany Wright was in the heart of Lavenham, before the latter got sadly overtaken with lucre and longevity. Another popular haunt was The Black Lion at Long Melford where many happy alcohol fuelled jazz evenings were enjoyed. Plus some shambolic and very wet boat trips along the river Bosmere. And the agreeable aftermaths.

However after a further forty five minutes I was forced to ring Wells Fargo again. Apparently Tonker had a little trouble in finding Hawkedon. Of course the silly bugger would, having never been let out of Mid Suffolk before and not possessing any maps whatsoever. Well he wouldn't, would he? He was only an effing taxi driver. Anyway I passed on extremely detailed instructions to Thin Lizzie from which even Fargo's worst couldn't go wrong. We just had time for another quickie before Tonker triumphantly arrived with a screech of tyres and a loud honk. I escorted a now very tipsy Tiff into the back of Tonker's newish 406 and got in the back with her, but not before I had caught Tonker's wicked smirk.

'OK Tommy?,' he asked a shade too brightly. 'And you madam?' Oh shit, he wasn't going to put his great big orifice of a mouth in it and spoil my perfect day, was he?

'Fine Tonker. Very fine.' Tiff gave me a more than reassuring smile. Luckily Tonker missed this one as he was for once concentrating on the road. I directed him back to the A143 horrible Haverhill road so even he couldn't go wrong on the return journey and settled back into my seat, waiting apprehensively for the inevitable crude little sally.

But I badly underestimated Tonker on this occasion, as he kept his big mouth firmly shut and even switched to Classic Gold radio for my benefit. Replete with unaccustomed alcohol and further relaxed with gentle music, Tiff soon fell asleep while I let the momentous events of the day wash over me.

Before I knew it, we were back in Rattlesden. I awoke a drowsy Tiff and escorted her to her front door. There she allowed me to plant a very firm kiss on her luscious lips.

'Thanks for a wonderful day Tommy. Take care and give me a buzz when you have a spare moment'.

And with that she was gone, leaving me standing there alone in the porch feeling like a lovesick teenager again. Eventually I reluctantly broke the spell and walked back to Tonker's car.

'Thanks Tonker.'

'You're welcome mate.' The old bugger never ceased to amaze me. No doubt he would give me fearful stick back in The Hutch but tonight he was The Good Samaritan in every sense of the word.

A quarter of an hour later he had dropped me back at my flat. The fare was twenty five pounds twenty pence and I gave him two twenties. He had earnt every penny.

'I never thought I'd say these words Tonker, but you're a bloody star. Thanks again and goodnight.'

'Wait till tomorrow Tommy,' was his not so enigmatic response, but he gave me a huge wink as he said it. The verbal gloves would be ripped off by then, but fair does. He had more than done his bit tonight.

Back in my flat I went straight to bed for once, more than intoxicated by a little thing called love and even Georgie caught the mood.

> Why force the backward heart on love,
> That of itself the flame might feel ?
> When you the Magnet's power would prove
> Say, would you strike it on the Steel ?

The Magnet's power was effing well working as Tonker might have said.

> When no one steps on my dreams there'll be days like this
> When people understand what I mean there'll be days like this
> When you ring out the changes of how everything is
> Well my mama told me that there'll be days like this.

9. AND THE HEALING HAS BEGUN

And we walked down the avenue again
And sang all those songs from way back then
And we walked down the avenue again
And the healing has begun.

It had indeed. For the second day running I bounded out of bed in very unTommy-like fashion and had a scalding shower.

And we walked down the avenue in style
And we walked down the avenue with a smile.

Emerging from my invigorating shower, I got renewed pleasure from the bright sun shining across the unchanging meadows. When you are well you see everything in every detail. When you are not so well you see nothing at all. Nothing in the whole wide world.

I had of course long given up the school rat run and so toddled out to work at my own convenience. However the punters proved to be as soporific as the weather and I was soon heading back to The Hutch for an unearned cuppa. Of course I expected a little bit of stick orchestrated by a back to normal Tonker, but was totally unprepared for the storm which followed.

As I entered The Hutch there was at first an unnatural silence and some very odd expressions on the faces of the assembled multitude. Then they hit me where it hurts most. Feelings.

Suddenly blasting out of the air waves was Mendelsohn's bloody Wedding March. I was then assailed by cat calls and various audible obscenities. And what did I do in the face of this unnerving situation? I blushed right down to the roots again like the guilty schoolboy of old. How I still hated myself for this juvenile weakness, even at the half century mark (as you can see, the healing had only just begun). And I was utterly speechless, me the mighty orator again reduced to a mute heap of rubble by a motley group of roadies.

'Give us a kiss, you old romantic.' Elise started the ball rolling. 'You certainly are a dark horse, aren't you? And what other dirty hidden depths are lurking underneath that posh exterior? In fact, behind all that Toffy Tommy tosh, you really are as randy as the rest of us.'

I tried in vain for the higher ground.

'That's all I would expect from you Elise. You obviously wouldn't know anything about love emanating from the heart.' But of course my patronizing remarks were swatted away effortlessly.

'In my very wide ranging experience Tommy, love comes from the groin. And coming is what it's all about, isn't it mate.' She should have been a beguiling barrister. Or a QC.

Again The Hutch collapsed and again I found myself blushing crimson under this withering full frontal assault. I may have had a way with words, but I was crap at the cut and thrust of actual debate. Especially with a hard-nosed and soft-breasted woman.

'Well she's certainly a fit piece of kit, I'll give you that Tommy.' A mini olive branch from Leonardo, even if I was a little bit miffed to hear my beloved described in such vulgar terms. On the other hand, she might have taken it as quite a compliment from such an annoyingly good-looking young man.

'Thanks Leonardo. I will remember you in my will. And now if you will excuse me ladies and gentlemen, I rather think I will partake of a coffee in the more rarefied company of the Café Gascon.' And then with as much deflated dignity as I could muster I retreated rapidly from The Hutch to further expletives deleted from the gleeful audience.

That's it Tommy. Revert to type. When in trouble, retreat into that little Walter Mitty world of yours and look through life with rose-coloured glasses. Where have you heard that before? How about Van and that old Ivory Tower? And now that you've nine tenths of your clumsy foot into that precious citadel surely you are not going to sound the retreat again, are you? That has always been your method of 'coping' with problems in the past and look where it has sodding well got you? You might enhance the situation by confronting your demons for once. And that doesn't mean the Charge of the bloody Light Brigade over the top routine which is your usual suicidal alternative. How about a halfway house? Think about that old half full glass mantra, not half empty. Oh yes, very droll. Who was this damned inner voice assaulting my eardrums?

> Then to the rolling Heav'n itself I cried
> Asking, 'What Lamp had Destiny to guide
> Her little Children stumbling in the Dark ?'
> And – 'A blind Understanding !' Heav'n replied.

A blind Understanding. I like that one Omar. Perhaps a little less thinking and a little more action might be in order. As Eric had been heard to utter on a number of occasions, 'thinking makes you constipated.' I had often pondered this apparent verbal crap from the mouth of the most garrulous taxi driver in Suffolk, but at last I think I had got his drift. Yes, a blind Understanding. Give it a crack Tommy. It can't do you any long term harm, can it?

Giving it a crack meant getting back to proper hard work after the temporary relief provided by the Café Gascon. All went smoothly till my last fare of the evening. It was always that fatal last fare that seemed to bring me so much grief.

The Scarecrow had sent me to Grave Road on the Hollesley estate at about eleven o'clock to take a punter to the docks area in Ipswich. The ominous street name should have given me an inkling of what was to come but fools rush in regardless of experience. Grave Road was a suitably dingy, badly lit cul de sac on the edge of this notorious estate. Pulling up outside number thirty three, I suddenly received my first feelings of disquiet. There was no sign of life at all and I didn't fancy getting out of the sanctuary of my car. Just as I was about to drive off with much relief, a bulky figure emerged out of the gloom. In got a Sonny Liston lookalike and off we went to the not so fair town of Ipswich. As usual I entered into innocent banter just to get to know a bit about my fare. I was more than a fraction disconcerted to hear that he had just come direct from the police station, having spent the whole day incarcerated there answering questions about an armed robbery. Apparently there wasn't enough evidence to detain my distinguished client any longer, and he had eventually been let out to my tender mercies. Thanks a bundle, Suffolk Constabulary. The drive along the A14 seemed an eternity as I felt his surly menace at far too close quarters. He was monosyllabic with me for most of the way except when he positively waxed lyrical about what he intended to do to his father-in-law when we got to Ipswich. Apparently 'the shit had shopped him.' Charming. Time to play the coward again. No I must rephrase that sentence very precisely. Time to be the coward. That's it, encourage him to take out his father-in-law. No shame, no pain.

All the time I was aware of this huge brooding presence next to me. For a man of letters not of action, this was a distinctly unnerving experience. It was not what he did but what he might do to me if I said the slightest wrong thing, whatever that might be. I felt so alone and so, so vulnerable. Shades of the schoolboy again. After an eternity we arrived at the Neptune Quay in Ipswich and Sonny paid up not like a lamb, but a veritable wolf in sheep's clothing. But there was still plenty of time for a nasty sting in the tail.

'Thanks mate. But you'd better pray for the old man though.' I thought a little thanks to someone up there might be in order, especially after I read in The East Anglian Daily Times a couple of days later of a brutal assault in the docks area by an as yet anonymous person but one that sounded suspiciously like it might be down to Mr Liston. I don't quite think that was what Omar quite had in mind by a blind Understanding. Or perhaps

187

he meant in his obscure way that I should have sympathy for 'her little Children stumbling in the Dark ?' Ah well, perhaps I'd better stick to the healing after all.

Talking of the latter, it was more than time to give Tiff that little buzz she had requested. I was up at the crack of dawn again the next day and had plenty of time for a leisurely shower and to put on my make-up before ringing her.

'Hi Tiff, it's me.' Not very Shakespearean I know but factual if nothing else.

'Hello darling.' Crikeys. Not Tommy dear in inverted commas, but darling. Where to go? Shit, I'm busted. I'm way out of my depth here.

'Hello luv, yesterday was great.' Even Marlowe would have winced at that one.

'Oh Tommy, you still can't hack it, can you? I do love you for better or the other.'

What could I say? The love of my life says she loved me. I just tingled all over. The girl of my dreams says those magical words. It must be a dream. No, I'm stone cold sober for once so it must be real. I just love her so.

> And we walked down the avenue in style
> We walked down the avenue with a smile
> And say it was all worthwhile
> When the healing has begun.

Our own special avenue had been The Promenade at Felixstowe where we used to enjoy many a wintry walk with a cutting east wind blowing off the black and forbidding North Sea. Tiff used to say that it would blow all my troubles away but it was the sheer splendid isolation of this apparently bleak walk that was so precious to us. We passed the fading Victorian splendour of the former hotels above the theatre, past the Ladies College, round the bend to the myriad row of beach huts, then the golf course and finally past the old Martello tower to The Ferry itself. All the time we would be immersed in typical lovers' conversations, like our plans for the future, the psychedelic music of The Grateful Dead or simply the present. Then quickly back to the Millers Tea-rooms for a rapid warm up with tea and crumpets. More golden memories.

So why had I walked away from Tiff with barely a backward glance? How to begin? I could say that we just drifted apart as young lovers do. I could say that I walked before I was pushed. Or that I was so jealous of a new and better looking rival with an even more impressive car that I didn't want to stay any longer and be subject to further exquisite agony. I certainly wasn't in the E Type league and I wasn't very good at coping with competition.

But none of the above would strictly be true. The truth is that I don't really know. When Tiff went up to Sheffield University it was obvious we would see a lot less of each other but it didn't in itself mean the end of our relationship. We could have kept in touch during term time and then have all the time in the world together in the hols. No need for students in those halcyon days to subjugate all their spare time to working and paying off student debts. The summer of love may have been left far behind but there was still plenty of time for a winter of sex.

189

But I was also an idle sod. While Tiff wrote regular letters of unrequited love, absence wasn't making the heart fonder for me and, to my everlasting shame, I never replied to a single one. It was also very difficult to get hold of her on the university phone. In the present climate of mobile phones and texting I wouldn't have any trouble at all, would I?

But these are utterly feeble excuses. The real truth was that I was just a selfish shit. I drifted into a number of casual sexual encounters and let Tiff drift away at the same time. How could I have been so stupid? My conquests were only Sutton Market slags and meant nothing at all to me. Conversely the slags might have said that I was just a Sutton Market shagger myself and was merely cheap sexmeat to them. It was always thus.

By the time I came to my senses Tiff was long gone. E Type man had driven her off at the rate of knots in a puff of exhaust and she was never to return. Until now. I wonder whatever happened to E Type man? Hopefully he disappeared down his own big end. I've told you before that women haven't got the monopoly on bitchiness.

But why the sudden softening? What had been the strange alchemy which suddenly had converted old friendship into new love?

> The vine had struck a Fibre; which about
> It clings my Being – let the Sufi flout ;
> Of my Base Metal may be filed a Key,
> That shall unlock the Door he howls without.

I had unlocked the Door to love without even realizing it.

Back to the blind Understanding. Perhaps Tiff had not only now felt ready for another relationship but had finally forgiven me for the unforgivable behaviour in my murky past? Or perhaps she thought I had been punished enough by Megan? Perhaps I would never know?

I resumed our up to date telephone conversation.

'How about a little stroll along The Promenade at Felixstowe this Sunday? I could pick you up at twelve if you're interested.'

'Of course I'm interested, you silly old fool. It will be like old times again, won't it? And good old times at that.' I had been forgiven. 'See you then.'

'And Tiff,' I essayed with difficulty.

'Yes Tommy.' I could feel her incurious tenderness down the phone.

'I love you too Tiff.' There, I'd damned well said it.

'I know you do. See you Sunday Tommy.'

I put down the phone with a whoop. It almost felt like a century at Lords. There's no fool like an old fool in love. And for love to be returned was heaven indeed. But in one important way the tables had been imperceptibly turned. When I knew Tiff of old I always felt in control. I had been three years older and that seemed to make a huge difference in those days. Now the difference in age meant nothing and it was Tiff who was pulling all the strings. And I was more than happy to be pulled along.

Another frantic Saturday night. There was certainly no time tonight to contemplate the vagaries of love, blind Understanding or even just the meaning of life. This was life in the fast lane in the true sense of the word as I hurtled from place to place, permanently twenty minutes late and increasingly flustered by impatient punters and other lunatics or slowcoaches on the road. Tonight I seemed to be either constantly overtaken by boy racers with a death wish or held up by geriatric meanderers who obviously had all the time in the world to reach their destinations. Well, I didn't and the latter didn't have to face abuse either. We seemed to have some extra special right ones tonight, and even someone with my legendarily laid-back nature would have struggled to keep his cool.

The first person to feel the wrath of my acerbic tongue was some helpless punter from The Bear who happened to mention innocently that I had a 'nondescript accent' and that I was, much worse, 'not one of us'. This gave me just the easy opportunity and soft target I had been looking for all evening.

'Actually, I happen to think that my voice is quite distinguished, which is a bloody sight more than can be said for your execrable estuary accent. And for the record mate, I happened to have been born here in Sutton Market, not on some crappy Thames mudflat like you were obviously ill-conceived on.'

After I had finished my little polemic, I happened to glance over at my young fare. His face was ashen and he looked totally devastated.

'Sorry mate, I didn't mean to offend you,' he stuttered.

And then I suddenly saw the light. What right had I to take out all my frustrated spleen on this totally innocent lad? Who gave me the right to play the verbal god? Pick on someone your own size. How about Elise? Not so lucid now, are you Tommy? For the record, play it again Georgie.

> What is your angry Satire worth,
> But to arouse the sleeping hive.
> And send the raging Passions forth,
> In bold, vindictive, angry flight,
> To sting wherever they alight ?

'Shit, I'm sorry. I'm just having one of those nights. Have this one on me.'

Out got a very confused teenager, naturally bewildered by my rapid mood changes but apparently more than happy to accept a freebie.

'Thanks mate. See you around.'

This time I refrained from making another sarcastic sally at his expense and contented myself with a very subdued goodnight.

I was just a pathetic flat track bully, picking my soft targets oh so carefully like the contemptible coward I had always been. As with the recent little incidents concerning Elise and Frank, when the going got tough I got the hell out.

But hold on a moment. This time I had recognised the nastiness of my ways just in time and had attempted a remedy by actually apologising. Tough word sorry, almost as tough as love.

And I had said them both this week. A new Tommy record. The healing had truly begun.

> And we walked down the avenue again
> And the healing has begun.

Feeling unjustly pleased with myself I set off for my next fare with a spring in my step and a metaphorical muzzle on my mouth. But to no avail. I just can't help myself, as the tart said to the bishop. Neither can I was the gravelly response.

My next punters proved to be a very pleasant couple taking their daughter and her fiancé out for a little treat to the restaurant at Silford Hall where they were apparently going to get married next month. It was certainly a very popular venue for weddings, and dare I say it, quite romantic. Unfortunately for everyone, I only had eyes for the husband's trousers. Perhaps I had better explain myself before you start wondering? But of course I forgot, you have been wondering for a while now, haven't you? But I digress.

'What revolting trousers. Even with my dark glasses on I can see that they are way over the top.' I took off the shades. 'Christ, they are still hideous.' The offending trousers were a kind of puke ridden mustard colour and even Chris Eubank would have struggled to compete with this particular peacock.

However the peacock in question proved that he could defend himself quite adequately without the assistance of any old former boxing champion.

'Good god, I didn't realize that I had ordered the Mafia. I

thought that we were meant to be going out for a meal, not a hit. Ha ha.'

Blimey this guy was good.

'In the light of your robust response I will overlook your sartorial misdemeanour on this occasion,' I riposted.

After that we got on like a house on fire, although his wife expressed slight reservations whether I would make the grade as a diplomat. On arriving at Silford Hall, the husband asked if he could make a return booking.

'No probs,' I replied brightly. 'What name shall I give.'

'Oh, I rather think that Colonel Mustard will suffice,' he twinkled. What class.

I picked them up again about three happy hours later. The women were in very merry mood and sung along lustily to some Classic Gold oldies. In the front of the car the Colonel and I had discovered a mutual passion in rugby and spent the whole journey in an intense discussion concerning England's prospects in the forthcoming World Cup.

I deposited the happy foursome in Priory Street which contained some of the finest old houses in the town. However such was my benevolent mood by now, I didn't even feel envious for once.

'Thanks for the laughs young man. Keep the change.'

Yup, I was healing nicely.

But not totally. I still had time to give a touch of sarcastic applause to some inconsiderate motorist who had incurred my displeasure. And I was well rewarded when he turned his car round and chased me all round the town till I managed eventually to elude him down an obscure side street. I also had great difficulty in explaining to The Fat Controller where I had disappeared to for those five precious minutes. Keep on running Tommy.

Back yet again to The Silford Hall Golf and Country Club, to give it its full name, eleven fifty pick up, this time to Ipswich, East Bergholt and Hadleigh, fare thirty three pounds, name of Lord. I arrived a bit early at quarter to twelve, plonked myself prominently in front of the entrance and settled into a bit of Van in anticipation of a few minutes wait. The disco music blasted out, other taxis came and went but there was no sign of my fare. It was now almost twelve o'clock and I was beginning to get seriously impatient. That stupid Fat Controller should never have taken it as a before midnight booking. Even if Mr Lord had come out dead on time, by far the largest part of the journey would still have been carried out after midnight. So I was already pissed off with them both as the fare should really have been fifty quid with the fare and a half premium.

While I am in pissed off mode, I must say that it always got me mad when some drunken dickhead complained about the fare with a 'you must be fucking joking mate'. To which my stock reply was: 'you want to drive pisspots like you round at three in the morning and see if is still a fucking joke. Mate.'

Still no sign of Mr Lord so I had a natter with one of the few drivers from Lone Star Cars that I was on speaking terms with, and commiserated with him about one of his fellow driver's prang the night before. The latter had written off his new Mondeo and had almost written himself off in the process. Luckily there were no fares with him at the time. However he was still badly hurt and apparently would be in hospital for at least three months. I didn't like the grumpy old so and so but even I wouldn't have wished that fate on any driver. There but for the grace of the god of The Road go all of us. A sobering thought even for Sandy. None of us had either injury or loss of earnings cover and would be totally stuffed in every sense if we had a major but not fatal crash. Probably best to put us down to go to the Great Motorway in the Sky, condemned to drive eternally round the M25. Not much change there then. Better stick around for a while but I still don't fancy the long term odds. If The Road doesn't get you, the punters certainly will. In the end.

Talking of punters, where the hell was The Lord? It was now quarter past midnight. What to do? I was feeling a bit knackered and the thought of an early night seemed seriously tempting.

As it was now well after midnight the fare and a half rate was clearly indicated so I decided to hang on to twelve thirty with the comforting thought that I would now be earning the not inconsiderable sum of fifty quid plus waiting time for my late night labours.

At twelve thirty one precisely, sleep was the winner and I started the engine. However just as I was about to drive away down the tree lined opulence beloved by estate agents, there was an explosive whack on my window. I eased the offending object down gingerly and Sylvester Stallone stuck his bloody great chin through the narrow gap. My Lord had arrived not with a whimper, but a bloody big bang. Sylvester obviously thought he was back in Nam, or would have done if he wasn't too pissed to think. Or could he think in the first place? He then eased his badly decomposing body into the front passenger seat while his two henchman and a lady got into the back, albeit not without difficulty and with a yawning amount of milk white thigh being exposed above the sensuous black stocking tops. And that was just one of the henchmen. It was obviously going to be a Rocky ride.

As mentioned before I liked to discover a bit about my fares on a late night journey, just to be on the safe side and to anticipate possible problems. I relaxed considerably when I found out that all my fares were from The Rutshire Building Society and that the fiercesome Sylvester was in fact the local branch manager. My mother always said I shouldn't judge a book by its cover and I hadn't realized how percipient she was. I would be OK on this one.

But not so fast, Tommy. I had already informed Rutshire Incorporated that the fare would now be a fare and a half but clearly hadn't been clear enough. This apparently small but potentially disastrous error became apparent a couple of miles down the road when I heard them discussing the fare and Sylvester said 'it would be about eight quid fifty each.' In true pantomime fashion I spoke on cue.

'Oh no it won't. The fare will now be fifty quid altogether, thanks to your dilatoriness.' I had decided to keep it simple in monetary terms if not in language.

198

They all ejaculated loudly that they hadn't seen me and they were waiting to be summoned by the DJ while they had an uncomfortable forty minutes propping up the bar. I don't like liars and retorted sarcastically.

'It's not surprising that you didn't see me right under your noses when you never even bothered to look out of the fucking window.'

This little sortie was enough to provoke Sylvester back on to a war footing.

'Whatdoyoumean, the agreed fare was thirty three pounds fifty.' He was all right on figures, but I supposed he should have been with all his Rutshiring. I patiently explained again the changed circumstances and he at least had the grace (and certainly the only grace he showed all night) to admit that the original quote seemed very cheap but spoilt it all by barking 'thirty three quid was the agreed price and that's all I'm fucking paying.' That was the signal for me to stop the car, fortuitously just before we turned onto the A14.

'That's fine, in that case I will take you back to Sutton Market and you can get another taxi from there.'

That's when things turned nasty and first I was subjected to a combined volley of particularly foul mouthed invective and then instructed by Sylvester to 'take us home before anyone gets hurt.' This prompted me to reassess the situation radically because, beneath my outward bravado, I of course hated unpleasantness of any kind. I had undoubtedly been threatened and Sylvester was clearly capable of doing me some major damage. I could see his naked aggression as I looked him in the eye and was told menacingly not to eyeball him. Perish the thought, one mustn't eyeball a branch manager of the Rutshire Building Society.

That thought gave me comfort and decided my plan of campaign. That vital piece of information concerning his employment so fortunately garnered was going to save me. However pissed he might be, surely an innate sense of job survival must preclude any physical aggression? To bluff or not to bluff, that is the question? Take a gamble Tommy go for it, an unknown but familiar voice inside me urged. And of course I had always been a gambler, whether on the horses, in business and to my eternal cost, with women. I felt rather than heard my disembodied voice strongly inform the company that I was going to take them back to Sutton Market.

Sylvester was positively steaming by now and shouted at me 'take me home pal and we'll forget all about reporting you to your company and the Taxi Authorities.'

I pointed out with a lot more conviction than I felt that I was self employed and 'didn't give a toss what you do or want. And I'm not your pal either, thank fucking goodness. I'm tired, I want to go home and go to bed. Its a matter of total indifference to me whether you get home or not. And by the bye you are all a load of drunken tossers.' Not very constructive I have to admit, but deliciously satisfactory.

But the pendulum had imperceptibly swung and though Sylvester reiterated that I must take them home, there was less conviction in his voice this time and a corresponding vastly reduced level of testosterone. Carpe diem, as all taxi drivers instinctively say. I suddenly saw an ingenious answer to the impasse.

'I'll tell you what' I informed the assembled and bewildered minitude. 'If Syl asks me nicely, I will take you all home at the previously agreed fare.'

After what seemed like an eternity Syl managed a very feeble 'could you take us home please.'

I was now revelling in the changed situation. What childish pleasure I took from that contorted visage as it struggled to emit the dreaded word. Milking the moment, I said that 'I still didn't quite catch that Syl. Again, if you please.'

A truly anguished please was my rich reward. Yet another victory for the Vietcong and a very smooth remaining journey round the Mekong Delta. In fact when Syl finally disembarked at Hadleigh he was almost contrite and managed a very nice goodnight after he had paid up with a totally unconvincing grumble.

Of course it was Sylvester's arrogance which had angered me most. He had treated me like dirt and I wasn't having that, was I? Or had he just treated me like an arrogant taxi driver? Arrogance against arrogance doesn't gel. The fact that I had been a suit myself who suited himself till a few years ago had of course nothing to do with it. When I bumped into people of the same ilk in this business I became irrationally irked. Discuss with Tiff on Sunday, Tommy. People in glass boxes shouldn't throw stones. Back to the neurotic drawing board and a little more healing.

But the fact that I could actually recognize my own arrogance must mean that I am getting a bit better. To even vaguely look at the situation from the opposition's point of view was a huge mental leap for me and must be worth at least a few celestial brownie points.

Yes, its certainly an absurd, mad bad old world. From Rutshiring to women's underwear, us taxi drivers certainly get around.

Take legs, bosoms and kissing for example, in no particular order of preference. Heterosexual male taxi drivers certainly have it made. We must see more pulchritude than in any other menial job. Over the course of a normal weekend, our blood pressure would sometimes reach boiling point. I just wish young ladies with short skirts would learn to negotiate with a trifle more elegance the admittedly tricky hurdle of getting into the back of the car. I also wished they would curb their language occasionally, or at least use a little variety. Sometimes the sheer crudity of their language made even me blush. It wasn't like that in my day. However after more than three years on The Road I had learnt to harden my heart and everything else from these pleasant and not so pleasant distractions. For heaven's sake, most of these girls were young enough to be my daughters, or even grand-daughters.

Bosoms were another matter. I just couldn't handle them, as it were. Since the catastrophic introduction of the Wonderbra and the subsequent less than spiritually uplifting variations, it was downhill all the way on the brassière front. British boobs were now pushed up so far by such ingenious corsetrie that they certainly were right up where they belong. I always wax lyrical at the most inopportune moments. Where was I ? Oh yes, bras. The girls of my flower power generation were of course far more at home with the burning of the bra and consequent no bra, no fee situation. If they were worn at all they were invariably of a delicate and beguiling lace variety. Being a purveyor of quality not quantity I was strictly a small boob man. So it was that I found it easy peasy to turn away from the singularly unpleasant vision of vast mammaries constantly gaping at me like unpricked balloons.

Kissing wasn't so easy to turn away from, even if I wanted to. My first one took me totally unawares. I had picked up this rather dishevelled young lady named Kirsty from Bosmere House, a refuge for homeless young people. She wanted to go to Ipswich to see an old friend who was in trouble. We got chatting and it transpired that her stepfather was in Norwich prison having been convicted of murdering her mother. Apparently he was a psychopathic bully who had taken a knife to his wife in a frenzy one drunken Saturday night. Make cannabis compulsory and lager illegal post-haste. Anyhow it also transpired that Kirsty was also pregnant by her uncle's rape. What a fucking mess. How the hell could I charge her fifteen bloody quid? Of course I didn't charge her anything at all. I was rewarded with a quick peck on the cheek and a murmured 'you're a good man, Tommy.' I don't know about that but I certainly felt good. Who cares if I am a gullible old fool? Perhaps the world would be a better place if there were more of us around.

My next unplanned kiss came in far less harrowing circumstances, I'm pleased to relate. I was outside the Copacana Beach night club at the usual two o'clock kickout time waiting for a recalcitrant client when I was approached by two charming young ladies. Could I possibly take them to the Bosmere Heights estate? Their respective boyfriends had deserted them and they were bloody freezing, to politely paraphrase their words. I never could ignore damsels in distress, especially if they were pretty. In three minutes flat I had safely deposited them at their destination. 'Thank you kindly Mr Taxi Driver sir, you're a veritable star,' and two chaste kisses on my cheek confirmed this unlikely fact. And two polite and literate fares for once. Who needs rewards in heaven?

Lastly, but only temporarily I hope, a distraught lady of a certain age. I picked her up from Sutton Farms chicken factory. She related tearfully that she had just heard that her newly born grand-daughter had been struck down with a critical illness and that she needed to go straight to the hospital to see her. Her anguish was pitiful to behold and I again naturally waived the fare. Thank you so much, she gasped and planted yet another grateful kiss on my overused left cheek. Hell, I hope Mr Smiley hasn't been keeping me under surveillance recently. He might just get the right idea. My reward was doubly tangible this time. I happened to pick up the same lady two nights later and all was well with her grandchild. Another indefinably good feeling. God, I'm getting there. The healing had seriously begun.

Mentioning kissing and healing brings me neatly back to Tiff and our Sunday afternoon outing. After my late night adventures with Syl, it was a rather weary Tommy who struggled out of bed that morning. After a hasty coffee, I followed that familiar but thrilling road to Rattlesden. And thrilling was the only way to describe Tiff on another golden day. She was dressed in a crimson red dress that was far too short for comfort but at last did full justice to those delectable legs. For once she had her hair done up in a bun with a more than appropriate ivory butterfly clip. In short she looked stunning.

'Oh Tiff,' was all I could manage.

I was rewarded with a full-blooded kiss full on my full lips and we were more than ready for the road. We had never been to Felixstowe in the summer before and that was something special which I wanted to do with her. Something new to break the mould and optimistically something brand new to bring to the memory bank.

We did our old walk down The Avenue again, but this time in warm sunshine and surrounded by teeming crowds of holidaymakers. But it didn't matter an iota as we were lost in our intimate world of love. Nothing had really changed and we talked animatedly about our plans for the future again whilst laughing blissfully about the past. And having completed the old circuit, minus the now sadly defunct Ladies College, we steamed passed the old Millers Tea-rooms which had been transmogrified into a tired bistro. From there a radical change of direction was called for in more than one way.

Back in the car, I decided to do the slow traditional tour of the Deben estuary via Waldringfield, Martlesham Creek and Woodbridge. Eventually we arrived at The Ramsholt Arms on the other side of the river. The latter public house must have the finest river views in Suffolk. Facing south west over the huge patio area, the massive skies met the lowering cattleland in rugged symmetry.

> Not distant far, a house commodious made.
> (Lonely yet public stands) for Sunday-trade;

Thither, for this day free, gay parties go.
Their tea-house walk, their tippling rendezvous;
There humble couples sit in corner-bowers,
Or gaily ramble for th'allotted hours.

After two pints of Woodford's finest, I was getting peckish. So
was Tiff. We perused the aphrodisiacal fish-filled menu and the
juices were going again. We both selected the sea bass and moved
easily onto the eminently acceptable house white. By the time
we had consumed the succulent fish and a couple of armagnacs
plus a token cup of coffee, the sun was beginning to set over the
now receding river. Tiff was enchanting as ever and I was as witty
as never before fuelled by the demon drink. The mud flats were
more than ripe, Tiff seemed more than ready to collapse into the
Ramsholts' comforting bedrooms but was the timing right? Was
it time for Tonker again or was it time for tonking?

I want you to put on your old summer red dress
Your Easter bonnet and all the rest
I want to make love to you yes yes yes
And the healing has begun.

10.   IN THE GARDEN

> The streets are always wet with rain
> After a summer shower when I saw you standin'
> In the garden, in the garden wet with rain.

No we didn't do it that glorious evening at Ramsholt. Something wasn't quite right. Too much alcohol perhaps? I wanted it to be perfect, and perfectly sober.

In the end I utilized an Ipswich private hire firm to get us home to preserve a bit of anonymity and to keep the marauding Hutch and tabloids at bay.

> Like baneful herbs the gazer's eye they seize,
> Rush to the head, and poison where they please;
> Like idle flies, a busy, buzzing train;
> They drop their maggots in the trifler's brain;
> That genial soil receives the fruitful store,
> And there they grow, and breed a thousand more.

Bastards. But Georgie had captured the latter's true essence even in his day, just as he did with a modern day former broadsheet.

As artful sinners cloak the secret sin,
To veil with seeming grace the guile within;
So Moral Essays on his front appear,
But all is carnal business in the rear.

Spot on.

Anyway Tiff seemed quite happy with the revised taxi arrangements and again we had a long, lingering kiss on the portals of Rattlesden Towers without the distraction of Tonker's long, lingering leer this time.

Thus it was that I entered The Hutch the next morning to lovely indifference, and able to indulge in a bit of quiet euphoria without any dirty distractions. Anyway the centre of attraction this morning was Nigel, The Boy Racer. He had apparently raced to Heathrow Airport in the early hours in a new official Wells Fargo lap record of eighty three minutes and fifty eight seconds for the one hundred and twenty mile journey. Nutter. Unfortunately, on arrival at Terminal 4, he had parked in the taxi loading zone area and popped out of the car for five minutes to make sure his fare had landed, or rather that their plane had. On his return he discovered to his horror that his car had disappeared. Eventually he had traced it to an impounded car stockade. Despite remonstrating with the relevant dogsbody he still had to pay one hundred and fifty pounds up front to get his car released. His humour wasn't improved either by Mr Dogsbody's reason for the impounding. Apparently they thought it might contain an Al Qaeda bomb. Bloody likely wasn't it with Wells Fargo Private Hire plastered all over the car? Since Wells Fargo couldn't organize a piss up in a brewery or even getting a car to the church on time, it was hardly likely we could arrange a sophisticated explosion at an airport. One quick phone call to The Fat Controller would also have established the car's bona fides. And if the nameless authorities thought there might be a bomb in the car, why take it to the pound? Surely a controlled explosion on the apron of the runway was called for? Sensible security or witless paranoia? As Dylan said so many years ago, it's for you to decide.

Neither was his VIP client very happy to be kept waiting and Nigel received the proverbial flea in his ear. But much worse he received no tip either. As the fixed fare was one hundred and twenty pounds Nigel had made an obscene thirty pounds loss for his five hours of endeavours, exacerbated as usual by a snarl-up on the M25 on the way back.

Nigel had just used the first five words in the film Four Weddings and a Funeral when I slipped into The Hutch.

'Why do we all persist in this bloody job?' Nigel wailed. 'After paying parking fines, speeding fines and clamping fines, there's not much left in the pot after expenses have also been taken into account.'

'And of course there is no danger money to reflect the inherent dangers of confronting other nutters on the road and general nutters,' I chipped in. They all stared at me, Tommy who was the chief perpetrator in inviting danger. 'Well at least I haven't reversed into anything recently,' I stupidly added.

Still it was no wonder Nigel was totally disenchanted and talking of getting out of The Waiting Game. He had been in it for over five years now and even his innate cheerfulness was beginning to flag badly.

'I've had it Tommy. I'm just pissed off with The Road. You work your arse off for what? Fucking nothing, that's what. No, not fucking nothing. Fucking minus thirty pounds. And then that bloody Smiley phones up QC to complain that I actually had the nerve to drive through that little taxi lane in The Thoroughfare and I've been given an official warning. What a wanker. What a bloody job.'

When somebody as normally mild-mannered as Nigel gets the hump in such a mega way, something is seriously wrong in the Private Hire firmament. Something had to give. Perhaps a Saturday night strike might get the message across. But of course we couldn't afford to miss out on our Saturday takings. I had taken three hundred quid on one gruelling double shift a few weeks ago in the course of which I did well over four hundred miles. Thus we were in a classic Catch 22 situation. Fucked if we did and fucked if we didn't.

Luckily the cavalry came over the hill at this critical moment in the unlikely form of The Singing Professor. Mr Mandrake was of course another old favourite from way back when. Also from way back when he had been a distinguished lecturer in history at Cambridge University. Now that distinguished brain had disintegrated into senility, he was a loose canon in the true sense of the phrase. I had to pick him up from his suitably odd house in Rotten Row and then do a little tour via a newsagent, Waitrose supermarket, Boots dispensary and then finally back to Rotten Row. All the time he was in the car I was regaled by his little ditties, the most notable being the infamous:-

We're on the road to Waitrose, hurrah, hurrah.

Followed later by the equally witty:-

We're going back to Rotten Row, tee hee.

I know it should have been very sad. But come on, he was happy and he made us drivers happy by helping us to escape from that bad old real world as well. Mr Mandrake was also much blessed not to have to return to that bad old world unlike the rest of us so-called normal people.

There were times I found my world almost as surreal as Mr Mandrake's, especially when aided and abetted by Leonardo's magic mushrooms. I had been trying to grow my own recently, but as yet my enthusiastic efforts had fallen on unfallow ground. I had also been more discreet with my use of the weed as I knew Tiff didn't approve. But that didn't stop the use of it and I could still safely disappear off the radar when I was back alone in the flat.

However, that same evening after Nigel's little setback I almost disappeared off another radar screen. The Fat Controller sent me on a late night pick up near the smelly village of Woolpit. Having eventually found the singularly elusive Nags Lane, I was now trying in vain to find the equally elusive Oak Tree Cottage. It was dark as pitch in the lane and I had never been much cop on the arboreal front anyway, even in broad daylight.

With increasing irritation I reached the end of the row of cottages. Time for a rapid three point turn and a resurvey on the return journey. However my rapid reverse was terminated by a loud thwack. Oh damn, what had I hit now? I drove forward gingerly a few yards and got out of the car to find out what it was.

I soon found a very solid piece of rounded stone on the grass verge of the last cottage in the lane, obviously precisely placed there to prevent urban prats like me from carrying out the delicate manoeuvre I had just carried out so carelessly. With a great deal of effort, I picked up the offending object and dropped it viciously into a ditch. However as I turned back to the car I noticed a tell-tale line of liquid caught in my rear lights. With trepidation I investigated the crime scene and even I could detect that the liquid was oil, not gold. Oh bugger, I must have cracked the sump. Forty three swear words later, my foul tirade was interrupted by a hesitant voice of a young lady about ten yards back up the lane.

'Is that Wells Fargo Cars?', continued the hesitant voice.

'It was,' I snarled back.

'Oh dear, have you got a problem? Can I help?'

I cooled off rapidly at her obvious concern. I was also very concerned that she might have heard all forty three of my swear words. It would be difficult to prove any mitigating circumstances this time if I was reported to Mr Smiley. I explained what had happened. By this time the young lady was joined by her boyfriend and they were both very sympathetic at what had happened.

Next the practical side. I radioed in for another car to be sent for the young lady. However before I could sign off I heard a huge guffah from The Fat Controller.

'You're not safe to be let out alone at night Tommy. You ought to stick to baby sitting or Tiff sitting. Ho ho.'

'Over and out, you great fat bastard,' was my unhelpful reply.

After that little contretemps I turned my attention to the AA. Miraculously they had a vehicle free in the area and would be with me in less than half an hour.

Next I was made to suffer at the hands, or rather the garrulous mouth of The Crafty Cockney who had come speeding in to the rescue of the damsel in distress and her boyfriend.

'Too much sex affecting your eyesight Tommy?' he jeered.

'Thank you Eric. I think we can do without the commentary tonight. This young lady wants to go back to Sutton Market post haste after our little delay. Goodnight. And I suppose I should thank you for helping me out.'

What a pompous bore I was.

'No probs Tommy,' he smirked unmercilessly. Oh no, more flack in The Hutch tomorrow. Why does it always happen to me?

The young man very kindly made me a cup of coffee while we waited for the AA man.

'By the way I was very impressed just then by the range and variety of your swearing.'

Oh shit, he had heard as well.

'And I just loved those five star Merde words. And all in that rich classy accent Anglais. Impressionant.

Oh no. Another bugger taking the piss.

Luckily the AA man arrived at that very moment and very efficiently set up his tow-pole.

'Its brand new,' he confided. 'Absolutely unbreakable.'

With this ringing endorsement of his equipment, off we went back to Sutton Market with my car suspended precariously behind and me apprehensively behind the wheel. Some years ago in France I had an alarming experience after yet another break down. My car, with me in it, were lifted up onto the first floor of the recovery trailer and off we zoomed down the Autoroute with me becalmed on high. Terrifying. This experience was almost as bad. You are steering totally unsighted a disconcerting few feet behind the recovery vehicle with its double flashing orange light also blinding you. Why do they have to be so bright? Anyhow we somehow got back to Sutton Market with no mishaps. Just one right angled left turn at the lights and we would be back in the comfort of The Hutch. Unfortunately I had never driven on a fixed tow before and didn't know you had to go with the flow as it were. Before I knew it there was the second great thwack of the night and my front lights went out. I hadn't got a clue what had happened but the AA man soon put me right.

'You bloody moron. You've broken my pole,' he stormed.

He then fiddled about ineffectually for about quarter of an hour trying to rectify the damage while a queue of hooting cars tried to get round the 'unnecessary obstruction'. All the time groups of revellers passed by with their unwelcome catcalls, laughter and derision. It didn't help either when I employed my usual casual 'V' sign tactics and some of the mob moved in for the kill. Then the police lumbered up and I got booked by PC Bunter for foul and abusive language. I think this warranted that old cliché that things were getting seriously out of hand.

While all this was going off the AA man continued to fiddle with his pole. He suddenly exploded into life.

'I've done it.'

'Congratulations, now you can get on with something useful,' I said sarcastically.

'I mean I've fixed my pole, you wanker.'

'Oh, I'm sorry, I thought you were the only one round here doing the wanking.'

PC Bunter now did something seriously useful at last by calling a very loud break and implanted his reassuringly large bulk in between us. He then directed us back to our respective vehicles and the convoy crawled back to The Hutch. Needless to say our parting was both silent and glacial. Time to join the RAC methinks.

'Oh hello Tommy,' chortled The Fat Controller. 'What kept you? Ha ha.'

'Thank you for your concern, TFC. I rather think I will be shuffling off home now.'

'Yes, I rather think you are safer on foot Tommy,' added Eric unnecessarily. 'But be very careful at the lights. Ha ha.'

So someone had seen the second debacle as well. Life wouldn't be worth living in The Hutch tomorrow. Then I brightened. Perhaps Sutton Market Motors would work at their usual speed (i.e. reverse) and the car wouldn't be ready for a couple of weeks. The heat should be off by then. But how would I get to Rattlesden in that case? Oh, life's a bugger isn't it? Time for another quick one, as the AA man might have said if he had a sense of humour.

It was still only half past ten so I had plenty of time to make useful inroads into Mauldon's best.

'Steady on Tommy,' said Graham forcefully. 'I thought you were a changed man now that you've got Tiff to keep you in order.'

'Only spiritually Graham. And talking of spirits,' I looking hopefully up to Graham's special armagnac.

'Oh no you don't, you pisspot. Or at least not till you tell me what's bugging you now. I think it's me who should be paid to be your counsellor, not Tiff. I would keep you on the not so jolly straight and narrow, that's for sure.'

I quickly brought him up to speed on the events of the last couple of days. When I had finished my little spiel he looked unduly pensive through his owl–like glasses.

'I don't understand you Tommy. You just don't get it, do you?

You've got the girl of your dreams positively swooning at your feet, however unlikely a prospect that is to me who knows what a useless waster you are. And here you are getting all itchi titchi about a stupid piece of machinery. What happened tonight is irrelevant in the grand scheme of things.' (Oh no, not another bleeding orator). 'All that matters is Tiff. Can't you get that into your thick head'.

'You're right of course Graham. By the way, isn't it boring to be always right? It's all right, you needn't answer that one. In fact I will take myself off home right now.' And off I jolly well went, leaving an astounded Graham speechless for once.

Over a wee glass of Madiran back at the flat, I planned my course of action. First I would face the music in The Hutch tomorrow morning. Then I would arrange to get the car fixed asap and then I would tackle Tiff. That was the plan anyway.

The next day I rose with a reasonably clear head and sauntered round to The Hutch. It was a typical August day in England. Sunshine and showers, with the showers in the ascendancy at the moment. Luckily I still had my old Barings Bank golf umbrella to protect me.

But I needed more than a golf umbrella to protect me from the verbal darts which rained down on me at The Hutch. First off the mark unsurprisingly was Eric.

'Morning Tommy, nice to see you are still in one piece. Which is more than can be said for that poor pole. Ha Ha.'

I winced under this friendly fire but there was a lot more to come.

'As you obviously have big problems with night driving Tommy, we have clubbed together and bought you some night glasses.' More hoots of laughter.

'Thank you Nigel. That is the least that I would have expected from you,' I replied in my most civilized manner as I examined some weird purple goggles that appeared to be a cross between ones used by Biggles and those in Flashdance. 'I hope they didn't set you back too much at Woolworths.'

'So pleased you haven't lost your sarcastic touch Tommy. The Hutch would be well poorer without it.' Oh no, even QC wanted a piece of the action, or rather destruction.

'And I'm delighted to hear you care so much about your troops, QC. How about giving us all a day off to show your appreciation?'

This counter attack only produced a wicked smile from that cunning face.

'Oh, I rather think I can safely give you today off Tommy. And tomorrow and the next day for that matter. However I have already rung the Ferrari mechanics and they have assured me that they will have Herr Schumacher back on the road again as soon as humanly possible.'

Oh no, I was even being whitewashed on the sarcasm front now. Things couldn't possibly get any worse, could they?

Enter The Fat Controller, stage right. Well, he would have entered if there had been room for that vast bulk in that confined space. However, although I couldn't control my bitchiness he still had the upper hand here, as I was about to find out to my cost.

'Oh Tommy, I forgot to tell you. A certain middle aged lady has been trying to get hold of you. You apparently have your mobile switched off as usual.'

'Thank you very much, messenger boy,' I replied nastily.

But TFC continued smoothly.

'If you have a spare moment in your busy schedule today Tommy, Mrs Tiff asked if you could possibly be so kind as to give her a tinkle.'

'What are you on today TFC? Verbal ecstasy?' I retorted.

But I said this much too late as my reply was drowned out by further catcalls. I exited rapidly stage left, but not quickly enough to avoid some lewd advice from Tonker. With relief I stumbled out of The Hutch and gave Tiff that tinkle in private that TFC had so mischievously suggested.

'Oh Tommy. Thanks for ringing back. I hear that your car is en panne. Why don't you pop over here this morning for coffee and a light lunch?'

Why not indeed? But first how to get to Rattlesden? I daren't go back in The Hutch and ask for a lift, although I was sure there would be several takers to give me a freebie on this occasion. I obviously couldn't use the Lone Star cowboy outfit or those bastard Omega Cars. Nor did I trust those shysters on the rank.

It was Tiff who came to the rescue.

'Tell you what Tommy. Why don't I pick you up for once? I'll be at your flat in half an hour.'

> And then one day you came back home
> You were a creature all in rapture
> You had the key to your soul
> And you did open that
> day you came back to the garden.

And there she was in her sporty little red Mazda with the hood down. The sky had miraculously cleared and a bright sun was shining directly down on Tiff. White suit again, lime green blouse and dark glasses. Perfect.

'Hi Tiff. You look great as usual.' I always resort to clichés when in trouble, but did at least manage two little pecks on those heavenly cheeks. She took off her glasses and fixed me with those enormous blue eyes.

'Let's go, you old bastard.' But her eyes twinkled.

Heavens, she was quick. And that was just her driving. I settled down blissfully in the passenger seat and let the world pass me by. Before you could say Jack Robinson, we were in Rattlesden. Her little cottage by the church looked a picture in the morning sun. I had of course never penetrated the inner portals of The Ivory Tower before. Tiff gave me a quick tour of the downstairs accommodation. Ultra modern kitchen with obligatory Aga, cosy beamed living room with large inglenook, tiny dining room and simple cloakroom. Exquisite.

'How about coffee in the garden Tommy?'

'Fine,' I replied weakly, but the tension crackled in the air.

'Go outside and relax while I make the coffee.'

I went outside as instructed but didn't relax. The small walled garden was totally private adjoining the churchyard. Tiff had obviously put her heart and soul into it as well as it was informally perfect. A rose covered pergola, York flagstones and a box hedge surrounding the pungent herb garden. Estate agents could do some real verbal damage here. Luckily Omar was on hand to save their blushes.

> I sometimes think that never blows so red
> The Rose as when some buried Caesar bled;
> That every hyacinth the Garden wears
> Dropt in its Lap from some once lovely Head.

But I didn't have my mind exclusively on flowers and herbs at that precise moment. Suddenly for no good reason I remembered going to tea for the first time at Tiff's parents' house in Lavenham all those years ago. I still squirmed at the memory of being inspected by them in their lovely garden with their lovely daughter sitting demurely next to them. I knew exactly what they were thinking. Had this long-haired lout been defiling their lovely virginal daughter? Their unspoken accusation hung in the air like the sword of Damocles whilst I had to sit there haplessly sipping unwanted tea and growing more and more uncomfortable under their stern stares. But Tiff hadn't been the slightest perturbed.

> They had one daughter, and his favourite child
> Had oft the father of his spleen beguiled;
> Soothed from attention from her early years.
> She gain'd all wishes by her smiles and tears.

Nothing had changed in that direction. And I was just as uncomfortable now. Without that comforting glass in hand feelings had to be faced head on. I felt as emotionally naked as the day I was born.

'A penny for your thoughts,' said Tiff, suddenly emerging with the coffee and startling me out of my reverie.

Not bloody likely. Not even for a million pounds. It was more than my life was worth.

'Black or white, Tommy?'

'Black please. And no sugar.'

'You really haven't changed, have you ?'

We then relapsed into uncomfortable silence whilst we drank our coffee. Eventually Tiff broke the uneasy peace.

'Right Tommy, why don't you come and join me on the garden seat?'

I got up awkwardly and joined her as commanded, taking my coffee cup with me as protection.

'Relax, I'm not going to eat you. I thought we might just have a gentle chat, that's all.' But then she carefully put down her own cup.

'Do you mind if I have a ciggie?'

'Of course I don't if it helps you to relax. And you do look as if you could do with some relaxing. Massages are very good at The Bodywave, or so I've heard.'

I looked at her face hard to identify a trace of irony in her words but all I saw was a warm, unquestioning smile. Not everybody is like you Tommy thank goodness, I silently reproved myself.

'Oh shit, I'm not very good at this Tiff.'

'At what Tommy? Having a simple conversation with a vaguely attractive middle aged woman in a congenial location? That shouldn't be too tough for a man of your vast experience.'

Again I looked at her to see if she was taking the piss. She wasn't apparently.

'The trouble with you Tommy is that you can't take anything at all at face value. Anything at all.' And then she turned her head to look at me directly. 'Why don't you let yourself go for once in your life. Go with the flow. And your feelings as well. What are you feeling now?' She smiled at me encouragingly.

'That I'm a very lucky middle aged man to be sitting intimately next to such a gorgeous creature,' I essayed tentatively.

'That's much better. Pray continue in the same vein.'

I stubbed out my cigarette vehemently.

'OK, you win again. I was just thinking that I love you right down to my very soul. And beyond. Satisfied?' I added belligerently and unnecessarily.

'Yes. Very, very satisfied,' she replied oh so quietly and docilely. Hell, I was like putty in her pretty hands. And then she kissed me.

> The summer breeze was blowin on your face
> Within the violet you treasure your summery words
> And as the shiver from my neck down to my spine
> Ignited me in daylight and nature in the garden.

Wordlessly she took my hand and led me back into the cottage. Back into the cottage and then up the creaky stairs. And then into the hallowed ground of her bedroom which was dominated by a huge four poster bed. She let go of my hand and turned to face me. She slipped off her white suit and green blouse to reveal underneath not that little black number I had glimpsed long ago at La Vieille Maison, but a voluptuous lime green lace ensemble. She also revealed that terrific body in all its proud splendour. There wasn't an ounce of fat anywhere, and I mean anywhere. She still looked good and knew it. And I now knew what it was like to be a true voyeur. Off came the bra. Breasts small, firm and pert as ever. Then she eased down her pants to reveal a fetching blue butterfly tattoo in a very fetching place. She slipped under the sheets. I ripped off my own offending clothing as quickly as possible with clumsy hands.

'Not so quickly young man,' she suddenly commanded as I made a dash to join her under those pristine sheets. 'You've seen my bits as it were. Let's see yours properly now. Men can be so prudish.' Her eyes were shining unnaturally brightly.

My no longer towering but cowering member would have withered completely under her penetrating inspection if it hadn't been bent on a little penetration of its own. I was left to squirm for a full half minute with a not so proud penis at full mast before she finally she let me off the hook.

'Pas mal. Now let's see if it still works. Come over here and let me check it out.' She was giggling like a mischievous schoolgirl as she said it but then suddenly, her mood changed. 'I want you Tommy. Now,' she finished huskily.

Despite the gravity of the situation or probably because of it, I sought the last refuge of the scoundrel.

'Well, fuck me,' I ejaculated.

The vision of my dreams was on the bed before me and I still didn't know whether to laugh or cry.

Christ, she was so desirable. I greedily wanted every bit of her. Every single bit.

'That is precisely what I intend to do to you, Mr Gainsborough. In spades. Don't say you weren't warned.' And then she was gone.

And you went into a trance

> Your childlike vision became so fine
> And we heard the bells inside the church
> We loved so much
> And felt the Presence of the youth of
> Eternal summers in the garden.

Some time later I resurfaced. Tiff was still sleeping peacefully beside me. I watched her 'countenance divine' in fascination for some minutes and reflected blissfully that the world had not only turned full circle, it had spun right off its ruddy axis. Life was good. No, life was great. I was the luckiest man in the world. Don't ever let her go now.

Just then the object of all my attention, all my affection and all my obsession opened her eyes and smiled.

'Ah Tommy, that was good,' she sighed. 'I didn't realize how sex-starved I was.'

Women are extraordinary aren't they? When you are in the mood they go cold on you, but when they are in the mood they are insatiable. Then they switch from passion to practicality like the flick of a switch. At least I wouldn't have to ask Tiff if she was on the Pill. I wouldn't, would I? Oh no, back to the dirty dog days of my youth. Well I'm the same age as our beloved Prime Minister so anything's possible, I suppose.

'What are you thinking?' she murmured, tracing her long nails down the small of my back. Help. Georgie!

> Inspiring thoughts that he could not express,
> Obscure sublime! his secret happiness.

226

Oh no, I was going to have to reveal my soul as well. Is that the true price of sex?

'I was thinking how much I love you darling.'

'Liar. Try again lover boy.' And then she moved forcibly on top of me.

I squirmed and then squirmed some more.

'I'm waiting Tommy. And I'm a very impatient woman when I want something.'

'Sorry matron.'

I received a sharp scrape down my front this time for my troubles.

'Oh, that was good matron.'

'Stop changing the subject again. Don't forget, I know your little evasions of old.'

I could never compete for long with her full-fronted approach.

'Oh no you don't, you randy bastard.'

That sharp rejection came after a tentative foray on my part at her full front hovering tantalizingly above me.

'I'm still waiting for your thoughts Tommy.' So masterful.

'OK, you win again Tiff.' Take a risk. 'If you really want to know I was wondering if you were on the Pill.'

She looked at me in amazement and then burst out laughing.

'That's so outlandish even by your standards Tommy, it must be the truth. You men can only think in ever decreasing circles and then disappear up your own testicles. Don't look so shocked. That's what I like about you. Your bashfulness, and one or two other things. Do you really think I would have set about seducing you today without taking precautions? Don't look like that. Yes, of course it was my decision, you old fool. If I had waited for you to finally make your masterful move, we would both have been well past it. Men always think they are in control. Women know they are. That's why we were designated to bear children.'

She stiffened suddenly. Behind the laughter I had struck a vital nerve. Whenever I said something serious or truthful, it just came out wrong. I wasn't very good at being pinned down, metaphorically or verbally.

'It's all right Tommy,' she continued at last. 'The subject had to be broached sometime. Why not today while the iron is still hot, as it were?'

My humour wasn't in her league but I tried.

'Carry on Tiff, I'm listening hard.'

After I had ducked a right uppercut thrown at me with more passion than accuracy, she continued in a quieter, more thoughtful tone.

'That was the main reason why I went so slowly with you. Actually William and I didn't have children because William was infertile. I knew that I was OK.' A long pause. 'Perhaps you can guess how I knew. But perhaps not. You are probably still obsessed by one or two other skeletons in your little locker as well,' she added waspishly. She turned to face me directly.

'Yes Tommy, the truth is that I had an abortion after I went up to Sheffield. It was your baby and you were oblivious as usual cocooned in your own self-satisfied, selfish world of pleasure.'

I tried to look penitent but was shocked to the core.

'Why didn't you tell me Tiff,' I croaked.

'I would have done if you had written just once' she replied dryly.

'What can I say ?'

'Not a lot if your past record is anything to go by.'

'I'm sorry Tiff.'

'Well, that's a start I suppose. It's all right Tommy, I've forgiven you now. But only completely in the last month I must add. It took thirty years but I did it in the end.' She softened her harsh words with a slow, soft smile. 'Counsellor heal yourself, as you might have said if you had known.'

Hence her sudden change in direction at Ickworth Park and punishing counselling sessions at La Vieille Maison before that.

They were meant to be punishing.

'What are you thinking now?' Hell, she was turning the mental screw, wasn't she?

'I'm a shit.'

'Yes, you were. But you're not now.'

'Yes I am.'

'Come on Tommy, it's a bit late in the day for flagellation. I said I had forgiven you and I meant it. Anyway you have certainly improved with age, just like the Madiran you are so fond of drinking. Otherwise you wouldn't be here today. And you certainly wouldn't be in my bed.'

Yes, she was still a very naughty girl. And I loved her so. I had been given a second chance. Yes, I was increasingly coming round to the idea that there was a god up there after all. At the very least I would have to concede that there were some very odd goings on indeed that a rational being alone couldn't explain.

Then there was silence again and not a lot of thinking.

After that little piece of extra curricular activity, we realized we were both ravenous. I looked at my watch. It was four o'clock. At the ripe old age of fifty I had finally found out how time passes when you are enjoying yourself.

It was time for Tiff to nail her colours to the culinary mast. And she didn't do a bad job for a woman. A nutty salad with extra virgin oil, new potatoes and a magret uncooked to perfection. Plus a bottle of Madiran. She had done her homework as well as her spade work.

'A toast. To a perfect day. Thanks for everything Tiff. And I mean everything.'

'A counter toast. To a reformed Tommy.'

We clinked glasses and devoured our little feast. A post-coital and post-prandial Dunhill was more than called for. However that would have to wait till we went outside. I would also have to do without the other of my main props.

'Sorry, no armagnac for you today Tommy. Just black coffee. We don't want anything to spoil our perfect day, do we? I'll call a cab in a moment. I rather think that Elise might be your best bet today, don't you?'

I looked at her again for a further trace of irony but there was none. We went back into the garden again to finish our coffee. The sun was beginning to go down rapidly in the west over the churchyard and God was right back in his heaven.

> In the garden, in the garden wet with rain,
> No guru, no method, no teacher
> Just you and I and nature
> And the Father in the garden.

11.   PRECIOUS TIME

Precious time is slipping away
But you're only king for a day
It doesn't matter to which God you pray
Precious time is slipping away.

Never did Van write truer words. But most of us still don't get the message. We'll do it soon, next year, sometime never. But never now. Go out today and live the dream. Tomorrow could be too late. This message was brought home to me in the most brutal way on that terrible Friday morning in mid September.

As usual I didn't rush out of bed that morning. Thus it was I ambled out to work about eleven o'clock in blissful ignorance of the tragedy that had just unfurled.

'Bandit thirteen to base. Ready to play TFC,' I jocularly called in.

'You'd better come in to the office Tommy.' It was the subdued voice of QC himself on the blower. What the hell was going on?

I zipped round to The Hutch to find virtually every Wells Fargo car parked haphazardly in the stockade. Virtually every one. But one significant vehicle was missing. With increasing trepidation I entered The Hutch to find this filthy den of din totally silent for once. Everyone was sitting round aimlessly just looking into space.

'What's happened?', I asked to nobody in particular but with increasing certainty at what might have occurred.

'It's Tonker.' It was QC who answered. 'He's dead.'

'What do you mean? What happened?'

'RTA on the A12 at East Bergholt about seven thirty this morning. That's all we know at the moment.'

'Anybody else involved?'

'Not that we know of.'

> Well this world is cruel with its twists and turns
> Well the fire's still in me and the passion burns
> I love a medley 'til the day I die
> 'Til hell freezes over and the rivers run dry.

Well, there would be no more medleys for Tonker and this hell of a world had fucking frozen over.

However, my fire was still there and the smouldering anger inside me welled up. The mighty Tonker was dead. No more effing laughs or expletives deleted. Our world would be a much poorer place without him. Because, behind all that bullshit and hard man exterior, Tonker was really as soft as puttee and one of the best and truest friends I had ever had, unlike those two-faced bastards in the City I had been brought up with. And what about Edna, his long suffering wife? She was the one who had kept the whole Tonker show on the rails. What would she do? Had anyone told her ?

'Does Edna know?' I asked QC harshly.

'I think so,' was his pathetic reply.

Suddenly that passion and anger that had been simmering in my soul exploded.

'You bastard QC. You killed him. I know he didn't finish his shift till after three this morning. Then the fucking school run. He hasn't had a day off in weeks. He was totally knackered. He must have fallen asleep at the wheel. I'll see you in hell. No I will do much fucking better than that. I'll make sure you get done for corporate manslaughter. That's if I don't kill you first.'

With that I lunged forward and threw my first punch since I had given up rugby almost twenty years ago. And it was a bloody good one. Right on that squodgy pug nose. QC staggered back and collapsed into one of his crappy sofas.

'Hold on Tommy.' It was Eric who inserted his large bulk between me and the prone figure of QC.

'That's not going to do anyone any good. We don't know what happened yet. And killing QC won't bring Tonker back.'

These sane words brought me back from the brink. I withdrew

but didn't apologise. I had nothing to apologise for. In fact, with only a bloody nose QC had got off bloody lightly in my opinion.

'I'll sue your guts Tommy.'

'No you won't QC because you haven't got any fucking guts.'

'You're fired.'

'Good.'

With that I stormed out, ripped off the Wells Fargo magnetic signs from the side of my car and hurled them in the general direction of The Hutch. Then I drove straight round to The Rising Sun for a bit of serious annihilation. After I had given a very cursory account to Graham of the tragedy and the subsequent events of the morning, he sensibly left me to it.

Left to it, I ruminated darkly over my beer. Only two weeks ago Tiff had seduced me In The Garden. There had followed two wonderful weeks with me allowed into Rattlesden Towers on all my time off. There was plenty of walking, talking and imbibing, and still plenty of precious time left over for sex. Tiff had obviously being reading some very rude literature on top of her counselling material as she came up with some very surprising suggestions. And we were even caught at it by Tiff's cleaner one Wednesday morning. I felt just like that guilty teenager again being caught in bed with the French au pair by my mother in the family residence thirty one years, two months and eleven days ago. Ah yes, I remember it vaguely. As I have asked before why should the young have a monopoly on sex?

Anyway they don't jolly deserve it. It's wasted on them. Except when I was young.

However I was never allowed to stay the night at Tiff's. What on earth would the neighbours say? Driving back late at night to my flat though brought back more delicious memories of those days long ago when I used to ship Tiff back to Lavenham in the early hours in the Morgan when her parents were asleep.

So just when I thought I had finally located that elusive Philosopher's Stone and love was all round, my world had come crashing down. Life may be a bugger, but death is far, far worse.

It doesn't matter what route you take
Sooner or later the hearts going to break
No rhyme or reason, no master plan
No Nirvana, no promised land.

Tonker and I had been through so much together. When I first joined Wells Fargo what seemed like a lifetime ago it was Tonker who took me under his wing. He taught this Private Hire virgin all the ropes and protected me from the nastier taunts of The Hutch till I was experienced enough and ugly enough to take care of myself. Yes I loved him in the purest sense of the word. He was probably the finest male friend that I had ever had in my life. Now my heart was broken and Tonker had gone to that great motorway in the sky. No, there was certainly no Nirvana or promised land.

Some five pints later Graham finally decided it was time to intervene.

'It may be an old cliché Tommy, but that doesn't mean it ain't true. Drowning your grief in booze isn't going to do you or anyone else any good. Why don't you do some real good instead and go round and see his widow as a sign of respect and of your much vaunted friendship with Tonker? It's the least you can do. Otherwise you're still that selfish old bastard as of old, whatever the supposed powers of Tiff's healing qualities.'

I looked at Graham through glazed eyes.

'Excellent decision Graham. Unfortunately I'm too pissed to go and see her now. I think I'll just go home and have a lie down for a bit.' That way I could avoid both the discomfort of any more of Graham's tough love and a tough meeting with Edna. I was a coward to the core.

After a couple of hours kip, I tottered up and made myself a coffee. I also lit a fag and looked out of the window. The orgasmic views were still there but blind men don't do views. Anyway views don't pay the rent and they certainly don't bring you happiness, do they?

Time for a silent toast to Tonker. A wee glass of Madiran was called for. To absent friends. Permanently absent.

> The mighty Spirit and its power which stains
> The bloodless cheek, and vivifies the brains.

Some time later and a bottle and a bit later, the phone rang.

'Hello darling. I thought you were coming round tonight,' Tiff started brightly.

'Tonker's dead. I won't be coming now.' But my slurred words didn't quite come out like that.

'You're pissed.'

'Yes, goodbye.' And I put the phone down and took it off the hook.

Why did I do it? The truth is that I just didn't know. Something inside must have told me to. Don't get too happy Tommy. Don't let anyone into your life. Why not destroy yourself instead? Wouldn't that be far more satisfactory?

A couple of days later there was a knock on the door. Well, I suppose it was a couple of days later because oblivion beckoned. I had made huge inroads into the case of Madiran and a few joints helped the process along nicely. I was going down again. And without a fight this time. Even Omar couldn't help me this time.

> And as the Cock crew, those who stood before
> The Tavern shouted – 'Open then the Door !
> You know how little time we have to stay,
> And, once departed, may return no more.'

It was Eric.

'Now listen Tommy, and listen good. Tonker died of a heart attack. The autopsy has just confirmed it. Swallow your fucking pride and go and apologise to QC.'

It's a tough one. Apologies. I don't like them. But I was in the wrong. What to do?

'Go on, swallow it. QC will have you back. Just fucking apologise, you arrogant shit for brains.'

Where to go? Apologize to that creep or just sink back into the cesspit of life?

In the end I bit the bullet and reluctantly walked the walk round to The Hutch.

'OK QC, I'm sorry. Satisfied?'

'Am I to take that as an unqualified apology Tommy?'

'Yes.'

'OK. I'll take you back. But just this once Tommy. Any more crap and you're out on your arse for good. And by the way, my nose isn't broken, but no thanks to you. Thanks for asking.'

I took the sarcasm bravely on the chin.

'Fair does QC. I deserved that. But I'll still miss the old bugger.'

'We all will Tommy,' replied QC quietly. 'And how about seeing Edna? She would love to see you.'

This time there was no escape. I went round to her little terraced house in Gas Works Lane.

'I'm so sorry Edna. We'll all miss the old sod.'

'Thank you Tommy. You always had a way with words. But where were you before?'

No answer.

'Tonker worshipped you Tommy. But at the moment of his death you betrayed him and let me down. You're a shit. And a Judas.'

'I'm sorry Edna.'

'Oh piss off, and return to your own kind. You don't belong here. Or anywhere else on this earth for that matter.'

Where to go now? Back to the bottle? No, that hadn't helped the first or the second time.

'Help me QC, I need to work straightaway.'

'Yes Tommy, I rather think it's time you worked your arse off at last. When you've dried out,' he added brutally.

'OK, QC. And you're right, of course,' I replied very subdued.

For the next month I worked like a demented dervish. Work would ease the pain. I didn't communicate with a fly, let alone Tiff. The post mortem confirmed the facts of Tonker's heart attack and my heart was fit to bust. Because:-

> Precious time is slipping away
> You know you're only king for a day
> It doesn't matter to which God you pray

Precious time is slipping away.

The saddest day of my life was Tonker's funeral. Even Omega Cars and Lone Star had buried the hatchet for the day and forty two taxis followed Tonker's hearse to the church. But Tiff wasn't there.

The service was too much. QC for once rose to the occasion and spoke very movingly. And then the hymns. But especially Tonker's favourite.

> I vow unto thee my country, all earthly things above,
> Entire and whole and perfect, the service of my love
> The love that asks no questions,
> The love that stands the test,
> That lays upon the altar the dearest and the best;
> The love that never falters,
> The love that pays the price,
> The love that makes undaunted the final sacrifice.

I broke. Me, who hadn't cried since prep school, was reduced to tears by the sheer bloody unfairness of that 'final sacrifice'. OK Tonker, to make sure your life wasn't in vain, I vow I'm going to fight back and beat those fucking demons. That's the least that I can do for you. Thanks for the memory. But I just hate that obscene coffin and all its connotations. I will remember you in all your corrupted flesh, not as one of God's blessed children.

> Ah, make the most of what we yet may spend,
> Before we too into the Dust descend;
> Dust into Dust, and under Dust, to lie,
> Sans Wine, sans Song, sans Singer, and – sans End.

What next after that oh so moving funeral? Tonker was buried under the Dust but now I needed company like never before.

Fortuitously, you never remain alone for long in The Waiting Game. Things just happen. Take the time I had to go to Colchester a couple of days after Tonker's funeral. Unfortunately it was absolutely pissing with rain when I was despatched to Colchester that September evening to pick up some VIP from the station. Equally unfortunately, just as I set out on my journey I leaned forward to reset the mileage clock. However at the critical moment I was dazzled by another car's offending headlights on full beam. As I clumsily tried to adjust the dial, I incompetently caught my hand in the steering column. The next thing I knew I had broken the stalk of the windscreen wipers and had to rely on manual power. Half way to Colchester the manual packed up altogether and I was obliged to spend the rest of the journeypeering impossibly through the windscreen. My concentration was absolute for once. Miraculously, I picked up said VIP at Colchester Station on time but then had to battle with the return journey. As I peered through the rain swept windscreen I wondered not for the first time what the fuck was I doing? Naturally my exalted client was a bit agitato for a while until I said I would radically reduce his fare due to technical problems. As I continued to peer desperately through the rain, I thought long and hard that I might also be on the road back if I indeed ever made the road back. However, finally I made it and dropped off said VIP in the centre of Sutton Market and reflected that I had done a bloody good job. No, I had done an impossible job. Full marks Tommy. Don't let the demons get you down.

To confirm the obvious I even got a well done from QC. Well, that was after The Hutch had another bloody good laugh at the expense of their resident mechanical expert as QC went on to say:-

'What's going to be your next mishap Tommy? I just don't know how you do it. Such a vivid imagination. From tyres to aerials to tow poles to stalks, you're in a class of your own. Perhaps I should appoint you as our resident comedian. You certainly know how to keep the troops happy. I know, we'll now call you The Joker. Ha ha.'

However I didn't mind in the slightest being the butt of their jokes. Even I was laughing again and boy, did it feel good? I was back in the groove. Then another massive cloud came belatedly back into view. I was hardly going to get a well done from Tiff, was I? In fact I would be bloody lucky to get a reply at all except for expletive deleted off.

Would she, could she, forgive me again? Well you'll have to face the music for once, won't you Tommy ? You had better give her the proverbial tinkle. Now. I plucked up unsuspected courage and picked up the phone. I dialled the oh so familiar number and it was answered almost at once. Oh no, perhaps Michael Douglas had made a play for Tiff in my avoidable absence. In a panic I almost put the phone down. But then she would ring 1471 and realize it was me and I would be even further down the plughole of love.

'Hello, is anyone there,' came that thrilling voice down the line that made me tingle all over again. I found my voice at last.

'Hello, it's me. What to say? Just one more last chance?' I tried to make it casual but I was sure Tiff would detect the tremor in my voice.

'Just give me one good reason why I should?', came the angry reply. No, it wasn't just angry, it was off the Richter Scale for scorned women. And there was a lot more scorn coming my way. I had no doubt of that inevitability and I wasn't disappointed. 'No, how about giving me fifty fucking reasons, to borrow your own filthy language ? And talking of really filthy things, your own behaviour must rank right up there with the dirtiest of them. OK, try me. And you'd better try bloody hard. I should imagine that your knees are getting pretty sore by now. Right, I'm listening avidly for your excuse this time and don't waste your time on any of your charming bullshit. I've had enough of your shitty behaviour. Right, you've got exactly one minute to state your case starting from now.'

On this slightly discouraging note, I tried to make my case. But what could I say that would make any difference?

'Ten seconds.'

Honesty, sincerity or humility. Would any of them work anyway?

'Twenty seconds. Lost that silver-tongued voice, have we?'

I had never been much cop at pressure, had I? I desperately tried to think of something to say that would swing her implacability. Anything at all.

'Thirty seconds. As you might have said if you weren't suddenly struck mute, precious time is slipping away.'

That did it.

'OK, you win Tiff. First, I am a double shit. No, make that a treble shit now. Second, I'm so, so sorry. Third, I will stop drinking like a deprived drunkard. Fourth, I love you completely and utterly, even to the tip of your acidic tongue. And fifth and finally, one more last chance. Please, please, please.' I hoped my absolute desperation and despondency would communicate itself adequately over the airwaves.

'Not bad for a condemned man Tommy. OK, just one more last chance. What you might say is your very own last chance saloon. Now listen, and listen good. La Vieille Maison next Thursday at seven thirty. Be there.' With that ultimatum still ringing loudly in my ears, the line suddenly went dead. I just prayed that our relationship wasn't dead as well.

I worked like the proverbial black that weekend. I pulled out all the stops in my locker. I charmed the young ladies in my car. I charmed the old ladies as well. I even charmed some of the male punters. In short I gave my everything. But would it be enough on Thursday?

At least I had a few visual delights to console me a little bit in the meantime. A sumptuous Italian girl on an English language course. In Sutton Market of all places. A very fit French girl selling French perfume. Things were looking up. And I liked looking up.

And then a long London run. Things were certainly looking up. A blond bimbo to Kensington. An expensive piece of piss.

The journey I mean. Unfortunately, said blond bimbo didn't know her delightful bum from her elegant A to Z elbow and I penetrated the inner sanctum of the Congestion Area just before the designated cut-off period. Never mind, my fare was one hundred pounds plus tip and the congestion charge was only five pounds. No probs. However when I phoned The Congestion Charges Agency the next day I discovered from a most unhelpful person from Delhi that I should have paid the charge the previous evening by ten o'clock. I was now lumbered with a forty quid surcharge on top of the basic five quid charge. What you would call a right result, if Arthur Daley was still alive that is.

Never mind, my humour was gradually attaining its equilibrium. But would that be enough to save the day or rather night?

Saturday as usual was tough. But there were also several rainbows. Pretty women, pretty widows and pretty girls. One mustn't totally lose one's sense of perspective. A young lady from The Post House. We discussed Spanish property selling and I rather contemptuously asked if she spoke any Spanish. She was Spanish! Exit Tommy stage left. Loss of dignity was irrelevant however because she was both beautiful and charming. The defence rests.

Tuesday night, work as usual. Nothing special happening. Double pick up at The Rose and Crown for me and Steve, one of the new drivers and a bit slow on both the uptake and the accelerator. I arrived first as of right and for once in a blue moon, both couples were waiting outside. I got out of the car very briefly to explain to the other couple that Steve would be along at his own convenience.

'He's a bit slow,' I added condescendingly.

I carelessly shot out of the car park just as Steve was carefully manoeuvring his ageing Astra in through the narrow entrance.

'Keep up the slow work Steve,' I shouted through the open windows. 'See you at Christmas.'

Two minutes later Rachel, a new controller as well, reported to me that Line Twenty Three (Steve) wanted to know if my surname, or either of my passengers' names, was Gainsborough. Still in clever clogs mode, I peremptorily asked why?

'He may have something of value for you,' she reported further.

'Oh, I don't think Steve has anything of value to me,' I replied smugly and had a good smirk with my fares.

Rachel then put Steve directly through to me on the two way radio.

'I think I've got your wallet Tommy,' said Steve diffidently.

My hand shot to my back pocket. It was empty.

'I'll be back at The Rose and Crown in two minutes Steve. Stay there.'

A minute later Rachel reported that Steve's fares were getting restless with the delay.

'I'll be there in ten seconds,' I lied.

Back at The Rose and Crown a minute later Steve silently handed me back my wallet.

'Thanks a million Steve. Here's a fiver. You've saved my life.'

A twisted smile crept on to Steve's battered features.

'I don't want your money Tommy. But you can kiss my feet.'

And kiss his feet I did in the middle of that benighted car park in front of the astounded punters and a few pisspots who had just come out of the pub. I even got a round of applause plus the odd ribald comment. But at least justice had been done and seen to be done, which is more than can be said at the Peasenhall Magistrates Court on any given day, and several other Courts round the country for that matter. Or even The Oval.

And the job still had its charms. So many really nice people amongst the isolated pisspots. I just love being called a star or a diamond. To paraphrase Oscar Wilde and Mark Twain very loosely, I can live forever on the odd compliment, or any sort of compliment for that matter.

'You've got an educated voice. You're not really a taxi driver are you ?' Two rather inebriated passengers in the car, one of them asking the innocent question.

Instead of taking this as an insult, I had at last learnt to take this as an inverted compliment.

'Or is this just a hobby after you retired with your millions?'

Still I didn't rise to the bait as I would undoubtedly have done until recently.

'No, regrettably I have to pay a few essential bills.'

This seemed to go down all right with these punters. They could at least understand bills if not exactly where I was coming from. But I was always fascinated by the fact that people thought that as I sounded educated I must be intelligent. Of course I am, but it ain't necessarily so.

Thank heaven for little punters, for without them what would little taxi drivers do? Two more punters from The Bear to the Copocana Beach. Not very far, but who cares? Anyway, one of them had his leg in plaster so all was forgiven.

'You sound very educated. Is this just a hobby?' Oh no, not another one. No reaction from me at first. I told you I had mellowed. Only after a long delay did I reply.

'No, I need the money. I'm fucking broke.'

'Fair does. In fact, you're not a bad old bloke after all. Keep the change.'

With that he handed me a fiver and disappeared into the ether, or at least the one without the crutches did.

Humility, that's still the key. And sobriety. And now the big one. Tiff.

I had never been so nervous in my life. Crucial sporting

249

encounters, my wedding day, court appearances, all paled into pathetic insignificance compared with my dinner date with Tiff. I would still have to pull out the performance of my life if I was going to be able to bring her back into my life. I had no illusions. Just because she had consented to come tonight didn't signify anything. I would have to woo her and win her for a third and final time. But I daren't even have a single drink at The Rising Sun to calm my nerves. Instead I had a special joint at the flat. I had recently found a new supplier of Morocco's finest. Shit, it was good. With a bit of Van this induced a much needed if brief feeling of euphoria. And, more important, my breath didn't smell of alcohol. I was devious to the end.

Still euphoric, I ambled round to La Vieille Maison. It was exactly seven twenty eight so I waited outside. As on our first meeting a year ago, Tiff was five minutes late, courtesy of Wells Fargo. As before, Eric's crappy Cavalier limped into sight. What next?

'Hello Tiff.' Be neutral.

'Hello Tommy. Let's go in.' No smile or hint of encouragement at all. Not that I was expecting any.

She was dressed all in black tonight. Black calf length skirt, black silk blouse, black broach and black tights. And undoubtedly black underwear, but I wouldn't be getting another glimpse of bliss tonight, would I ?

'What should we drink tonight Tommy? Mineral water perhaps?'

'Whatever you want Tiff.'

'Oh no, don't get pathetic on me Tommy. I think champagne is called for on such an auspicious occasion. I mean you're sober for once. Surely that is a pretty good reason to celebrate. I think The Widow is called for, don't you ?

She wasn't going to make it easy for me was she? But of course I richly deserved her sarcasm and her scepticism. My track record was after all a trifle disappointing, even by Premiership footballers standards.

'OK Tommy, you kick off. You were always very keen on sporting metaphors, weren't you?'

Shit, this was going to be a tough night.

'Let's wait for the champagne, shall we darling?'

'Don't you fucking darling me Tommy. I am still waiting for an eloquent account of your movements over the past month. And I don't mean your fucking bowels.'

'OK Tiff, destroy me. I deserve it and understand it. After all, I'm the original past master at destruction, aren't I? But usually I only do self destruction. I don't know what to say at all. Where to begin?'

'Try the beginning Tommy.' Bloody hell, she was tougher than tough tonight.

'I funked it Tiff. When the going gets tough, Tommy gets going. Right into his fucking rabbit hole until it's all over. A rabbit hole that always happens to be well stocked with alcohol by some stroke of good fortune. Good fortune for who you may well ask? I'll tell you. Good fortune for that scared little boy who never quite grew up and was never ready for the real and nasty world. So to protect himself he put on an impenetrable mask of words, sarcasm and superciliousness to shield him from anything unpleasant. And as for actually letting people into his emotional life, Gainsborough's just don't do feelings, period. Captain Oates had the right idea.'

'Have you ever thought of growing up Tommy. And growing less selfish. Other people have problems too, or haven't you noticed? In fact I had a little setback myself. Not everyone reaches for the bottle or disappears into the burrow at the slightest sign of trouble. You're a big boy now. Why not try and face that brave new world? Look on the bright side. It doesn't always have to be nasty and scary. Why not share your problems with someone for once?

'Is that an invitation?'

'No it's not, so don't get too excited. And 'it' is about all that does excite men. Except for sport of course. If they could let a bit of real emotion into their lives, they might find it quite exciting and a source of great comfort as well. Talking about emotions, what are you thinking about at this precise moment?'

And with that she bored those big blue eyes right through my heart. She always had that ability to put me on the spot.

'Oh shit Tiff, I'm not very good at this.'

'That's no answer Tommy. Try delving into that vast vocabulary of yours for something a trifle more convincing will you please. Now start again.'

'You're a hard woman Tiff.'

'No I'm not. Proceed.'

'To tell you the truth.'

'Ah, that sounds promising.'

'Give me a chance Tiff.'

'Sorry, but it's nice to see you do the squirming for once.'

'What am I thinking about? Obsession, that's what. Whether it's work, women or sport, I'm an obsessive. Taxi driving may be a crappy job but if I'm going to do it, I might as well do it to the best of my ability. Like being on time, like making no mistakes, like having maps for Africa. I have to do it well. That's why I'm so crappy with the pisspots. I hate imperfection, especially imperfect drunken males. That's also why I gave up all sport so early. I just wasn't good enough. Light years from perfection. Women. They've got to be pretty on the outside as well as the inside. That's why you're perfect Tiff. A trophy bird with brains. I want to own you. I want to devour every bit of you. That's not healthy, is it? And don't dare mention jealousy. I'm obsessed with you. And that's not healthy either, is it? But is it also real love?'

'Crikeys Tommy, you do have some feelings after all. OK, you've passed the first test with flying colours but what about avoiding that big black hole in future? A touch more difficult for you methinks.'

'I just don't know Tiff. Why do I keep jumping into it? Obsession again, I suppose. I just love jumping in. How to avoid it in future? Perhaps the deep undying love of the girl I love. Will that do the trick?'

'Yes it will Tommy! I didn't mean all that crap earlier. It was because I still love you despite everything. And I mean absolutely everything. We were made for each other. I've always loved you, even when I was married to William. Look, I've said it now. I am the one who is emotionally naked now. Marry me, you bastard.'

Luckily the champagne that had tactfully been put on ice during our little tête-a-tête arrived in the knickers of time. I like that. Saved by the champagne bell.

'I didn't know it was a leap year.'

'No. No more verbal games Tommy. Marry me'.

I carefully lit a Dunhill. Or I would have done if it wasn't brutally ripped from my mouth.

'No props Tommy. And no guru, no method and none of Van's not so jolly teachers either. Marry me.'

'Yes.' Crikeys, I'd said it. And was I happy ? Had I imagined it? How many joints had I inhaled at the Mill Flat? 'Yes, of course I will, you angel's dream.'

'I don't know about that. I rather hoped that I was a certain old man's dream. Or rather a very young at heart middle-ged man. However I'll certainly marry that man for better or worse. But not in white.' How could one resist such an irresistible sense of humour?

'OK, for better or worse Tiff. And I do like your worst.'

'Bastard.' But she was smiling as she said it.

'Cheers. To The Widow.'

'I'm so happy Tommy. I've been so lonely the last eighteen months.'

'So have I. In fact, I've been lonely all my life.'

'You can have your ciggie now. You certainly need it. Mrs Gainsborough. Yes, I like it. A touch of class wouldn't you say?'

'If you say so, my dear. I knew you were only after my name.'

'Bastard again.'

'Your language really has declined, hasn't it? You should be more careful of the company you keep.'

'Oh yes, I always take precautions now, luckily for you.' Another wicked grin.

Madame Corbière arrived for our order.

'I'm very sorry Madame Corbière, I've quite lost my appetite.'

'Never mind cheri, we will bring you something succulent to rekindle your appetite. Plus your Madiran comme d'habitude.' Plus a very knowing smile. At least the French understand love. And speak perfect idiomatic English into the bargain.

And she was as good as her word and I did manage a little bit of culinary bliss. A perfect piece of foie gras with a wafer thin brioche followed by shank of lamb and tarte limon. Sex off the bone. I swear Tiff came at least twice.

'When shall we get married?'

'As soon as possible Tommy. Church, chapel or registry office?'

'Oh, I rather think that Rattlesden church will do nicely. That should keep the neighbours quiet.'

'You really are incorrigible Tommy.'

'Does that mean I'm sexy ?'

'We'll see.'

Time for coffee.

But compliments of Madame Corbière, more Veuve Cliquot as well.

'Félicitations. I couldn't help but hear the odd word. And the even. Yours isn't the first proposal here by any means but it is the first by a lady to my knowledge. Félicitations again and bonne chance.'

Isn't the French language perfect on such occasions? English just can't live with it. Bonne chance, bon appetit, bonne route. Vive le Francais. Vive La Vieille Maison.

'To us Tiff.'

'To us Tommy.'

> Precious time is slipping away
> You know she's only queen for the day
> It doesn't matter to which God you pray
> Precious time is slipping away.

12.   MADAME GEORGE

> Down in Cyprus Avenue
> With a child–like vision leaping into view
> The clicking clacking of the high heeled shoes
> Ford and Fitzroy and Madame George.

Yes, Tommy was back in love that golden autumn. In love for ever and ever in that autumn that seemed to go on for ever and ever. Golden autumn days were followed by golden autumn nights. The brilliance of the autumn colours was matched by Tiff's radiance and her permanent 'child–like vision' leaping deliciously into my salacious view. Nothing could stop me now. Nothing could possibly go wrong with Tiff walking beside me. Or could it?

The only minor cloud I could visualize on the immediate horizon was a teeny weeny financial one. Or should I say clouds. Bills. I had as usual been riding a bit of a financial tightrope. Car service, four new tyres, new alternator and then, most painful and expensive of all, a new clutch. The 406 had given me sterling service over one hundred and fifty thousand miles, but was now obviously feeling a bit tired and fed up with all the abuse I had heaped on it over the years and had decided that it was now time for me to be relieved of some sterling of my own. But the Peugeot's revenge wasn't sweet on me at all as this all happened in the course of twenty eight ruinous days. A kind of quadruple financial whammy if your English standards have declined so dramatically to induce the necessity to invoke such foul language. Yes, my finances were declining nicely. Or rather, my account had gone into orbit light years over the all powerful Provincial Bank's authorized overdraft limit. My extravagant little sorties with Tiff hadn't ameliorated the situation either. She had raised a single eyebrow once or twice in response to my continued firm declarations that the financial situation was pas mal but wisely hadn't pursued the matter. She knew I was rather prickly to say the least concerning money matters since my bankruptcy. We hadn't discussed the latter either. Tiff also knew that was a subject that was strictly off limits, although an off licence was more than OK of course.

However, when Mr Mainwaring from the bank phoned to discussed to discuss my 'situation' as he so delicately put it, I knew that I couldn't divert him quite so easily.

'Mr Gainsborough, did you know you are more than eight hundred pounds over your agreed overdraft limit?'

What a stupid question. He well knew that I knew and knew that I knew that he knew. Well two can play verbal games and I was the king of those, wasn't I?

'Actually I was just about to give you a buzz,' I replied over casually. 'Slight blip on the cash flow front. Could you possibly extend my credit for a month or so to tide things over?

But Mr Mainwaring wasn't in a jovial or forgiving mood. Banks don't do jovial or forgiving.

'We have already been very generous with you already considering your blemished record Mr Gainsborough,' he replied unctuously. 'What appears to be the problem now? Why are you so overdrawn again? Haven't you learnt anything at all from your chequered past?'

His condescending manner blew my very limited self-control clean away.

'Because I'm not earning enough fucking money, you stupid man. Ever heard of Ivory Towers? No, I didn't think you had. You are too busy putting the squeeze on little people like me. Why are you so concerned with my measly eight hundred quid when I read the other day that your bank have just written off eight hundred million pounds to save some Banana Republic. That wasn't very prudent, was it? And what about that one million pound first prize for the World Tiddlywinks Championship? I suggest an urgent meeting with the Chancellor is needed to bring both prudence and sanity to your miserable organisation.'

'I don't find your attitude at all constructive, Mr Gainsborough. And you know full well it wasn't tiddlywinks. You will be hearing from me in due course, and don't expect any clemency after your little outburst.'

'That's if you've still got a job to write from, you wanker banker. Why don't you just bugger off to India before you are pushed off there,' was the worst I could muster with my double bore shotgun.

Talking of shots, I knew the situation was serious but even I hadn't suspected that I was to be shot at dawn. Not The Listening Bank at all but The Shoot on Sight Bank. Pour encourager les autres pauvres, I presume. Perhaps they ought to rebrand themselves as The Wells Fargo Bank and then we could all come under their corporate cowboy umbrella. Oh no I'd forgotten, there already was a Wells Fargo Bank. I wonder how they made their fortune?

In high dudgeon, I belted round to The Hutch. No Tonker of course, a permanent cloud under the horizon. The Hutch was still a subdued place, even a month after his death. It had lost its magic for me now. Perhaps I ought to go solo. I don't think so would be The Provincial Bank's predictably dusty response. Oh well, better grind on as the miller said to his mistress.

However the sun kept shining and the punters kept coming.

'Tommy, could you pick up a Mister Pasher Bay from The Turkish Delight restaurant and take him to Ipswich please.'

After a quick double take I deduced that The Fat Controller was more likely to be referring to a certain Pasha Bey who was going to be my exalted Turkish fare. On arriving at the restaurant I was greeted by two gentlemen who were involved in a furtive conversation in some foreign tongue. Eventually they both came over and the proprietor asked me in halting English to take his friend to The Pier Restaurant in Ipswich. Unfortunately, my fare apparently spoke little English either, and even my multi-lingual skills didn't extend to Turkish. Thus it was a very subdued journey to Ipswich and I switched on the radio to pass the time.

I still hated silence in the car, especially for a longish trip. For some reason I still felt uncomfortable to have a taciturn passenger with me in the front, even after all my time on The Road. Some debate on 5 Live was waging boringly on about the monarchy so I switched to that old favourite, Classic Gold. Bad Moon Rising by Creedence Clearwater Revival. That's better. Funnily enough, that record was number one in the hit parade when I had my twenty first dance. Who had I been going out with then? Oh yes, the vivacious Roxanne. I had received the red card shortly after that but I went quietly and still have very fond memories of her. I wonder whatever happened to her?

Where was I? Oh yes, old Pasha Bey, and we had already arrived at the docks.

'Where now?'

In response to my question, Old Pasha brought out a dirty old scrap of paper with the address scribbled on it. I looked at it carefully and eventually deciphered it was The Pier Pavilion, not The Pier Restaurant.

'It's Felixstowe you want, you Turkish twit.' Oh dear, it looks like I am going to fall foul of both the Race Relations Board and Mr Smiley in one unguarded sentence. Oh bugger, and bang goes my hopes of winning the prestigious Courteous Cab Driver award for the third year running.

'What is this twit ?', old Pasha asked carefully.

'Oh don't worry your dusky head Pasha. I will take you on to Felixstowe as well if you like.' I was as sarcastically good-natured as ever after my little outburst, even if the old bugger didn't look as if he could put two drachma together, let alone twenty five quid.

Off we whizzed down the A14 to Felixstowe, where the sun was still twinkling on a remarkably benign North Sea. As usual Georgie was on the money, even if I wasn't going to be.

> Turn to the watery world ! – but who to thee
> (A wonder yet unview'd) shall paint – the Sea ?
> Various and vast, sublime in all its forms,
> When lulled by zephyrs, or when roused by storms.

Certainly, the sea was lulled by zephyrs at the moment, but was I being lulled into a false sense of security at the moment? Old Pasha could be anything, even a terrorist for all I knew or cared.

I finally dropped Pasha off at The Pier Pavilion and wished him good hunting, totally tongue in cheek of course. I was soon put in my place by his effusive thanks for my endeavours, although he just managed to refrain from calling me effendi.

And then he unpeeled a huge wad of notes, all of them fifties. I had only received three of these big ones during all my time on The Road, one of them from an anonymous Afrikaner who wanted his full forty seven pounds change. Yup, those old Voortrekkers are pretty mean with their money as well. He got both footsack barrels on that occasion. Anyway old Pasha must have had at least fifty fifties in his wad. He casually peeled off one of them and in perfect English and now without a trace of an accent spoke positively magisterially to me with just a hint of a smile. Or was it just a look of Balkan contempt?

'Keep the change sonny. I rather think you need the money more than I do.' And with that he was gone. Gone either to Illegal Immigrants Anonymous, or back to finish his latest film. Who cares? No probs, I just love a guy who can beat me at my own game in my own language and a foreigner to boot. What class. England nil, Turkey five.

God certainly has a funny sense of humour. That same evening TFC sent me to a certain Crabtree Cottage, Rattlesden Road, Drinkstone.

'You shouldn't have any problem finding this one, should you Tommy? I should think you could do a Mastermind quiz on this particular area with your eyes wide shut. Don't deviate on to rumpty tumpty Rattlesden mind you. We don't want our Top Gun straying from the straight and narrow, do we? Ha ha.'

Had TFC been studying his Thesaurus or Shakespeare in his spare time? He was certainly becoming disconcertingly more eloquent with age and girth. Perhaps he had just been resorting to the real Philosopher's Stone like me and it was rubbing off in more than one way?

The pick up time was eight o'clock, so I had almost half an hour to make the short drive to Drinkstone and find my destination. All the time in the world, or so I thought. Forty five minutes later, I was in a lather. I had already been up and down this infernal road three times all the way to the edge of Rattlesden and back without success. I called up The Fat Controller.

'TFC, have we got a telephone number on this one?'

'Sorry Tommy, we haven't. Struggling, are we? Well, keep hunting. You have managed to bring down one deer in the area so a second shouldn't be much of a problem to a man of your capabilities. Tee hee.'

Oh no, even TFC was taking the parochial piss. This was too much for a man of my standing. Quarter of an hour later, I still hadn't located this bloody Crap Cottage and the steam was coming out of my ears. I was just about to retire hurt when a torch approached me. When it got closer I saw that there was an old lady behind it together with an aggressive looking Alsatian.

I wound down my window.

'Can I help you, young man? I have observed you going up and down the road for a while now, and I was about to call the police when I noticed your Wells Fargo signs. You are a taxi aren't you?'

'No madam, I'm a burglar casing the joint as they say. Are you worth casing? And by the way, in case you haven't noticed, I'm not a young man. I'm glad you're not involved in an ID parade.'

'I don't like your tone. In fact I think you are a very rude man. Do you want assistance or not?'

'I'm sorry. I was well out of order there, but I've been going up and down this damned road what seems like for ever. You don't happen to know where a certain Crabtree Cottage is by any chance, do you ?'

'As a matter of fact, I do. But it will cost you.'

I looked at her sharply but even in the darkness I could see or rather imagine her eyes twinkling.

'Well, you asked for that. Young man.'

'Why is everyone taking the piss out of me today? What have I done wrong?'

'Oh, I rather think you bring it on yourself, don't you?'

'What's your name? Miss Marple by any chance?'

'Touché. As a matter of fact, the property you are looking for is about two hundred yards back up the road on the right hand side just past the second thirty mile an hour sign. It is set back well from the road so you wouldn't have a hope in hell of finding it in the dark, to be fair to you. Although why I should be fair to such a rude man I don't know.'

But again I sensed rather than saw the humour in her voice.

'You are really a remarkable old lady. Many apologies again.'

'Be humble. Oh, and dip your lights in future. I was quite dazzled out there.'

'Point taken Miss Marple. Thank you and a very good night to you.'

She raised her hand in acknowledgement and retreated to

her humble abode.

But I wasn't so forgiving to the residents of Crabtree Cottage. As I drove into a very dark and narrow entrance drive I espied a tiny sign on the open gate. The ideal place to be seen at night. I arrived in front of a chintzy thatched cottage and deliberately waited inside the car. Let the mountain come to Mohammed. The mountain turned out to be a smartly dressed yuppie couple in their early thirties. Neither did it help that I noticed a new BMW and Range Rover parked casually at the end of the drive. When I'm Chancellor of the Exchequer I will give the latter a right financial hammering. I think their owners would well deserve it. Anyway, the yuppie couple got into the back of the car together, but not before they had received the full power of one of Tommy's megawatt scowls.

'Who was the idiot who booked this taxi? Didn't they think it might have been advisable to give a few directions or did they think that they were so famous that they didn't need to give any instructions? What is your name by the way? Beckham by any chance? Oh sorry, I forgot. He's just buggered off to Spain. So who are you?'

'No, Wilkinson actually. And please don't speak to us in such an offensive way. We'll have to speak to your boss about this little episode.'

'You can talk to Jesus Christ and all his disciples for all I care, Mr Wilkinson Actually. As a matter of fact, I'm self employed so I only have to answer to myself. And Mammon of course, which you should know all about. Sutton Market Grange wasn't it? Having a nice little din–dins with the trophy wife, are we? It's all right, don't bother to answer that one, it was just a rhetorical question. Oh sorry, they don't do rhetorical in The City, do they? Hedging and ditching would be more your line, wouldn't it?'

Yet again there was a deliciously icy silence in the car during our little trip to the Grange. I drove right up to the entrance hall and indicated rudely to the Wilkinsons that they could get out.

'How much?', asked Mrs Wilkinson as hubbie was still sulking.

But I was more than ready for them and employed the classic Scotsman tactics again.

'No charge. And before you whine why not, it is my golden rule never to charge people of your plutocratic ilk. I wouldn't want to stain my hands with your soiled money.'

'Go to hell,' was Mrs Wilkinson's feeble final riposte.

'I will take that as a cancellation of the return journey. Bonne nuit et bon appetit.'

Oh yes, I had put another shot over the bows of the rich but did I feel any better at the end of it? And did I feel poorer? You bet I did, in more ways than one. Envy isn't a very nice trait, is it?

Life should have been perfect but something was badly wrong. There was also a real viciousness in my tongue that wasn't there before. On my good days I merely tried to take the piss out of the pompous. Now I wanted to destroy them. My anger was all embracing. And that was all I wanted to embrace. Lead into gold my arse. I was effortlessly turning gold into lead. What a perverted alchemist I had turned out to be. And what about that Healing Game Van had been wittering on about? What was wrong with me? Was I going down again?

Back at the flat I tried to analyse the situation, over a couple of glasses of Madiran of course. When staying with Tiff I carefully controlled my alcoholic intake, but when I was on my own nothing had changed. In fact I probably drunk even more than before to compensate for being deprived while with her. Was the dreaded ruby liquid more important than Tiff? Another cloud, and the most insidious one of all? Ah, that's a tough question. Cue Omar.

> And as much as Wine has played the Infidel,
> And robb'd me of my Robe of Honour - well,
> I often wonder what the Vintners buy
> One half as precious as the Goods they sell.

Well, wine had played the Infidel all right, but was it going to rob me of my Robe of Honour as well as Tiff at the death?

But talking of death it was Tonker's death that had affected me most. I had lost all interest in The Road since his accident. It was no longer fun but just a bloody hard and unrewarding sweat. Surely a man of my multi talents could find a proper job again? Yes, the fucking mythical Philosopher's Stone was well and truly buried in my eyes. Like poor Tonker. It just wasn't worth dying on The Road for a few measly quid, was it? Time to move on. But to what? Tiff was comfortably off of course, but I couldn't bear to be merely a kept man. My pride wouldn't allow

269

it. That was where the pressure was coming from. I had to financially compete with Tiff. I was barely earning more than ten thousand measly quid net. Pathetic. I was earning more than that twenty five years ago. How could I hope to financially support such a sophisticated lady? But what else could I do now? I was on the wrong side of fifty and ageism was strongly against me. You're not allowed to be sexist, racist or religist in this so called liberal island, but you can be ageist as much as you like. You haven't got a hope in hell of finding a good job unless you are young and dynamic, whatever the latter adjective really means. I suppose it must mean that you're solely in charge of the fireworks on Guy Fawkes night. Anyway, who would want to employ a bolshie bugger like me?

I would have liked to quit straightaway. But, of course, I couldn't. Mr Mainwaring wouldn't allow it. Nor would the car leasing company. I still had six months to go on that front. Six months. The six weeks to Christmas would be six weeks too much. In fact six minutes would be too much the way I felt at that moment. I just didn't want to get back into the car anymore. The vibes just didn't feel right. What to do then? Have another couple of glasses of course. Come on Georgie, help me.

> Lo ! proud Flaminius at the splendid board,
> The easy chaplain of an atheist Lord,
> Quaffs the bright juice, with all the gust of sense,
> And clouds his brain in torpid elegance.

Oh yes, the High Priest of the taxi world had always been good on elegance. Unfortunately I was also pretty torpid by now as well. The second bottle of Madiran was already open on the table and I was almost done for.

Ten minutes later, the phone rang. It was Tiff.

'Hello darling. How are you?'

'Pas mal. And you, my lovely firm breasted one?'

'Tommy, you haven't been drinking again, have you ?' Tiff came back sharply. She had always had a keen ear amongst her other more attractive features.

'No of course not. I've only just got home. I'm a bit zonked that's all.' Lying came easy to me now.

'Oh sorry, you sounded a bit funny there. Well, I won't keep you. See you Thursday, usual time and place. Love you lots.'

'Bye darling.'

I put the phone down slowly. Lying may have been easy but it didn't mean it was painless. I was already cheating on Tiff, not to another woman but to the far more insidious Grape. Blow me away Omar.

> While the Rose blows along the River Brink,
>   With old Khayyam and Ruby Vintage drink,
>   And when the Angel with his darker Draught
> Draws up to Thee – take that, and do not shrink.

No, I certainly didn't shrink from drink in any form. But dark thoughts were drawing up to me and I couldn't escape them however hard I tried. I wasn't destined for happiness. I didn't deserve Tiff. Edna was spot on. I was a shit of the highest order. That inner voice that whispered 'destroy yourself' wouldn't go away. Where oh where was that 'darker Draught'?

Thursday night. Dinner with Tiff. I still couldn't shake off that terrible feeling of foreboding. Christ, I damn well tried to be the old carefree Tommy but it just wouldn't work. I even tried to alleviate the situation by ordering the most expensive wine I had ever bought in my life, a 1995 Chateauneuf du Pape, price sixty five smackers. Very symbolic I thought. You can't get away from the old bugger can you? But no god or religion or pope was going to save me tonight. The sheer papal power of the wine only served to get me pissed again double quick. Well, I didn't need much topping up, did I?

Suddenly Tiff exploded.

'What's bloody wrong Tommy? I thought we were meant to be in love. Some love. No, don't turn away. That would be too easy. Look me in the eye, you bastard. Now, what's really wrong?

I looked at her blankly. I felt nothing. Nothing at all. I tried with all that was left of my fading strength to summon up even a little emotion but nothing happened.

'I just don't know Tiff.'

'Oh you don't know eh. Well, I'll fucking well tell you in that case. You're an alcoholic, that's what. I naively thought I could save you. No, not save you. Help you rather, but you're too far gone now. You don't know eh! I'll tell you what you can do. Report directly to Alcoholics Anonymous tomorrow and don't come back till you have passed Go and completely dried out. Goodbye Tommy. I just hope it's not adieu.'

Tears were pouring down her cheeks, but all I could do was to turn away from those accusing eyes and continue to look into space blankly. And feel blankly.

'Oh Tommy,' she wailed.

And with that she was gone. Gone for good, leaving me with a bill that my plastic could barely bear. I couldn't bear to look Madame Corbière in the eye either as I paid it. I could feel her accusing look boring right through me as well, and to show her contempt for me she didn't even wish me bonne nuit or bon anything else. Where now? Round to Graham's? No, that wouldn't work. The Rose and Crown would be better. I would be safely anonymous there.

> On an inn-settle in his maudlin grief,
> This he revolved, and drank for his relief.

Of course I was an alcoholic. I just hadn't ever wanted to confront that simple truth. I had been a consummate actor all my life but it was me who was stripped naked at last. It was the beginning of the end. No Tiff, no teacher and no guru. They had all failed me when it came to the crunch. Or rather I had failed them utterly.

> Dry your eyes for Madame George,
> I wonder why for Madame George,

Oh the love that loves the love that loves
To love the love that loves to love that loves to love.
Say goodbye to Madame George.

Goodbye Tiff. Goodbye, goodbye, goodbye, goodbye, goodbye, goodbye. No more golden summer memories. No more golden autumn days returning. Or no more golden anything for that matter. The love that loves the love that loves was over for the last time. Over and out. As I was.

Of course I wouldn't register with the other AA. All their finding God crap and their nonsensical mantras. 'My name is Tommy and I'm an alcoholic.' Fuck that for a game of soldiers. Bugger The Waiting Game for that matter. I would go through the motions but nothing mattered now. Nothing at all. How about suicide? No, I hadn't even got the guts to end my miserable existence. Well, you'd better keep driving then Tommy, right on and on till the end of The Road, wherever and whenever that might be.

I became a recluse again. The Hutch was out of bounds. So was The Rising Sun. I drunk myself stupid whenever and wherever I could. If you are going to be an alcoholic, you might as well go the whole hog. I began to suffer from the most terrifying repetitive nightmares. All my sins came back to haunt me in those dreadful dreams. In the first one I was driving interminably round and round the M25 except for the very occasional pit stop at one of those awful service station places which always seemed to metamorphose into The Hutch. But a very different Hutch to the one I was used to. The crappy exterior was still the same but inside it was like a spotless new hospital room, and the only inhabitant was a ghostly Tonker lying on a hospital bed with a beatific smile on his face. I always tried to speak to him to say how sorry I was but no words ever came out. Then I had to return to driving round and round that infernal motorway alone. And then I woke up. Hell.

In the worst of my dreams Tiff, Megan and Roxanne were all gathered round my bedside. No, it wasn't my bed. I was looking down from high on my body lying alone, apparently asleep, on Tiff's massive four poster at Rattlesden with the three women weeping round the bed. Then I was always woke up in a mucky sweat before I could discover what had happened to me. What had happened was that I had begun to lose touch with any sort of reality. My mind was outside my body. I couldn't take any more of this. Those demons had won in a canter. At last Peter Grimes really came into his own.

> Still there they stood, and forced me to behold
> A place of horrors – they can not be told –
> Where the flood open'd, there I heard the shriek
> Of tortured guilt – no earthly tongue can speak ;
> 'All days alike ! for ever !' did they say
> 'And unremitted torments every day' –
> Yes, so they said' – But here he ceased, and gazed
> On all around, affrighten'd and amazed ;
> And still he tried to speak, and look'd in dread
> Of frighten'd females gathering round his bed.

Yes, Georgie had finally done with me, but was I finally done for?

Saturday November 22nd, 2003. A good day to remember for some. And a bad day to die for others. I reflected mournfully that Kennedy had been shot exactly forty years ago. All I can remember of that terrible evening long ago in England was of a very young public schoolboy waiting with dread to be beaten for talking after lights out. Yes, a very bad day altogether.

It was now eleven thirty in the morning. England had at last won the Rugby World Cup Final against Australia in an epic match. Unfortunately, I had a hangover of epic proportions so couldn't get too excited about it all. In truth, nothing in life excited me any longer. Unlike Willy-John Macbride, that great Irish and British Lions rugby player, I would never utter those immortal words 'now I can die happy'.

Very, very reluctantly I dragged myself off to work for the sixteen hour slog of the Saturday graveyard shift. No salutations to The Fat Controller. Just a terse ready to play. But of course I wasn't ready to play at all. Neither was I mentally or physically ready to work. I just wanted to lie down and sleep far from any madding crowd. Very appropriate for a madman.

Despite this inner turmoil going on in my head, I went off into battle for the last time to face the barbarians. I battled monosyllabically with the usual pisspots, dickheads and thickos, plus the occasional nice and normal fare. No matter, they all came alike to me now and I wouldn't have recognised any niceness, let alone reality even if it had reared up and kicked me in the bollocks. I had pulled up the drawbridge of life on them all. I was also drowning in the cesspit of insanity.

Then about ten thirty, I had a pick up from The Bear. No name, but we were going to Orford on the coast again so at least it would be a lucrative fare. Not that that mattered either. The

Inland Revenue had finally caught up with me and I had to find over five thousand pounds within twenty eight days or they would send in the bailiffs. Yes, send in the clowns. I knew all about these comedians from my earlier bankruptcy days and I didn't fancy bumping into them again. But again, why should the mighty Revenue bother about such a measly sum when they seemed to be totally immune to the huge fiddles and VAT frauds amounting to millions of pounds? Mr Mainwaring had also followed up his verbal threat with a very threatening missive. I had twenty eight days (it always seemed to be twenty eight bloody days) to repay not only the excess overdraft figure but also the agreed two thousand pounds limit. As I had finally exhausted the patience of Messrs Mastercard and Visa as well, my financial future looked none too rosy. There must be a vast black hole somewhere where I could either extract vast sums of money from, or at least jump into. Yep, the latter alternative seemed far more desirable.

Back to The Bear. After about five minutes impatient waiting, I was just about to drive off when a very colourfully dressed North African looking gentleman with an acoustic guitar got in the back of the car. One glance at him and I realized at once that my 'Angel with his darker Draught' had finally arrived.

'Good evening. Orford village please,' he said in heavily accented English. Of course he could be related to old Pasha Bey but I rather doubted it in this case.

We got chatting and I found out his name was Zini and that he did indeed originally come from Algiers. However, he had apparently travelled extensively throughout Europe and had lived in Portugal for several years. He was at present doing research in

England for some obscure project, funded of course by The European Community. How he qualified for the grant heaven only knows, although Zini probably thought that it was appropriated manna from his particular nirvana. Zini was very charming in that flashy Arab way, but beneath the polished veneer I could detect his quiet aura of menace. He positively exuded it. But this time I wasn't afraid at all because he was going to do the deed that I hadn't the guts to carry out. I knew that. He knew that. And we both recognized that the other knew that too. QED. By this time we were approaching the little village of Campsey Ash although in somewhat differing circumstances to that golden autumn day returning only just over a year ago. There was one similarity to that happy day though.

'Would you like a spliff Tommy. I think it is traditional, n'est ce pas?'

Pourquoi pas? If you are going to die, die high.

'I don't mind if I do Zini.'

So he expertly rolled a joint for us both. We then puffed away companionably while Van and Astral Weeks lamented in perfect harmony with an imperfect situation.

Say goodbye, in the wind and the rain in the backstreet,
In the backstreet, in the backstreet.
Say goodbye to Madame George.

In the backstreet, in the backstreet, in the backstreet.
Well, well, down home, down home in the backstreet.
Got to go, say goodbye, goodbye, goodbye.

We had driven through Tunstall village and were now entering the dark and forbidding form of Tunstall Forest. In the backstreet of Suffolk in the wind and the rain.

'Turn off here Tommy.' Zini indicated a small track to the right. 'Keep driving till I say stop.'

I did as I was commanded. The track was very muddy and narrow and we passed a couple of dimly lit cottages. Deeper and deeper we went into the forbidding depths of the forest but still I felt no fear. It was as if my mind and spirit had been completely disinterred from my body by some strange osmosis. I no longer had any will to live but felt strangely serene at last. My pathetic failure of a life was coming to a suitably bathetic end. Nothing else mattered now. What are you thinking about Tommy? Nothing my beloved. Nothing at all. It doesn't matter anyway. Nothing matters now in the wind and the rain in the backstreet of life. Fuck the world. Fuck fuck fuck the whole fucking wide world.

> In the backstreet, in the backstreet, in the backstreet,
> Well, well, down home, down home in the backstreet.
> Got to go, say goodbye, goodbye, goodbye.

I sensed rather than saw the knife come out and immediately stopped the car.

'Do it now.'

I felt the razor sharp edge of the knife on my throat and waited supinely for the end.

Ah, with the Grape my fading Life provide,
And wash my Body whence the life has died,
And in a Windingsheet of Vine-leaf wrapt,
So bury me by some sweet Garden-side.

***Thirty nine taxi and private hire drivers
have been murdered in the last fifteen years.***